D0960634

the love song of IVY K. HARLOWE

ALSO BY HANNAH MOSKOWITZ

Sick Kids in Love

Break

Invincible Summer

Gone, Gone, Gone

Teeth

Marco Impossible

Not Otherwise Specified

A History of Glitter and Blood

Zombie Tag

Gena/Finn

Salt

the love song

song

of IVY K.
HARLOWE

HANNAH MOSKOWITZ

Entangled Publishing, LLC
10940 S Parker Road
Suite 327
Parker, CO 80134
rights@entangledpublishing.com

Entangled Teen is an imprint of Entangled Publishing, LLC.

Visit our website at www.entangledpublishing.com.

Edited by Lydia Sharp and Jen Bouvier
Cover design and illustration by
Elizabeth Turner Stokes
Interior design by Toni Kerr

ISBN 978-1-64937-049-5
Ebook ISBN 978-1-64937-050-1

Manufactured in the United States of America

First Edition June 2021

10 9 8 7 6 5 4 3 2 1

entangled teen
an imprint of Entangled Publishing LLC

To Gale and Randy,
who luckily will never read this.

Author's Note: *The Love Song of Ivy K. Harlowe* includes themes, imagery, and content that might be triggering for some readers. Scenes depicting alcohol consumption, drunkenness, drug use, and drug overdose appear in the novel.

American Addiction Centers offers free and confidential guidance to those suffering from addiction.

Call the hotline: (866) 929-9301 or visit americanaddictioncenters.org.

If you or a loved one is experiencing a medical emergency, such as overdose, call 911 or go to the nearest emergency room. Do not call this hotline number for an emergency.

September

It's just about midnight on a Friday night and I'm spending it the same way I usually do: trying to figure out whether a girl who could not be less interested in me is gay.

She's about five feet away from me, leaning back against the bar and tapping her nails—a little long—on her rocks glass in time to the music. Her hair is hacked off, but that might not mean anything. The fact that she's here at Kinetic on a Friday night doesn't necessarily mean anything, either. Providence doesn't have a dedicated lesbian club, so Kinetic's population consists of mostly gay guys, a lot of straight girls, and, every once in a while, a girl who doesn't look at you like she thinks you're going to rear up and bite her if you dare to say hi.

Not that I ever do. There's a lot of comfort in telling yourself that every girl who doesn't immediately fall in love with you is straight. I'm good with staying in that comfort.

Besides, there's safety in numbers, and my friends have all abandoned me. Alyssa, who has about as little luck with girls as I do but with the addition of some inexplicable optimism, is over at the other end of the bar, buying drinks for a girl who's definitely going to smile sweetly and kiss her on the cheek and walk away in a minute or two.

Melody and Diana are the mate-for-life types and I can't see them, but they're for sure over on one of the couches in the back, making out like this is their only opportunity to do it. And Ivy...

Well.

Ivy is where Ivy always is, in one location or another: the center of everything going on, silent and calculated, moving so perfectly, it's like the music is following her and not the other way around, locked in eye contact with the second-hottest girl in the room.

Ivy's hair is cherry-Coke brown in the bouncing lights of the dance floor, and she's poured into a black tank dress that rides dangerously high up her thighs as she moves. She's looking at the girl she's with like she's the only person in here — Ivy always does — but every-fucking-one else in here, including the maybe-lesbian I've been eyeing for the past half hour, is looking at her.

Ivy has freckles and dimples and bright-green eyes, and with someone else's energy, she'd be adorable, but there is nothing cute about Ivy. She is ice and hot metal and electricity. There is something about her where you know she could ruin your life in a word if she wanted to, and she always, always might want to. She is, without fail, the hottest girl in the room.

I'm mostly here to drive her home. Usually with whatever girl she's chosen for the night licking at her neck in the back seat of my shitty secondhand sedan. It's actually my parents'. They just lend it to me. For this.

Alyssa comes over, draining her cocktail down to the ice, the rim tapping against the nose of her glasses. She's wearing a T-shirt and jeans because she wants people to think she's not trying too hard, whereas I'm wearing a

T-shirt and jeans because I'm here half the nights of my damn life and the novelty of dressing hot for no reward wore off sometime in the first year. Besides, I've never been a real femme, like Ivy is, though I don't have the commitment to go full butch, either. I just exist in this kind of gray area. But I have dozens of piercings and some big colorful tattoos, so it's not like people don't know I'm gay.

Alyssa sighs and sets her glass down heavily on the bar next to me. She passes for straight, incidentally, and guys hit on her a lot because she has long eyelashes and dark curly hair and big tits, but she's a whole six on the Kinsey scale and has, for whatever reason, never had much success with girls. It's kind of a running joke at this point. But probably not all that funny to her.

"No luck?" I yell over the music.

"She had to go meet her girlfriend."

"Of course. Didn't there used to be single lesbians in Rhode Island? Where the hell did they go?"

"Not Boston," Alyssa says. She's about to start her sophomore year at BU, heading back up there on Monday. From what she's reported back, last year wasn't the wild queer utopian collegiate experience she'd been promised. It's not like my townie time spent here working was any better.

"Maybe they're invisible," I say.

"Maybe *we* are." She nods toward the dance floor. "Doesn't look like everyone's having trouble." Ivy's now lip-locked with her target, her fingers digging into her waist.

I say, "Ivy having trouble picking up a girl, wouldn't that be one of the signs of the apocalypse?"

"I think it's more like an urban legend. The Providence

version of Sasquatch is Ivy Harlowe not getting laid."

I ask the bartender for a water—I have a fake ID, obviously; how else would I have been coming here since I was seventeen? But I have to stay sober enough to get Ivy home—and Alyssa opens up Tinder and starts scrolling through nearby girls. It feels a little like cheating at whatever the fuck it is we're all here to do, but it's a good way to check who around you is a girl interested in girls.

I can tell from the nonchalant way Alyssa keeps glancing up at one girl dancing with a group as she's scrolling through at lightning speed that she's looking for her specifically—which, of course, doesn't mean she's going to kill her chances with anyone else. She's swiping right on everyone.

All of a sudden, Ivy's here. She leans across the bar and orders a whiskey, then returns to her feet next to me, stretching like a cat. Ivy's tall anyway, almost my height, and in her five-inch heels she somehow walks in as easily as slippers, she towers over Alyssa like she's a different species.

"What are you doing here?" I say. "You're wearing a lot more clothes than I thought you'd be next time I saw you."

Ivy shrugs carelessly, the strap of her dress incidentally slipping down one skinny, bronzed shoulder. "I lost interest. It was too easy."

"Too easy to bring a girl home with you," Alyssa says, deadpan. "Something bad needs to happen to you someday. Nobody can be this lucky."

I give Alyssa a look—"lucky" isn't a word I'd use to describe Ivy's life—but Ivy either doesn't hear her over the pounding bass beat or charitably pretends not to.

"I need a challenge," Ivy says, raking her fingers

through her hair. She has that kind of wavy, shiny hair that always lays right and never tangles. "At this rate, I'll get stale, and we can't have that. If I'm going to be stuck in this shit town forever, I have to find a way to stay sharp." Ivy's in college, too, at the University of Rhode Island on full scholarship, but she commutes the half hour each day to campus from the crappy house that she shares with her mom, whenever she's actually around.

"Here lies Ivy, ruined by too much sex," Alyssa says. "I don't need to wish anything bad on you. You're going to get struck down for blasphemy."

"Lightning strike in the middle of the club," I say.

Ivy retrieves her drink and takes a sip, scanning the crowd. "Where's the married couple?" Ivy says the word "married" the way my mother says "Republican." Always has.

The couple in question is Melody and Diana, our resident polyamorous power couple and the last two members of our motley crew. We met them as a unit here a couple years ago. Alyssa's been my friend since tenth grade algebra, and Ivy...well. We go way back.

"Couches," I say. "They're not going to get off each other for hours. Melody scored some E somehow."

"That bitch never shares her shit. I'm so over it." Ivy cranes her neck over my head at Alyssa. "Hey. What are you doing?"

Alyssa holds up her phone.

"Let me see," Ivy says, and she squishes in close, snaking her arm around my waist. She smells like lemon and jasmine. "Oh God, not her. She has this awful girlfriend and they're always trying to pull in some unsuspecting victim."

Alyssa hesitates but finally swipes left.

"No," Ivy says on the next one. "Way too filtered. Who knows what she actually looks like."

Left again.

"Oh, she's good. I slept with her last summer. Nice apartment. Gets a little clingy, but…they all do. Saw her in line for the bathroom about an hour ago if you want to track her down."

Alyssa swipes right. "No match."

"Hmm. That's a shame." Ivy raises her drink to her mouth, then lowers it and narrows her eyes when Alyssa swipes to the next girl. "Hang on. Who's that?"

According to the name at the top of the profile, it's Dot. She has black hair, long and wavy, and, at least in her profile picture, pouty copper-red lips and big eyes with perfectly winged liner. She's looking artfully away from the camera, one hand holding her hair back from her face.

"She's in here?" Alyssa says. "She is not twenty-one."

"Neither are we," Ivy says, looking around.

"And by the time we turn twenty-one, maybe she'll be eating solid foods and sleeping through the night."

"Her profile says eighteen," Ivy says. A year younger than us.

"I will take a vow of celibacy if she's eighteen," I say.

Ivy laughs. "And that'd be different from your current state how?"

"Hey."

The song changes, the crowd on the dance floor shifts a little, and Ivy points across the room. "There."

I'm surprised Ivy recognized her, honestly. The girl standing on the edge of the dance floor with a death grip on her drink and a scared shitless expression on her face doesn't exactly match the Tinder profile, but, you know, who among us ever did?

Alyssa groans. "God, Ivy, leave her alone. She's the dictionary definition of 'baby gay.'"

Ivy finishes her drink. "So she needs to feel welcome."

"That girl is not going home with you," I say.

Ivy gives me a brief kiss, and my whole world is peach lip gloss for a moment. "Famous last words," she says, and she tweaks my nose and saunters across the dance floor, bodies parting for her like the Red Sea. She heads straight to Dot without faking any kind of nonchalance, and immediately she's bending down a foot to say something in her ear.

I always wonder what she says to girls. Maybe when you look like that, it doesn't matter.

Dot nods, and Ivy steals her drink and takes a sip—it's some pink thing—then makes a face and sets it aside. She takes Dot's hand and pulls her slowly out to the dance floor, and Dot follows without resisting, a look on her face I know way too well. I've seen it on every fucking lesbian in the state at this point. The wide eyes, the slightly parted lips. It's the face you make when Ivy chooses you.

"She is pretty," Alyssa says.

"Ivy likes older girls," I say. "I don't know why she's pretending like she wants to teach a new dog old tricks."

"Imagine Ivy being your lesbian welcoming committee," Alyssa says. "I can't decide if she'd do more scaring off or converting."

"We could put her on recruitment and find out."

"Hmm, yeah. Send her to Boston."

I turn back to the bar—I really don't need to watch Ivy's indoctrination program; I'm an old dog and they are old tricks—and order something stronger.

A guy comes up with his boyfriend and compliments Alyssa's glasses, and she starts talking to him about face shapes and polarized lenses and online discount codes like they've known each other for years. Alyssa could find friends in a vacuum. I try not to look at Ivy and Dot, but every time I do, it's like I've been fast-forwarding through a soft-core porno. First their hands are on each other. Then they're kissing. Then Ivy is hiking her leg up to wrap around Dot's little waist and pull her closer.

They're back over to me before my drink is finished, Ivy's hand on the small of Dot's back, Dot's eyes on Ivy. "This is Alyssa and Andie," Ivy says to Dot, her voice smooth. "We're ready to go," she says to me.

I look at Dot. Her face reminds me of my brother psyching himself up for a roller coaster. I sigh. "Hi. Andie."

"I'm Dot," she says.

"Do you want to go home with her?"

Ivy raises an eyebrow at me, but Dot takes a moment. She looks up at Ivy, and something in her eyes is... calculating. Like she's seeing how the whole night is going to go from here, and I want to tell her that she has no fucking idea, that she's in way over her head. Because who wouldn't be, with Ivy?

But what do I really know about it?

"Yeah," Dot says after a moment, and she turns back to me. "Of course."

Alyssa's enjoying her new friends and eyeing a new group of girls who just came in and says she'll catch a ride home with Melody and Diana whenever they release each other, so I leave with Ivy and Dot, spilling out of the club and toward the lot two blocks away where I left my car.

We're up on College Hill, and the street's covered with Brown and RISD kids standing in line for cheap pizza or stumbling back to their dorms. Dot's a little slow in her high heels, and she lags behind Ivy, who snarks to me, "Do you really think I didn't make sure she wanted to come?"

"Can't be too careful."

"I can rescue my own damsels, thanks. Or is this interrogation thing a new role you provide?"

"What, you mean along with my taxi service? And only if they look like they were born during the Obama administration."

Ivy glares at me and slows down to take Dot's hand.

They get in the back seat together and are all over each other before I've even started the car. Christ. I roll my eyes and adjust the rearview mirror so I don't have to look at them. "Yeah, you're welcome for the ride," I mumble to myself, wondering, like I always do, why the hell I always agree to do this shit.

God, I don't even agree. I volunteer.

I weave us around the college kids, down the hill, into the lights of the city, and south to good old Elmwood, the neighborhood where Ivy and I have lived since we were little kids making pillow forts and mixing nail polish colors and teaching each other how to kiss. Or I guess she taught me.

I don't really wonder why I volunteer for this shit. I just wish I did.

Elmwood's one of the shittier parts of the city, and I kind of expect Dot to try to back out when she sees where we're headed. She wouldn't be the first prospective girl of Ivy's to do it, and she doesn't exactly look streetwise. But she doesn't care, or maybe just doesn't notice, with her face and hands otherwise occupied, feeling up my best friend in my back seat, and there's no protest as I turn onto Ivy's block.

And then immediately stop, because her street is crowded with police cars, firefighters, and a bunch of people gathered on the sidewalk.

"Ivy," I say.

"Mmm," she says, her hands on Dot's waist, their lips together.

"Ivy."

She pulls away and shoots daggers at me in the rearview mirror. *"What?"*

"Your house is on fire."

There's a second where none of us moves, and then all three of us scramble out, leaving the cars open and beeping in protest as we run down the rest of the block, weaving through the crowd until we're on the sidewalk. The shithole formerly known as Ivy's house is smoking pathetically, one wall completely gone and the others not much better, bits of charred roof and furniture strewn into the front lawn. The firefighters are packing up their equipment, ready to go.

Holy shit.

Somehow what comes out of my mouth is, "How many fucking times did your landlord say he was going to fix the wiring?"

"Oh my God," Dot says. "Was anyone in there?"

I shake my head. "Her mom's in Costa Rica. Fuck, Ives. You could have been in there."

Ivy's staring at the house, her eyes slightly narrowed like she's trying to figure it out.

"God, wow," Dot says. She puts her hand on Ivy's arm.

"I'm glad you're okay."

"She's not okay," I snap, because who the fuck is she to be here, to be part of this, to act like it really matters to her world whether this person she's known for half an hour burned alive or not? "She could have died. If this had happened last night, she would have been in there."

"But I wasn't," Ivy says flatly.

"Still... God, all your shit. All your school stuff. Your clothes." All the crafts we made when we were little, her half of the construction paper heart that says BEST FRIENDS FOREVER, though fuck if I'm about to say that in front of Dot. I take her hand. "Ivy."

Ivy's still looking at her house like she's making a decision, and I think about Dot's face at the club when she was looking up at her. Two natural disasters in one night.

She's so fucking beautiful, in the streetlight and the smoke.

Her mouth quirks up into a smile. "Good," she says quietly. "Good. Burn it all down."

Ivy doesn't want to talk to the cops tonight—she says she'll take care of that tomorrow—so we get out of there before anyone can ask us to identify ourselves. I doubt it'll end up being much of an investigation. The wires in that house had been sparking for God knows how long, and it's not like there was anyone to gain anything from burning it down. And despite the number of girls in this town Ivy's loved and then left, I don't think anyone *actually* wants to kill her. I could be wrong.

"Why's your mom in Costa Rica?" Dot asks. We've driven the car a few blocks away, and now we're sitting against the hood just...decompressing.

"She's teaching yoga to starving orphans," Ivy says.

I expect that to confuse Dot, I don't know, but she just smiles a little. Ivy digs around in her purse for her vape pen, takes a long pull, and then gives it to Dot even though I hold out my hand.

Dot hesitates.

"Just hold the button and breathe in," Ivy says.

"Is it pot?"

Ivy laughs. "Yeah. You don't have to; it's okay."

"I just never have before." She pauses one more second, then wraps her lips around it and breathes in.

"Hold," Ivy says. "Hold. Pull in a little fresh air; don't breathe out... Good. You're a natural."

I roll my eyes and take the pen.

"Andie used to always cough when she was your age," Ivy says.

Dot clears her throat, obviously trying not to cough. "I'm not as young as I look," she says.

Ivy chuckles. "Good. How old are you?"

She pauses.

"Oh, come on," Ivy says. "You think I'm going to go back to Kinetic and tell them you snuck in? If they started kicking out everyone who wasn't twenty-one, they'd go out of business."

She rubs her skinny arms to warm up. "Seventeen. I just turned."

"When?" Ivy says.

"August fifteenth."

Ivy laughs a little more. Her birthday's the sixteenth. I

guess she thinks that's cute or something.

"How old are you?" Dot says.

Ivy takes the pen from me and pulls a long drag. "Nineteen." She doesn't mention that she just turned, too. Ivy's six months younger than me, which seemed like a decade when we were younger. She was the little one. I was supposed to take care of her.

It's almost laughable now, except that it's not.

Dot's mesmerized. "Are you in college?"

She nods. "URI."

"What are you studying?"

"Fashion merchandising," she says, still holding her breath.

Dot climbs onto the hood of the car. "The next-generation Anna Wintour."

I don't know who that is, but I guess Ivy does, because she watches her, finally exhaling. "Yeah," she says after a beat. "We'll see."

"How long have you been going to clubs like this?" Dot asks.

We both know what Dot's really asking here—how long has Ivy been a professional lesbian—but Ivy just says, "Awhile."

"This is sort of my first time," Dot says. "Being out like this."

Ivy keeps her eyes on her. "I figured."

They have this long moment of just looking at each other, and Dot is still sitting on my car, and to be honest, any patience I had for this little lesbian mentorship program is just about out. "Okay, Cinderella," I say to Dot. "Where can I drop you off?"

Ivy turns to me. "We're going to your house," she says

like it's obvious.

"*We're* going to my house. She's going home."

"I'm not going home," Dot says. "I told my parents I was sleeping over at my friend's house."

"Okay," I said. "So where's your friend's house?"

"I can't show up there at one in the morning."

"She's coming with us," Ivy says, fixing me with a hard stare.

I chew the inside of my cheeks.

"C'mon, Andie," she says with a little pout. "We don't have anywhere else to go." She puts an arm around Dot and tugs her in close, and she comes willingly, her chin tilted up and her eyes on Ivy.

God. What the fuck else can I do? The kid clearly came out tonight with no plan outside of finding someone to whisk her away for a night—and can we just take a fucking moment to roll our eyes at the fact that not only is she successful her very first night out, she's fucking *Ivy Harlowe* successful. Ivy's newly homeless and has just been through some kind of trauma, whether or not she knows it, and my mom is the type who would eat me alive if she found out I let her go to a hotel or something after that instead of bringing her somewhere safe.

My mom is also the type who doesn't give much of a shit about casual lesbian sex under her roof, which sounds like a good thing until you need an excuse to not let your best friend fuck a stranger in your brother's old bedroom.

Goddamn it.

"You want to come with me?" Ivy says to Dot, softly, with the kind of tenderness she'll give one girl for one night and never again, and Dot nods without breaking eye contact with her.

One night and never again. God. Fine. If Dot doesn't want to let me save her, so be it.

I drive the five minutes between Ivy's house and mine, which isn't exactly a palace, either, but at least it's probably not going to catch fire at a moment's notice. We leave the lights off and rush quietly up the stairs so we don't wake up my parents, and Ivy, as predicted, leads Dot straight to my brother's room. I guess I should be grateful she didn't assume she was getting mine. Max moved in with his then-girlfriend, now-wife four years ago, so his room has become sort of our makeshift guest room, complete with his old clothes still in the dresser and Bruins posters on the walls.

Ivy says something in Dot's ear and leaves her standing in the center of Max's room with her arms around herself while Ivy comes over to the doorway. She smiles at me, leaning her head against the doorframe. "Thank you," she says, her eyes soft and twinkly.

"Yeah, whatever."

She smacks a kiss on my cheek. "You're my favorite."

"I know. Have fun."

She glances back at Dot. "Oh, I will."

Ivy goes back into the room, leaving the door slightly open, and I don't go right away even though I know I should. I watch Ivy slide up to Dot and speak to her softly, and when Dot nods, Ivy lifts her chin with two fingers.

And then she does something weird, something I've never seen her do, and I've seen Ivy kiss hundreds of girls: she hesitates. Right before their lips touch, she pauses, glancing up from Dot's lips and into her eyes, and there's something so un-Ivy-like in the way she looks—*nervous*—that I convince myself it's a trick of the light or something.

They're kissing a minute later, Ivy's hands in Dot's hair, gripping the back of her head, Dot's fingers searching the hem of Ivy's dress, and all of a sudden I don't want to watch anymore. I close their door and go to my room, where Ivy and I have had a thousand sleepovers and never had sex.

I get out of my clothes and wash the glitter off my face and flop down on my bed and try to ignore the noises from the next room. And when that doesn't work, I turn up the music on my phone, reach over to my bookshelf, pull out one of my favorite romance novels, and lose myself in it until I fall asleep.

My parents have already heard about Ivy's combusted house when I come down to breakfast the next morning, even though Ivy herself is still in bed. My mom's a nurse, which is like having access to the world's fastest tip line. She knows what's going on in Providence before it's even happened.

"I told you that place was a death trap," she says, spatula in her hand, my father's GREATEST DAD apron around her waist. "Don't know how many times I told Ivy, hire Mike, get him to fix that place before you explode." Mike is our handyman who my mom might believe has magical powers. "And look what happens."

"I'm not sure it really exploded," I say. "More of a gentle boil."

Dad turns the page in his newspaper, his reading glasses balanced on the tip of his crooked nose. "How's

Ivy handling it?"

I shrug. "It's Ivy."

"I assume she's here," my dad says, and Mom laughs.

"She's here, all right," she says. "And I know exactly what she was doing. Unless that was porn someone was blasting at two a.m."

"How do you know that was Ivy?" I say. "It could have been me."

Mom gives me a look. God. You know it's bleak when even your mother is disappointed in your sex life.

"I don't know if she's still here," I say.

"Ivy?" Dad says.

"Not Ivy," I say. "The girl."

She is. She and Ivy come downstairs when we're halfway through pancakes and eggs. They're both wearing my brother's clothes; Ivy looks hot as hell in an old tied-up button-down and a loose pair of chinos rolled up above her spike heels, her hair slicked back, and Dot's just drowning in a Red Sox T-shirt and an old pair of gym shorts, her makeup from last night smudged around her eyes. Dot freezes when she sees my parents, but Ivy saunters over, kisses my mom's cheek, and steals a piece of bacon from the paper-towel-covered plate by the stove. "Morning."

"Hmm," my mom says, studying Dot. "And who's this?"

"This is, um." Ivy looks at Dot like she might be seeing her for the first time. "Spot, or something."

Ha. But also ouch.

"Dot," she supplies quietly.

Ivy is unbothered. "Right. Dot."

"Well, Dot," my mom says. "Why don't you sit down and eat something?"

Dot looks like she'd sooner disappear into the floor,

but she sits down anyway, twisting the hem of my brother's shirt in her tiny hand. "Thank you," she says.

My mom serves her and Ivy some pancakes and Ivy a reproachful look for good measure, which she answers with a cheesy smile. "So. Dot," my mom says. "Is that Korean?"

"Mom," I snap, while my dad chokes on a laugh. She means well, she just is missing a certain brand of tact. She might give Ivy a lot of shit, but the two of them are cut from the same shameless cloth.

"Um, it's just short for Dorothy," Dot says. "And I'm Vietnamese."

"Are you in school?" Mom asks.

Dot nods, sipping her orange juice. "I just started my senior year."

"Oh, really? Where, Brown? RISD?" my mom says, knowing full goddamn well it is not Brown or RISD.

"Um, I meant high school."

"High school," my mom says to Ivy. "Isn't that interesting?"

Ivy butters a piece of toast. "Not particularly."

Dot says, "I do want to go to RISD, though," and Ivy glances up at her.

My dad, who's able to, unlike my mom, sense basic human discomfort, clears his throat and reaches into his pocket. "Please ignore my wife," he says. "She likes to practice interfering in Ivy's love life in the hopes that she'll someday get to do it for Andrea's."

"Thank you," I say, while Ivy cracks up. "Thank you for that."

"Hope you don't mind I borrowed these," he says to Ivy, dropping her keys into her hand.

"Going through a gay woman's purse," Ivy says. "Isn't that a hate crime?"

"You lose jurisdiction when you come home in the middle of the night and leave your shit strewn all over my kitchen," he says.

She smiles at him. "You went and got my car."

"It's in the driveway."

"You lovely, lovely hate-crimer. Are you seeing anyone?"

This is all business as usual for me, minus the whole fire thing, but Dot's watching like this is the best movie she's ever seen.

"House looked pretty scary," Dad says. "You doing okay?"

Ivy shrugs. "Sure. It'll be good. Fresh start and all that. Lived in that shithole for too goddamn long." Ivy's mother is rarely home—she's always traveling, chasing whatever artist's colony or get-rich-quick scheme calls to her that month—so Ivy's been alone in that house for a while.

"What's the plan?" Dad says.

"Get my own place, finally," she says. "Maybe something closer to school. Might take some time, though, especially since I have to replace everything."

"You can stay here as long as you need," Mom says, and Ivy beams up at her, that smile that gets her anything, that got my father to walk ten blocks at the crack of dawn unprompted to go pick up her car. Ivy Harlowe, to quote a song she loves, has the world on a string, house or no house.

We eat and make small talk for a while, Dot still watching us in amazement, and after a little while, Ivy checks the time on her phone and wipes her hands on her napkin.

"I've got to go," she says with a dramatic sigh. "I have a fire inspector to speak to. You think insurance will pay for all my shoes?"

"Do you even have insurance?" I say.

"I don't know. A girl can dream." She stands up and looks at Dot, and I think we're all expecting her to leave her here stranded—wouldn't be the first time I've given some abandoned girl a bus schedule—but she says, "Come on. I'll drop you off at your friend's house."

Dot's as surprised as I am. "Yeah?"

"Yeah, come on."

Dot thanks me and my parents while Ivy gets her purse and hands Dot her discarded club clothes, and then Ivy kisses me and says she'll see me tonight and they leave. I can hear their voices through the open window as they walk to the car but can't make out what they're saying, then something makes Ivy laugh and give Dot a gentle shove.

"Huh," my mother says. "Never thought I'd live to see Ivy voluntarily spend time with a girl after her tongue's out of her twat."

"Jesus Christ, Mom, God created euphemisms for a reason."

"'Twat' is a euphemism. How did we end up raising Miss Fucking Manners?" she asks my dad, who shrugs and takes his meds.

"Anyway," I say. "I wouldn't call Ripley's yet. She's giving her a ride, not exactly picking out matching towels."

Mom snorts. "Ivy in a relationship. That would be the day."

"Yeah," I say, watching her car back out of the driveway, Dot fiddling with the radio.

"Don't you have work?" my dad says to me.

"I'm going, I'm going."

My family owns a strip club, which never really stops being a strange thing to say to people, even when you've grown up around it your whole life. It's called Davina's, after my dad's mom, who founded it with my grandfather back in the early seventies. Rhode Island used to have extremely lax sex work laws, and people were really taking advantage of that, opening up these intense, anything-goes clubs, and Davina's was meant to be kind of a counterpoint to that. It's just topless dancing, nothing all that scandalous, and it's bright and bubbly instead of dark and sensual. There are cardboard palm trees on the walls for some reason, and we get a lot more bachelorette than bachelor parties, if that gives you an idea.

It's how my parents met, too. My dad was the assistant manager, in his twenties, and my mom was a dancer here when she was in nursing school. Dad took over the business after my grandparents retired to Colorado, but he has bipolar disorder and the stress of running the place wasn't great for him, so he's mostly stepped back and let my brother manage everything for the past five years. Now Max handles the finances; his wife, Catherine, hires and corrals the dancers; and ever since I've been out of high school I've been responsible for the day-to-day operations of everything that goes into the place besides the dancers themselves, so think kitchen staff, security, DJ.

You might think that growing up around a topless bar is some kind of lesbian fantasy, but we have great benefits and wages for our dancers, which means once people start working here, they tend not to leave. Most of them have been around for years. They're like my aunts.

Melody, of Melody and Diana fame, is our newest dancer. A few years ago, she found out what we pay and then applied the second she turned eighteen. She's already here when I show up that morning, even though we don't open until one on Saturdays, sitting on the reception desk in her street clothes. "Where'd you go last night?" she says. Her curly hair is loose and wild down her back, and her long, rake-in-the-tips legs are crossed over each other.

"Taxi service."

"I heard Ivy slept with a high schooler."

"Mm-hmm. But over the age of consent." I checked last night, thinking maybe it'd be illegal so I could scare Ivy into kicking Dot out. No such luck.

"I didn't even sleep with high schoolers when I was in high school," Melody says.

"That's a depressing statement in a number of ways," I say.

"Hmm. Does it help to clarify that it's because I wasn't sleeping with anyone?"

"Ah, now you're speaking my language."

She clicks her tongue. "We have got to get you laid, Andie. How long has it been?"

It's starting to feel like the people in my life have some sort of financial stake in how long I'll keep my legs closed. "Decades," I say. "Is Hailey coming in?" Our front desk worker. Not the most reliable, but our staff manager is a coward about firing people. And is me.

"Uh, she was texting me this morning complaining about how hungover she is, so I would be surprised if she shows up."

"Great."

"I think Max was looking for you."

I head past the bar and the small stage—the main stage is around the other side, where the booths are bigger and the shows are more elaborate, but the small stage is more casual and low-key and some people prefer just to sip their drink and hang out—back to where my brother's office is. He's wearing a blue shirt a *lot* like the one Ivy stole this morning, which I decide not to mention to him. It looked better on her, but it's not really a fair fight. Max looks like me but with short hair, which is unfortunate for one of us, and I choose not to think too hard about which.

"Hey," I say.

"Do you have kitchen inventory from last week?" he says.

"I don't, but I will. Is Catherine here?"

He nods. "In the other office. Interviewing a new girl."

"We don't need a new girl. We can't pay a new girl."

"We always need new girls," he says with a sigh, moving to a new bit of paperwork in the stack in front of him.

"I need to see if she can spare anyone today," I say. "I don't think Hailey's coming."

"I cannot put someone at the front desk again when they're supposed to be dancing," he says. "They will mutiny." You still get a share of the tips working the front desk, but you lose the opportunity for stuff like private dances, which is where a lot of our workers earn a decent chunk of their nightly take-homes.

"I need someone at the front," I say.

He gives me a look, and yeah, I'm sure it's a big mystery how this is going to end up resolved.

"I'm out of here at six," I tell him. "Unless you want to pay me overtime, find someone else for the night shift."

He waves me out of his office. Charming guy, my big brother.

It's not like it's my first time doing intake, and it's not exactly challenging work. You sit there, collect the cover charge, point toward the bar or the main stage, tip off security if anyone looks like they might be trouble. You have to deal with assholes who think they have a shot of seeing you naked just because you're a woman inside the club, but honestly I'd prefer they get the record set straight on that, with me, before they go off and try to harass our bartender or the servers. I've got my brother here and many, many security guards. I'm not scared.

And honestly, we very rarely get any sort of significant trouble here. Like I said: it's not that kind of place. Cardboard palm trees. The real demanding patrons are at the charmingly named Girl Dungeon a few blocks over, not at Davina's with our bright-pink walls and Wednesday night specials on Slippery Nipples.

Still, if I'm going to get a share of the tips tonight, I need to bring in what I can, so I go back to the dressing room to get ready with the dancers before we open. Catherine, my sister-in-law, comes over and hands me her lipstick without a word.

"How'd the interview go?" I say, quietly so the other girls won't hear.

"She was experienced and amazing, so I think she's probably going somewhere else."

"Nobody pays what we do," I say.

"Trust me, I saw her. We can't compete with the tips she'd get at a full-nude place."

"Don't think about it," I say. "It" meaning: how much more money we could make here if our dancers bared all.

"Yeah. I try not to." She looks tired.

I have to take my post at the front desk pretty soon after that, so I sit down and put my feet out and get comfortable. I stopped at the library on the way here, thank God, so I actually don't mind sitting here as much as I usually do, especially since early afternoon isn't exactly our busiest hour. I smile and take the cover charge from the occasional customer and, besides that, dive into a new release from my favorite author, Ella Gennesy. She does pretty much the same thing with every book and I love it. Wrong-side-of-the-tracks heroine meets bored rich boy, sometimes the other way around. There's banter and electricity. There's some big misunderstanding. And everything works out perfectly at the end.

I know I should branch out, but also…why? What reality is better to lose yourself in than this one?

I get a text from Ivy at around three. So I'm done with the fire inspector, she says.

How'd it go?

Well…turns out it was arson.

What??

i'm fucking with you. it was the gas line. Womp womp.

I hate you.

they're giving me a tiny bit of money. Meet me at Sloan's after work. Gotta start the rebranding.

Okay. I hear the chime of the door opening. Gotta go.

I put my phone down and…okay, this is immediately

like something out of one of my books, because one of the prettiest girls I've ever seen has just graced our motley strip club with her presence. She's white with short blonde hair—natural dark blonde, not like my bleached-out disaster Ivy convinced me would be hot—and she's wearing black skinny jeans and a dark-blue tank top. Somewhere between twenty and twenty-five, I would guess. Freckles on her shoulders.

She hooks her thumbs in her belt loops on the way over to me. "Um…hi," she says.

I pull my bottom lip between my teeth. "How can I help you?"

She flashes me a half second of very, very beautiful smile. "Do you guys do, like…events?"

"We do! Our specialty." Trick of the trade: anything a customer asks for that we can in any way toss together is our specialty. Though our parties are genuinely kind of great.

"Okay. My best friend from high school is getting married and I'm the maid of honor, so…apparently it's my job to set these things up. Is there someone I need to talk to about that?"

"There is, and it's me."

Her eyes glimmer. "Fantastic."

"Let me pull out a pricing sheet for you, okay?" I duck under the counter and root around in our disorganized file cabinet. When I finally find our rate sheet and straighten back up, the girl seems even less comfortable than she did before. A few of our dancers are walking from one stage to the other, and she's trying to look casual about shielding her eyes like they're an eclipse, but you can only look so casual about being afraid of strippers.

"I'm guessing this isn't your favorite maid-of-honor duty?" I say, handing her the sheet.

There's that smile again. "Sorry."

"Nah, it's okay. Naked ladies aren't everyone's thing."

She laughs. "No, I'm a big fan of naked ladies," she says.

There it is. You learn ways to fish.

"Meeeeee too," I say. You also learn to do that.

She looks at me for a second too long, and God, right now I'm glad I let the strippers do my makeup. After a moment, she says, "I don't know, I know it doesn't make me cool or whatever, but I just take this stuff really… seriously. I don't mean any disrespect at all to the people who do it or anything like that. I know it's just a job."

"Sure," I say.

"But for me, it's…" She shrugs. "I don't know. I take sex very seriously."

Could you demonstrate that for me, please? I swallow. "Nothing wrong with that."

"No," she says, watching me. "I don't think so, either."

"Tell me you fucked her," Ivy says.

"Yes. Right there on the reception desk."

She sighs, rooting through a rack of clothes. "I hate that I know you're being sarcastic."

We're at Sloan's, this hole-in-the-wall thrift store Ivy discovered years ago. We both get all our clothes from here now, and somehow she always looks like she walked off a runway and I always look like I walked out of…a hole-in-the-wall thrift store, but hey, there's a reason she's the one in fashion.

Ivy's always had an eye for this kind of thing, even when we were kids. She used to cut up her dolls' outfits and make these avant-garde dresses, and she was always wearing ties as belts or knotting her hair up in scarves or turning her old comforter into a circle skirt, stuff like that. In middle school, she got her first sewing machine and filled all her notebooks with sketches of dresses and shoes. But fabric's expensive, and Ivy likes stability too much to go into something artsy. Hence applying for fashion merchandising at URI instead of design at RISD.

"I gave her my number, at least," I say.

"Christ, what is this, the fifties?"

I hug the hangers I'm holding to my chest. "She asked for it so smooth on her way out the door. Like she wasn't even nervous at all."

"Why should she be?"

"Some people get nervous sometimes, Ivy."

"Sounds fake." She holds up a floral dress. "Maybe I should do like a sundresses and cowgirl boots thing. Like Miley Cyrus, post-appropriation."

"Sounds a little sweet."

"I'm six degrees of separation from every dyke in this town. No one's mistaking me for sweet."

"Sex-peration."

"Cute." Ivy looks at the tag on the dress and puts it back. "So is she hot?"

"Very. Kind of a butch-lite librarian vibe. It's really gay."

"What's her name again?"

"Elizabeth."

"Elizabeth," Ivy tries, like it's a new and unfamiliar name. "What's she like? This shirt would be cute on you."

"I don't really know; I only talked to her for a minute."

"Well, maybe she'll call and you can ask her all sorts of fun getting-to-know-you questions. If you were a rock, what rock would you be?"

"She texted me already. I don't know if I'm going to answer."

Ivy looks at me like I'm speaking another language. "Why wouldn't you answer?"

"I don't know. She was wearing, like, jewelry. Like stuff that costs money. And her hair looks like it was cut by someone named Gustav who smells like pine cones and gives sage life advice. Not Bonnie at the Hair Cuttery."

"Bonnie does good shit," Ivy says. "And now Elizabeth just sounds old."

"Twenty-two." I took her license for the party registration.

Ivy roots around a shoe rack. "Hmm. Old."

"Well, we can't all be cradle-robbing."

"What?"

"Last night…?" Christ, imagine having so much sex that you have to be reminded the next day.

"Oh. She's seventeen. Two years apart isn't exactly an exciting scandal. Your mom is how many years older than your dad, again?"

I nearly choke on nothing. "Did you just compare your one-night stand to my parents?"

She shudders but then says, "I'm just trying to speak your heteronormative hopeless romantic language." Ivy thinks I need to read more books about lesbians. She's probably right.

"Mm, I appreciate the sacrifice."

"I'm going to need to rinse my mouth out now. And

not in a fun way."

I try not to laugh. "Gross."

She holds up a pair of pants. "These are hot. Wear these on your date."

"Yeah, if I had your legs, maybe."

"Your legs are gorgeous."

I look away so she won't see my reaction to that. I clear my throat. "And I told you, I don't know if I'm going to go for it. She hates strip clubs. I'm, like, genetically part strip club."

"She came to Dav's and told you she hates strip clubs?"

"No, she didn't…she didn't say she hates them, she said she thinks they, like…trivialize stuff."

"What's stuff?" she says, looking inside a pair of boots.

"Sex, I guess. Or, you know. Sex-related stuff."

"Just generally?"

"Yeah, she thinks it should be treated with more, like, respect."

Ivy squints at me.

And I squirm. "What?"

"I mean…it's *sex*. The thing where you're sweaty and jiggly and making gross squishy noises and rubbing up against another sweaty and jiggly person, right? I'm just making sure I have our topic right here."

"I thought you liked sex. Isn't that your whole deal?"

She rolls her eyes. "I love sex, obviously. And loving it required seeing through all the bullshit that it's something huge and significant and *meaningful*. It's just fun. Anyone who says sex is supposed to be serious is trying way too goddamn hard. And this is why people get their little hearts broken. They buy into this cultural myth that sex is anything more than doing something that feels fucking great for a little while."

"They say it's better when there are feelings involved," I say, not that either of us has any idea. I've slept with all of two girls ever, and both were so long ago that who knows if that's even how people are having sex nowadays, and Ivy, of course, has never had a feeling she couldn't shake off.

"Bullshit," she says, predictably. "Like, okay, take me and what's-her-name last night. That was some fucking phenomenal sex."

It's been a while since I've heard Ivy describe her one-night stands with anything more than a shrug and a dirty remark, so that's kind of weird. "Seriously?"

"Yeah, she's got a future. But it's, you know, not with me, because we didn't make up any shit or pretend it meant something it didn't. We had a really, really great time, and now we've both learned a few new tricks to bring on to other people. Her more than me, of course. But no hurt feelings, no sad little heartbreak, just a good time. Because I'm not buying into Miss Elizabeth's little myth that sex is some sacred act."

"You learned tricks from a virgin."

"I'm saying. She's got promise. Come on, I want to try this stuff on."

We haul our load to the fitting rooms, tell the bored girl who's very much not watching for shoplifters that we're sisters, as if she cares, and go into a room together. Ivy pulls her shirt over her head and I try not to watch the way her waist stretches, her ribs rippling like piano keys.

"Try the pants first," she says. She pulls a dress over her head, this light-blue cotton thing with sunflowers all over it. I'd look like I was wearing a tablecloth, but Ivy, of course, instantly looks Parisian chic.

I shimmy myself into these too-tight pants while Ivy messes with the sash on her dress. "It's pretty," I say.

"Can you zip me?"

"Yeah." I move behind her and start working the zipper up. It's old and feels delicate, so I go slowly. She smells faintly like her perfume from last night, and her hair falls down to her bra strap in those perfect dark-red waves.

It's just not fucking fair.

"You think I can do it?" she says quietly, after a minute.

"Do what?"

I feel her take a deep breath under my hand. "Replace everything," she says. "Start over."

I finish zipping her and wrap my arms around her waist, resting my chin on her shoulder and looking at our reflection in the mirror. She's stunning, so much more stunning in these crappy fluorescent lights than I could ever be anywhere. And she's right here, warm and quiet and smelling like mango. I breathe.

"Of course," I say. "You can do anything."

She leans her forehead into my cheek. "Not without you," she says, and I try to memorize the moment.

"Well, you never have to," I say.

She turns her face to mine and kisses me, softly, and I cling on for a lot longer than I usually do. I don't know. Glimpses of vulnerability from her just do something to me. Give me some kind of pointless hope, even after this long.

She pulls away eventually, laughing a little. "What are you doing?"

God. "What? Nothing."

She studies me for just a second, then shifts away from me and twirls a little in front of the mirror. "It's cute. I'm going to get it. Even though it's a summer dress."

"Fuck the rules."

"Fuck the rules. And you have to get those pants. And wear them on your date."

I crane my neck to look at my ass in the mirror. "I don't know."

"Your vagina's going to go on strike soon if you don't use it."

"I don't think I'd notice."

She snorts. "Just go out with her, fuck her a few times, it'll be great. What reason do you have not to? Can you get me out of this dress?"

I swallow. "Yeah."

Our group text with the girls lights up pretty soon after that, and we end up meeting everyone at Mama's, this bar up on College Hill with cheap drinks and incredible tater tots. It's not technically a gay bar, but the queers unofficially claimed this place back in my parents' day—I mean, come on, it's called Mama's; that's not for straights—and it stuck.

Alyssa tried to stay home to pack before she heads back to school, but we dragged her out and now she's mostly stressing about not having it done, so we're getting her drunk. Melody's still at Dav's working, but Diana, Melody's partner, twist-outs and Boston accent, is here, drinking mai tais and showing us pictures of the Airbnb in New York where they're running off to celebrate the anniversary of their first…something.

Ivy nurses her drink and tries to not look nauseated with either disgust, because we're talking about relationships, or jealousy, because we're talking about New York. She's already kind of over us and is searching the room for some new stranger to bring back to her place—my place—but we know what we're getting into when we go out with Ivy. Not five minutes later, she's out in the corner, making out with some girl, when Diana turns the topic back to Elizabeth and whether or not I'm going to text her. "Why the fuck wouldn't you?" Diana says.

Alyssa laughs. "You know why not."

"God, Andie, seriously? Still?"

"It just doesn't seem like… This doesn't feel like the time," I say.

"It hasn't been the time for what, fifteen years?" Diana says. "When is it going to be?"

"No, I mean, she's living in my house now. I don't want to… If there's a chance something's going to actually happen, it's now. If this was, you know, if this was a story, this is when it happens. She realizes the girl next door has been there the whole time." I may be a drink or two deep at this point.

"Things happening usually require one person telling the person who has *no idea* that they're in love with them," Diana says.

"And have been," Alyssa adds, "for fifteen years."

"I'm just saying, it doesn't seem like the right time to bring someone else into this," I say, right as Ivy slides back to the table, apparently bored of her conquest.

"Into what?" Ivy says.

I say, "Hiring a new dancer," with the smoothness of someone who's been telling lies of omission to her best friend for fifteen years. The conversation continues cleanly enough, despite the eye rolls from Diana and Alyssa, who are so sick of my shit, but a few minutes later, Alyssa glances at the door and chokes on a laugh. "Uh-oh. Look who's here."

Diana looks, her huge brown eyes scanning the doorway. "Who?"

It's Dot. Her hair is French braided, and when she gets closer—which she does right about immediately—I can see the deep-blue glitter eye shadow perfectly circling her eyes.

"Ivy's girl from last night," I say quickly. What the hell is she doing here?

Diana whistles. "Someone's got a fan."

Dot comes up to Ivy's side and smiles at her. "Hi."

"Hey," Ivy says—not unfriendly, but not exactly inviting, either.

It's enough for Dot, though, who immediately pulls up a chair and settles at the table between Ivy and Diana. She turns that smile on all of us. "Hi. I'm Dot."

Diana thinks Ivy's indiscretions are hilarious—I swear she and Melody have some kind of bingo board at home where they track all the outrageous things Ivy does—so she is all over this. "Dot. Hi, sweetie. Look how adorable you are!"

"Thanks!"

"Soooo what brings a hot young thing like you to a place like this?"

She shrugs. "Just checking out the scene." She reaches for a sip of Ivy's drink, but Ivy snorts and moves it away from her. She's honed in on a girl on the other side of the bar who's huddled with some friends on the minuscule dance floor. Dot's not even a blip on her radar anymore.

If Dot notices, she doesn't seem bothered. She asks Diana about herself, which of course leads to answers about Melody, and in a minute, Dot's exclaiming over the Airbnb pictures. Alyssa and I make faces at each other.

"This is amazing," Dot says. "I love New York. I'm thinking of going there for college, if I don't get into RISD."

"What program at RISD?" Diana says.

"Painting. I want to be a makeup artist, so having a BFA would be awesome." Well, look at us planning ahead. Way, way ahead.

"Ivy almost went to RISD," Diana says.

Ivy snorts. "No I didn't."

Dot watches her.

"You'd be a great makeup artist," Diana says. "That eye shadow look is incredible."

Dot turns to her and grins. "I do YouTube videos!"

"Oh yeah?"

"Yeah, I want to be, like, one of the big ones. I don't have that many subscribers now, but yeah…that's my goal. There aren't a ton of Asian-American girls doing videos in English, so it felt like, I don't know. If you can't find it, make it, right?"

"Majoring in painting sounds amazing," Alyssa says. "My parents would be all over me. *How are you going to earn a living?*"

"Oh, mine are," Dot says. "It's that, all the time, just in Vietnamese. My parents have this shrimp boat business and my older brothers all get up at five a.m. to help with that, and I just… No thank you."

"Waking up at five a.m. is probably not for everyone," Diana says diplomatically.

"I'm guessing these parents don't know you're at a bar with a bunch of dykes," Alyssa says. Maybe I should call them.

"Uh, yeah, no," Dot says. "They're…very Catholic. I told my mom I was bisexual when I was fourteen and I think we both just pretend it didn't happen."

"Fun!" Diana says.

"Eh, whose parents ever reacted well?" Alyssa says.

Diana laughs. "Andie's." I roll my eyes a little, but of course she's right. My parents are also Catholic, but I'm guessing not the kind Dot's talking about. My parents knew I was gay before I did.

Dot turns to me with wide eyes. "Oh my God, Andie, your parents are amazing. Oh my God. You are so lucky."

Oddly, I don't feel that way right now. "Yeah, they're something, all right."

Dot says, "No, they're, like… God. They're so amazing."

"They're amazing," Diana agrees.

Dot says, "They saw me coming downstairs with Ivy and they were, like, totally fine with it. If mine knew I was having sex, God, I can't even think about it."

She is clearly fucking dying for Ivy to give her any sort of response to her mentioning them having sex. Some kind of acknowledgment, anything. But Ivy hasn't looked at any of us in a while. She's still watching that girl on the dance floor, and pretty soon after that, once the conversation's turned to how old we all were our first time (nineteen for Diana, eighteen for me and Alyssa, and fourteen, although she doesn't volunteer that now, for Ivy) she gets up abruptly and goes to the bar. Better position to scope out her prey.

Dot makes a big show of pretending not to notice,

asking Diana some more questions about her anniversary and Alyssa what she's studying instead of painting—Alyssa can't even draw—and I sigh and get up and follow Ivy over to the bar.

"Makeup videos, huh?" I say to her.

Ivy doesn't look away from the dancing girl. "What?"

"Dot?"

"Who?"

"Oh my God, Ivy."

"Oh." She shrugs and takes a sip of her drink. "Yeah, apparently."

"That's, uh…kind of shallow."

She raises an eyebrow. "Yeah, I guess she's not saving orphans in her spare time like the rest of us."

Fine. "So you realize you're being stalked, right?"

"What?" she says, eyes narrowed on the girl.

"Can you pay attention for a fucking second?"

She sighs and turns to me. "She asked me this morning where some cool places were to hang out, I told her here. It's not exactly shocking she'd come out here. She's a baby gay. She's exploring."

"She thinks you're going to take her home."

"Well, I imagine she'll find out I'm not when I don't."

"You're not going to talk to her?"

"And say what? She doesn't expect anything of me. I never gave her a reason to."

"You just said it—she's a baby gay. They get attached."

"And they get over it." Ivy finishes her drink. "She'll be fine. And she's not my responsibility if she isn't."

Sometimes I forget how easy this is for her. She's never cruel about shaking people off, but she's never felt bad about it, either. And I just don't understand that. I don't know how to not feel like I owe everyone everything all the time.

Ivy goes out to the floor, dancing by herself, sidling up close-but-not-too-close to the girl. Alyssa comes over and nudges me.

"Here's a concept," she says, and oh boy is she drunk. "What if you juuuust…tell her?"

I turn back to the bar to get a new drink.

"No, don't get something here. Me and Diana want to go to Kinetic. Melody's gonna join after work. You coming?"

Back at our table, Diana's gathering her shit together, but Dot's watching Ivy and looking goddamn stricken, and I'm only human for fuck's sake.

And it's not as if I don't know that feeling.

"Someone needs to tell Dot not to wait for Ivy," I say.

"Why do I feel like you're going to say that someone is you?"

"Hopefully because I'm a nice person. Let me get something out of this."

"You are a nice person. You're also the person who always cleans up after Ivy." She tugs on my sleeve. "Let your duties down for one night. Come dancing."

"I'll meet you there later."

She sighs and kisses my cheek. "Yeah. Okay."

I order two rum and Cokes—that's what I drank when I was in high school—and bring them back over to our table, where Dot is scrolling through her phone and trying desperately to look nonchalant. I sit down across from her and slide one glass to her.

"Thank you," she says softly.

I give her a minute. "You okay?"

She shrugs, but a second later she says, "She barely even noticed me."

I almost feel bad for her. "Yeah…that's Ivy. She, uh, moves on."

"She's staring at that girl in blue. She's not even hot."

"She's pretty hot."

She sulks.

"Well, what did you think would happen?" I say. "You'd walk in here and she'd forget every other girl exists?"

Dot looks at me incredulously. "Have you seen me?"

"Wow, okay, they make them confident these days, I guess." I take a deep breath. "Look, Dot. The thing about Ivy is, she's sort of a onetime experience. She's a lot more interested in the hunt than anything else."

"That's not true," Dot says. "She didn't exactly have to hunt me, or whatever. I didn't really need convincing. And trust me, that was fine with her."

"Yeah, but…"

"You weren't in the room," Dot says. "You didn't see her face. You didn't hear her—"

"I'm not saying she didn't have a good time," I say. "I'm just saying she doesn't like to give anyone a chance to get attached. Ivy doesn't really do the feelings thing."

"But it's not like it was just sex and then it was over. We talked after. We slept all curled up together, like… You don't do what we did without feelings," Dot says.

"God. You really, really do. Especially if you're Ivy."

Dot watches me, tracing her finger around the rim of her glass.

"Trust me," I say. "I'm telling you this for your own good. Ivy Harlowe is not your girlfriend. She's just a good story."

Dot shakes her head slowly. "You're jealous."

Hang on. "Excuse me? I'm trying to help you."

"Bullshit. You think the way you look at her is subtle? You're jealous, so you have to minimize what she and I had. You weren't there. You don't know."

I feel hot and breathless and fucking furious, watching this kid try to tell me about Ivy. About me. "I know that 'what she and you had' is exactly what she's had with a hundred other girls."

She shrugs easily. "A hundred other girls aren't me."

"Wow. All right. Fuck you, do what you want. But if you think I'm jealous that I'm not one of Ivy's toys she uses once and throws in the trash, you're even stupider than you seem."

She stands up, glass in hand. "Thanks for the drink."

God, fuck this. I have friends to go meet, and Ivy has a girl in a blue dress to take home. There is literally no reason to concern myself with this kid any longer. Hope that ego doesn't hurt when it hits the ground.

I do turn and take one more look on my way out, though. Dot's moved to the bar, her eyes narrowed on Ivy, and just then she pushes off it and heads to the dance floor. She goes straight to a girl near Ivy and starts dancing with her, and it's immediately clear that she knows what she's doing where dancing is concerned if, from what I can tell, literally nowhere else. She moves easily, carelessly, her body sliding like it isn't quite solid, and I see the girl Ivy's been talking to notice her right before I turn around.

I'd be embarrassed for Dot if she were a little less annoying, but, well. Can't say my heart's breaking that she's going to get shot down at close range instead of just watching from a distance while Ivy picks up someone else like every other heartbroken lesbian in Rhode Island has at some point in her sexual development.

So I walk the two blocks to Kinetic and dance it out with the girls for an hour or two, but I'm tired before too long and this shifty-eyed girl I am very much not interested in won't get her shifty eyes off me, so it's not too late when I get home. Only to discover Ivy in the stairwell, like she couldn't even make it all the way into my brother's room, half dressed and wrapped around…

"You've got to be kidding me," I say.

Dot tucks her forehead into Ivy's neck and starts laughing.

"Can I talk to you for a minute?" I say to Ivy.

"Seriously? I'm kind of in the middle of something."

"You're kind of in the middle of my hallway."

Ivy whispers something in Dot's ear, and she nods and goes into my brother's room and shuts the door. Ivy leans against the wall, way too nonchalant for someone in a bra and a yanked-down sundress. The same dress I'd zipped up in the dressing room.

Dot must have unzipped it now.

"Can I help you?" she says to me.

"What the fuck are you doing?"

"Foooreplay?"

"You're sleeping with the same person twice? You don't…do that."

"I don't believe this is some contract I've signed," she says. "She's cute, she's a nice girl, she's great in bed, she wanted it, and I wanted it. Did I have to start running everyone I sleep with by you when I moved in? Is *that* a contract I signed?"

I can't believe this. "She's stalking you."

"You're awfully loud when I'm drunk."

"She's going to get even more attached and you're going to be stuck with her." And God, Dot's just going to be reeking of *I told you so* tomorrow morning, and I don't think I can take that on an empty stomach.

Ivy laughs, the kind of genuine laugh you don't get out of her all that often. "I'm really not concerned that I won't be able to shake off a seventeen-year-old when I want to."

"She's going to get ideas," I say. "She's going to think it means something."

She kisses me, sloppy and too short.

"This is not one of your romance novels," she whispers, her face still close to mine. "It's just a girl fucking a girl."

With that, she goes back into Max's room. I hear soft voices and not quite as soft laughter.

Ivy never does this.

This is not…this is not how Ivy sleeping with the same girl more than once for the first time ever was supposed to go.

So I go to my room, kick my shoes against the wall, and take out my phone.

And I text Elizabeth: hey.

October

"Are you more of a white wine or a red wine person?" Elizabeth asks me.

I'm more of a cheap beer person, but I feel like that isn't the right answer. We're at this restaurant called Clair de Lune, which even townie-me knows is the place that college kids' parents take them when they come to visit. There are tablecloths.

We've been texting for the past three weeks, but now it's the first weekend in October and the date is actually happening. She's been busy, with wedding prep and veterinary school, and I've been making up things I was doing so it would sound like I, too, have a life, every time she takes a while to answer a text and I convince myself she's ghosting me, because why the hell is a twenty-two-year-old in veterinary school who looks like *that* and has the money to bring me to Clair de Lune *not* ghosting me?

"Um…whichever is fine," I say after an awkwardly long pause.

"White goes best with shellfish," she says. "If you know what you're ordering."

"Uh, yeah, I like shellfish."

"Perfect," she says, and she turns to our server and orders a bottle of something fancy-sounding.

We're sitting by the window down by the river with

this gorgeous view of the downtown skyline. Elizabeth is wearing a slinky black jumpsuit and her hair is slicked back. Her nails are painted.

The wine comes, and she hands it to me to taste, and I say it's good when to be honest it just tastes kind of tolerably bad to me the same way all wine does, and then I order shellfish because I guess I'm supposed to. I'm trying to figure out if I've ever been on a dinner date like this before. I didn't know people still did this. Elizabeth looks so comfortable, settled in her chair like it's her living room. I can't get over the way she holds the wineglass, how her wrist is so loose and casual, how elegant her fingers look.

She smiles just with her eyes and says, "Tell me about your day."

There is no answer I can come up with that's worthy of being looked at like that, and certainly not anything close to the truth.

"Just same old, same old," I say. "Worked. One of our dancers is leaving, and it's sad because she's been with us for, like, five years, but she's going back to school to teach, which has been her dream forever, so we can't really be mad."

"Following her bliss," Elizabeth says.

"Yeah."

"How about you?" she says. "What's your dream job?"

"Are you saying most little girls don't dream about being the staff manager of a strip club?"

She smiles.

I wish we could just talk about her instead. "I don't know," I say. "I was never…you know, the kid who had a dream job. I think I'm going to probably end up in some job that I'm fine with, but I don't feel like I'm ever going to… Like, Ivy, my best friend — "

"I know who Ivy is," she says, and I bite my cheek. Yeah. It's possible I've mentioned her in texts one or two times. Or a hundred. Who's counting, right?

"Yeah," I say. "So she's in school for fashion merchandising and that's, like…she's going to be a big deal. And she's always wanted that. She's driven." I take a sip of wine just to shut myself the fuck up. "Did you always want to be a vet?"

She nods. "It's one of those childhood dream careers. Vets, doctors, firemen, and meteorologists."

"When I was a kid, I wanted to be a stegosaurus," I say.

"Also good."

"Still working on that, I guess."

"So what are you passionate about?" she asks me.

I laugh a little. "What?"

She smiles. "It doesn't have to be something you can make into a career," she says. "But I'm sure there's something you really care about. I like hearing what people really give a shit about."

Even I'm not socially stunted enough to think *Ivy* is an appropriate answer here. So I go with the other answer. "I like love stories."

"Mmm." She sips her wine. "I assume you don't mean those, you know, the supermarket paperbacks."

"Oh, um…"

She holds her hand out. "Oh, shit, I'm sorry."

"No, I mean…you're right. They're embarrassing."

"Everyone deserves a guilty pleasure," she says. "I'm sorry. I bet they're really fun."

"I mean, not just those," I say, and she nods and probably thinks I'm about to say I also read leather-bound

Russian literature or some shit. God. "Like...okay. So my parents?"

"Okay."

"They've been together for ages. They met when my dad was eighteen, I think. And my mom got pregnant with my brother and that wasn't planned and my dad just stepped right up, and, like...they still make each other laugh all the time. They tell these stupid jokes and they just, like, delight each other. And my dad...he's had some setbacks. It hasn't always been easy. And my mom's been there for him the whole time and he always makes sure she knows that he notices. They're just good to each other."

There's a moment where she doesn't say anything, just watches me really intensely, and I'm totally nervous until she says, "I love that. That real shit. What it actually looks like."

I nod.

"Yes," Elizabeth says decisively. "Yes. That's very good."

I feel myself exhale.

It gets easier after that. Probably helps that the food is so unbelievably good that it's hard to focus on anything else, even if I do have a seriously intimidating number of forks.

It also helps that Elizabeth does most of the talking, and she's so damn *interesting.* Her family moved around all the time when she was growing up, and she's lived in China and New Zealand and the Philippines. She's only in Providence because she went to Brown. Meanwhile I've barely ever left Rhode Island and the closest I've come to college was when I felt up a girl wearing her sister's Johnson & Wales sweatshirt.

But she doesn't ever tell these stories like she's judging me or even like she expects me to match them, but just like she's letting me in on a secret. She lowers her voice and sends me these small smiles, and it's like every time she finishes telling me about the fish markets in Manila or the dragon boats in Hong Kong, those stories sort of become my stories, too, just a little bit. She tells me them like I deserve to hear them. Like I've somehow earned them by sitting here and babbling about my parents and stumbling my way through eating an entree she pays for.

My dad needed the car tonight and Ivy was out, so I took an Uber to get here, but Elizabeth drives me home. Ivy's car is in the driveway when we get back, so I assume there's a strange girl in my house. Ivy's been living here for three weeks now, so I've gotten pretty used to the parade of shame every time she fails to sneak someone out before we get back. She's supposed to be saving up for her own apartment, but she's going to go broke paying cab money for club girls to get out.

I must not roll my eyes internally enough, because Elizabeth laughs and says, "What?"

"Sorry. Nothing."

She turns off the car and just says, "Hmm."

I don't know what's supposed to happen now. If this were a romance novel, we'd magically lean in toward each other at the exact right time. If this were one of my friend's lives, we'd already be fucking in the back seat.

"Thank you for the ride," I say.

"Of course." She smiles gently. "Come here."

Oh. I guess that can happen, too.

So I scoot closer to her, and she kisses me, softly at first, and then hard, her hands in my hair, the kind of kiss I feel all the way down to my feet. And there's something so fucking hot about that, as if she meant to kiss me formal and controlled but she couldn't, she got carried away. As if in some reality, it's possible that someone like me could overwhelm someone like her.

She smells like vanilla and peppermint and her dress feels cool under my hands like some sort of very expensive water, and oh, I like this. I like this a lot.

When was the last time someone kissed me who wasn't Ivy?

I'm about to invite her in, I'm so close, when she pulls back and kisses me one more time, short, soft. "I'll call you?" she says.

Oh. Right. Classy shit. Not having sex on the first date. I've heard about this.

She waits until I'm inside the house to pull away, and I kind of…float around for a while, making enough noise in the kitchen that maybe Ivy will realize I'm home and wrap it up. I can hear voices upstairs, hers and—surprise surprise—one I don't recognize. They're finally coming downstairs about ten minutes later, a tall, half-dressed girl with curly hair and Ivy in one of my brother's T-shirts, when the doorbell rings.

"Are we expecting more?" I ask Ivy.

She cranes her neck to see out the window, then laughs and rolls her eyes. "Ah, fuck."

"Don't tell me—" I say as I open the door, but sure enough, there's Dot, winged eyeliner and red lipstick and French braids and jeans and a T-shirt, holding a reusable shopping bag. She raises an eyebrow at Ivy's girl, who pushes past her and out the door like she's afraid of being caught.

"Something tells me you can do better," Dot says to Ivy. "Hi, Andie."

Ivy sits on the stair and leans her head against the banister. "I told you, you cannot just show up here."

"At my house," I say.

Dot holds up the bag. "I brought ice cream."

Ivy sighs. "Okay. Come in."

"Ivy!" I say.

"She brought ice cream!"

"I hope you think of that ice cream fondly when she's murdering you," I say, shutting the door behind Dot as she skips in.

"She's not that kind of stalker," Ivy says. "She's the nice kind."

Variations on this theme have happened a few times over the past few weeks. I have never seen someone this goddamn persistent, and Ivy for some reason keeps… letting it happen. She turns Dot down about half the time, but that never seems to convince Dot not to just try again next time, somehow, and then hell if the next time she doesn't just shrug and let Dot in or bring her home from the club or say she's going home with some other girl and then in the morning, who's making scrambled eggs but *Dot*.

If she weren't still screwing other girls constantly, I'd be afraid she'd been body snatched. Or that Dot was drugging her.

"We're not having sex tonight," Ivy says to Dot over her shoulder, on her way to the kitchen.

"Yes, I imagine you're tired," Dot says diplomatically.

Ivy gets bowls out for ice cream, and I sit down at the kitchen table while Dot leans against the counter and watches Ivy. I say, "I've got to wonder if this would have worked for every girl Ivy's blown off if they'd tried it. Maybe you can't reject someone who just flat-out refuses."

"I never claimed to be lazy," Dot says.

"Yeah, or subtle," I say, which is supposed to be a little bit of an insult, but fuck if she doesn't laugh. And Ivy does, too! Christ.

"Your foundation looks weird," Ivy says to her, handing her a bowl.

"I know, it's breaking up around my nose. I'm trying it for a review video. Not going to be a winner. Did I tell you about that eyeliner stamp?"

"Mm, no time," Ivy says. She points to me with a spoon as she sits down at the table, Dot right on her heels. "I need to hear about Andie's date."

"Ooh, you have a date?" Dot says. "When? I can do your makeup."

Dot has not seemed to realize I am not her friend any more than she's realized Ivy is not her girlfriend.

"It already happened," I say. "I did my own makeup."

"Of course," she says smoothly. "It looks great. Where did you go?"

"Clair de Lune."

"Oh shit, that place is nice." Dot nudges Ivy. "How come you never take me anywhere like that?" she says, and I just about choke to death on my ice cream. Seriously, who the fuck does this girl think she is? Who asks that? Who asks *Ivy* that?

Ivy somehow manages to just roll her eyes. "Because I don't date," she says, with the voice of someone who's told an overeager seventeen-year-old this many, many times. "And I don't need to pay a hundred and twenty dollars to have sex."

"We didn't have sex," I say.

Ivy says, "Ah, the other problem with dating."

"You said we weren't having sex, either," Dot points out.

"Yes." Ivy slides a spoonful of ice cream into her mouth, smiling. "And for free."

"Elizabeth's, like…amazing," I say. "She's lived all over the world. She speaks three languages."

"Hey, that's one more than you," Ivy says to Dot.

"And two more than you!" she says back.

"She was telling me all about her life and… God. I have no idea why she'd be interested in me at all."

Ivy looks at me with an eye roll. "Because you're amazing, obviously?"

I am so not about to blush in front of Dot. I will not. "Come on," I say.

Ivy ticks things off on her fingers. "You're gorgeous, you're smart, you're funny, you're a great friend, you care about your family. And I'm not feeling real great about someone making you feel like that shit doesn't matter because you haven't lived in Antarctica."

"No, it's not her," I say. "She didn't say anything like that."

Ivy shrugs, digging into her ice cream.

"Oh, what?"

"Nothing, I just think she sounds kind of…pretentious."

Here we go. "She's not pretentious," I say.

Dot says, "I think she sounds pretentious."

Shocking. "Ivy could say she sounded like she's secretly

a mermaid and you'd agree with her."

"She has good judgment," Dot says, gazing at Ivy all fucking doe-eyed.

The truth is, Ivy's always critical when I date someone. And…I mean, it's not ridiculous to think that maybe that's because she wants me for herself, right? That's not really a stretch. She probably hasn't even admitted it to herself, but someday when she's going to be ready to fix whatever it is about her that her mom or her dad or society broke and stop chasing everything that moves and actually feel something…she probably doesn't want me to be with someone else, right?

I'm not saying it's sweet of her or even something tolerable; I'm just saying, there's basis there.

But it does get kind of exhausting, so I change the subject pretty quickly after that, and then they stop paying attention to me whatsoever, because Dot mentions some weird, obscure artist Ivy likes that she'd probably Googled on the way here so Ivy would think she was interesting, when, like, when has Ivy ever cared if the girls she sleeps with are *interesting*, but okay, Dot.

I go out to the back porch to water the plants and come back inside just as my parents are getting home. They have season tickets at this rinky-dink community theater because they're both total drama geeks, and so once a month they go out to dinner and a play and they get all dressed up and excited about it every time. It's cute.

They say hi to Dot, and Dad asks her about school while Mom asks Ivy if she's taken the trash out yet (she has). Dot smiles and charms and gives cute answers to my parents' questions but before long says she should probably head out. Ivy waves with her spoon and, once

Dot gets up, brings her dishes to the sink and washes them and puts them away. She never lets them just sit in the sink like the rest of us do. I don't think she's used to having a dishwasher still.

"Sweet girl," Mom says as the door closes.

"Yeah, she is," Ivy says. "How was the play?"

"Amazing. They had a six-year-old in the cast and goddamn could that girl sing."

Dad comes over to get a glass and touches Ivy's elbow. "You should have seen the costumes."

"Oh yeah?" she says, and he starts describing them to her and she's immediately on her phone trying to find out who the designer was.

I'm tired, all of a sudden, so I slip upstairs to my room and flop down on my bed to waste some time online. There's a knock on my door a few minutes later, and my mom's there, taking off her makeup with a wipe.

"Sounds like you had a good time," I say.

"We did. And how was your evening?" As far as she knows, I stayed here and watched TV with Ivy. You can't tell my mom about a new girl too early. It just means too much to her.

"Fine."

She studies me.

"What?"

"I'm just wondering, again, if my instinct to invite Ivy to stay here wasn't the best."

"What are you talking about?"

"I don't know if having her here is good for you."

"I'm with her all the time anyway."

She gives me a hard look. "Which is the problem."

"You have a very active imagination," I say. "You

should put it to good use."

"Well, maybe I should give her some kind of... I don't know. What do you call a curfew when it's not about staying home but instead about not inviting a sex parade of young women through my foyer?"

"A sex parade?"

"I don't know what you kids call it nowadays."

"I'm used to Ivy's sex parades," I say. "This isn't news. It doesn't bother me. And I'll have you know I had a date tonight, so get ready for me to start, y'know, marshaling my own parades." Sometimes you gotta bite the bullet.

Her eyes light up. "Andrea Jean. A date?"

"Miracles happen."

"Well." She comes in and sits on the foot of the bed. "Tell me everything."

"I will tell you nothing, because you'll start picking out wedding venues."

"I'll remain calm."

I sigh deeply and say, against my better judgment, "She's a vet student."

Mom clasps her hands together.

"Oh my God, Mom."

"A doctor."

"She's not a doctor."

"A white coat. That's a doctor."

I flop backward on the bed.

"So how did it go?" she says.

"She's nice."

"And...?"

"And she's nice. And I'm going to see her again. So you don't have to make my best friend homeless to be a good mother. Ivy's never-ending ability to find new eligible lesbians is not a problem just because it's here instead of at her place."

Mom watches me.

"Nothing's changed," I insist.

She's quiet for too long, then she says, "I like Dot," with her voice very even.

"Yeah, apparently everyone likes Dot. Who knew obnoxiousness was so endearing."

She raises an eyebrow.

I laugh. "What, you think I'm jealous of Dot? Sorry to wreck yet another theory, but she just came over tonight with ice cream. They didn't even sleep together."

My mom pats my knee and stands up. "That," she says, "is exactly my point."

I get a night off work the next Friday and Elizabeth has a light day of classes, so we end up meeting at this café by the URI vet school. There's a bookstore nearby that she loves, and she's showing me secondhand copies of something by someone that are apparently really rare—I don't know, but I like the way her eyes light up and her voice gets fast when she talks about it, and I think about what she said about passion itself being more important than the subject, and I think I'm getting it now—when my phone rings.

I check the screen, and of course Elizabeth sees it, too, so of course it's Ivy, complete with the picture that pops up whenever she calls, one of the two of us looking really hot before we went out one night, making goofy sexy faces at the camera.

"One second," I say to Elizabeth. "Sorry."

"You're fine," she says.

Ivy is excited in a very undignified, very un-Ivy sort of way. "Andie. Andie."

"Um…yeah?"

"I got it."

"Got what?"

She gives this aggrieved sigh; that's more like it. "The internship."

"Ivy! Holy shit. Holy shit! I thought you weren't finding out until next week."

"Yeah, so did I. Then they called."

"Oh my God. Oh my God."

"I'm getting *paid*. I'm getting my own fucking place without your parents' sex noises through the wall or the sketchy people my mom brings home."

"Just the sketchy people you bring home."

"Exactly. I'm actually doing it. I did it."

"You're amazing." I look over at Elizabeth and say, "Hang on," then lower the phone. "Ivy got this internship she applied for."

"That's cool," Elizabeth says. "Doing what?"

"Working as a buyer at Nordstrom," I say. "She's going to help choose what they sell, what goes on display, what's on sale…everything." I shrug. "It's totally her dream job."

"I thought you said she wanted to be a designer."

"No, she used to when she was a kid, but she's way too practical." And right now she's yelling my name into the phone. "Sorry," I say to Ivy. "I'm back."

"Are you with someone?" she singsongs.

"It's fine. Sorry."

"No, no, don't apologize." She sighs theatrically. "Thing is, I was about to invite you out to Kinetic for a very special night of celebration, but I would *hate* to interrupt..."

"No, you're not..." I glance at Elizabeth and turn away from her as subtly as I can. "Of course you're not interrupting."

"Andie. Are you on a date?"

"Shut up."

"And this is how you talk to me, on the day of my internship. It's fine. The party will continue without you. Somehow I'll survive without my best friend in the world."

"God, shut the fuck up. What time?"

"Nine," she says. I can *hear* her smiling. "Think the vet will still be awake, or will she have taken her teeth out by then?"

I hang up the phone and turn back around to Elizabeth, who's leafing through a poetry book.

"Everything okay?" she says. I must look as nervous as I feel.

"So I know we were going to go to your friend's restaurant tonight—"

"We can reschedule," she says. "You want to go out with your friends; it's okay."

"Come with me," I say. Without even thinking.

I've been coming to Kinetic since I was old enough for the bouncers to at least pretend they thought I could possibly be the age on my fake ID. I know this place like I know my own house. Every nook where no one will bother you, which stall in the bathroom is tacitly agreed to be for hooking up, what drink to bring the DJ to get her to play the song you want. In high school, I brought a few girls here for the first time, mostly bi-curious ones who wanted to see what it was like, but maybe because I meet most of the meager number of girls I hook up with *here*, it's been a long, long time since I met someone who didn't know Kinetic just as well as I do.

"Seriously, *never?*" I say to Elizabeth in the car.

"Never."

"You've never been to Kinetic. Not even when you were in college? It's practically all college kids."

"I'm really not a club person."

"I know, but I figured you discovered that by going to clubs."

"I know what clubs are like; I've seen *Euphoria.* Where the hell do I park?"

We park, finally, and make the hike to the club, which is simultaneously more and less annoying than usual— less because I'm not in my club clothes and therefore not wearing heels, more because I haven't pregamed and therefore am not drunk—and show our IDs and sweep into Kinetic along with a pair of very nervous-looking boys.

Elizabeth looks around without saying anything, and I'm suddenly so self-conscious of this place, like it's mine or something. I'm embarrassed by the pink lights around the drink specials and the way-too-young guys making out on a pillar next to us, like I put them there.

It's stupid, because it's not like she's insulting it, but I guess some part of me remembered the first time Ivy and I came here and we looked around like Dorothy entering the Emerald City. I wanted Elizabeth to be enchanted by this dirty, magical little place.

But it's fine.

I point to the bar. "Those are my friends."

Melody and Diana are making out against the bar while Ivy laughs at something Alyssa says, a glass hanging carelessly from her hand. She's done a good job replenishing her wardrobe since the fire, and she's wearing these incredible spike heels we found for eighteen dollars at Sloan's. Her hair's teased up and her eye makeup is kind of smudged heroin-chic to match, and I suddenly very, very much regret bringing the girl I'm dating to see the two of us together when I'm in jeans and sneakers. What the fuck was I thinking? Girls have come with me and left with Ivy over a lot less.

God, she looks beautiful.

Ivy sees me and holds her arms up like *ta-da*, and I go over and hug her. "You're incredible," I say.

She grins and sips her drink. "And someone besides you finally sees it." She studies Elizabeth over the rim of the glass.

"Hi," Alyssa says, and I hug her, too.

"This is Alyssa," I say to Elizabeth. "She's basically our moral compass."

"Which means I spend a lot of time roasting Ivy," Alyssa says.

I say, "Well, someone has to." And Lord knows it won't be me. "And that's Diana and Melody, if they ever come up for air. And this is Ivy."

Ivy offers her hand limply, and the dread in my stomach gathers some additional force.

"Congratulations," Elizabeth says to her.

"Hmm." Ivy slings her arm around my neck. "To you, too. Andie's amazing, isn't she?"

"Cut it out," I say, batting her off.

Ivy sighs. "Just doing my job."

"Where's the president of your fan club tonight?" I ask her, to change the subject.

"Who?"

Elizabeth orders a glass of wine, which makes Ivy stifle a snort of laughter into her wrist, and I chew on my thumbnail and shake my head when Elizabeth asks what I want, because suddenly anything seems like taking sides. Ivy finishes her whiskey and smoothly buys a drink for a hot girl who's come up next to us and strikes up a conversation, her back to the rest of us, and Elizabeth raises her eyebrows at me.

"Yeah, she comes here for business, not pleasure," I say. "Or I guess, business and pleasure."

"I've heard you're not supposed to mix them."

"It's working okay for her."

"God, I can't hear anything in here." She slips her arm around my waist, and my heart flutters.

"Do you want to dance?" I ask her, but before she can answer, Melody and Diana split apart and they're all over us like I've never dated anyone before, but it's cute how excited they are and they're being sweet. Alyssa's being nice, too, asking Elizabeth questions about vet school and complimenting her jean jacket. Coming from anyone else, I might think she was being flirty, but this is just Alyssa. Honest and unafraid. I think that's what scares girls off, honestly. Lesbians aren't known for being straightforward when they like each other. Alyssa will tell you unprompted.

Ivy's still talking to the hot girl. And Elizabeth keeps

glancing at her and then back to me. I should have known Ivy would take the opportunity to be extra bratty, extra her, but part of me thought she'd be on her best behavior for meeting my girlfriend for the first time. Part of me is deluded.

Her concentration does finally get broken, though, but not because of Elizabeth. We've only been here for a blessed twenty uninterrupted minutes when in comes: you guessed it.

Dot saunters right up to our group and leans across the bar with a smile. Her hair's blown out and wavy and she has on the tightest, tiniest jeans I've ever seen. "Whiskey lemonade?" she says.

"The fuck are you doing here?" Ivy drawls. "I thought you had basketball practice."

Melody laughs a little and gives Dot a hug. A hug, like they're friends! They've only met, like, five times, on nights when Dot pops up just like this. Jesus Christ. "Basketball?" Melody says, sizing Dot up, or what there is of her.

"It's a small school," she says. "They take what they can get." She turns back to Ivy. "And that ended hours ago."

"Mmm," Ivy says.

Dot tilts her head, looking at Elizabeth. I roll my eyes. "Elizabeth, Dot," I say. "Dot, Elizabeth."

"You weren't kidding about them not checking those IDs carefully, huh?" Elizabeth says.

"No one comes to clubs like this after they're actually twenty-one," Dot says, like she's some sort of expert, and twenty-two-year-old Elizabeth and I exchange looks.

"Dot's very enthusiastic about Ivy," I explain.

"Yeah." Elizabeth raises her drink a bit, toward Ivy. "Who isn't?"

Ivy shows her teeth in something like a smile.

Alyssa tugs on my arm and shows me some texts from this girl she's been pursuing. This girl is so not interested. Honey.

"Oh shit," Diana says. She grabs Melody's arm and points her chin toward the door. "She's here."

Dot says, "Ooh, who?"

"This girl Diana's obsessed with," Melody says.

"Oooh, yeah," Dot says. "I've seen her before."

"She's in my hot yoga class," Diana says. "She is…very bendy."

"So you've got an opening!" Melody nudges her. "Go see if she can help you downward dog."

Diana whines.

"Oh my God, I am not going home with you again and listening to you lament that you didn't go for it. *Again.*" Melody kisses her. "Go have fun."

"Getting rejected is not fun."

"You sound like me," Alyssa says.

"Oof. That'll get me off my ass," Diana says, and she heads over to the hot-yoga girl while Alyssa tries to make her pouting look ironic. I give her a squeeze around the waist.

"I'm confused," Elizabeth says.

"About what?" Ivy looks after Diana. "Damn. Hot yoga is right." Dot flicks her, and Ivy knocks her hand away without looking at her.

Elizabeth turns to Melody. "Aren't you two together?"

"Yeah! For years."

"But she…"

Melody shrugs. "Well, yeah. We're open," she says, like it's the most obvious thing in the world.

"Wow," Elizabeth says. "That's…very bold of you."

Ivy's finally found something that interests her. "I'm sorry," she says. "Are you surprised by non-monogamy? At a queer club?"

"I don't like that word, first of all," Elizabeth says.

Ivy laughs. "Oh my God."

"But yeah, I think the goal eventually is to find a person who you want at the exclusion of anyone else. There's a reason that's been the standard for centuries."

"Yeah," Ivy says. "And the reason is straight people."

"Gay people are just as capable of committed, loving relationships as straight people," Elizabeth says.

"Amen," Alyssa says.

"I'm capable of jumping off a bridge," Ivy says. "Doesn't mean I should."

"Isn't the point that we can be as good as straight people?" Elizabeth says.

Ivy looks at her like she's an unfamiliar species. "No," she says, nice and slowly. "The point is that we're *better* than straight people."

"And not being monogamous is better," Elizabeth says.

"Yeah. Than just about anything."

I know I should step in here, because Elizabeth and Ivy are looking at each other like they're about to spring on each other wild-animal style, but that would require having some idea of whose side I'm on—I don't love everything Elizabeth's implying, and objecting to the word "queer" feels very…dated, but I'm not with Ivy on her staunch brigade against monogamy, either. Dot, of all people, catches my eye, and she looks…sympathetic? She's probably just sad at yet another reminder that she's never going to be Ivy's one and only. Not that I need one of Ivy's hookups feeling bad for me, yikes.

Luckily I'm saved from having to think of anything to say, because Melody checks her phone and grabs me by the sleeve. "Niya's doing it," she says.

My stomach goes cold. "She's not."

"She is. Says she's doing it right now."

Shit. *Shit.* Niya's easily the most popular dancer we have, brings in the closest thing we have to crowds every time she's in, and she's been cutting back her hours more and more each month to take more shifts at other clubs that bring in more money. And she keeps saying she's going to leave for good.

We cannot lose her.

"You need to get down there," Melody says. I'm Niya's favorite and she's told me a bunch of times I'm the only reason she's stayed as long as she has. "You gotta do something."

"Like what, write her a fucking check? There's nothing I can do." But of course I have to try. I turn to Elizabeth and wrap two fingers around her wrist. "I have to go."

"What's up?"

"Strip club crisis," I say. "I can take an Uber—"

"No, I can bring you," Elizabeth says, which is sweet but also I kind of expected it, because it doesn't exactly seem like she's hitting it off with my friends. Still, she tells everyone it was nice meeting them and Ivy shakes her hand again, even more limply than before. I shoot Ivy a look to show her how very much I don't appreciate how firmly she did not stay on her best behavior, but she just smiles at me. I feel kind of bad for bailing on her celebration, but hey, getting in a fight with someone about monogamy has got to be one of Ivy's top five ways to commemorate an occasion.

The streets are loud and we're walking fast, so I'm saved from having to talk until after we pull out of the parking lot. At which point Elizabeth immediately says, "So."

"I don't know why I thought this was a good idea," I say.

She glances at me. "What was a good idea?"

"You meeting my friends."

"Hey." She puts her fingers around my wrist, like I did back in the club. "I like your friends."

"Oh, bullshit. You and Ivy were about to have a duel."

Elizabeth's quiet for a minute, then says softly, "She's protective of you," which is not what I was expecting.

So I laugh. "What?"

"Ivy. She was being...possessive, I guess."

I squirm. "We've been best friends for, like, ever."

"You're sure that's it?"

"What? Come on."

"The way she looks at you..."

"Ivy Harlowe is not interested in me," I say. "Trust me."

"But you want her to be," Elizabeth says.

I can feel my heartbeat in my ears. "This is ridiculous," I say. "I'm with you."

She nods a little, staring straight through the windshield, and I put my hand over hers on the gearshift.

"For the record," I say. "I'm not on the same page as her. About the monogamy stuff. I'm not, like, completely against it."

"So, uh, what page are you on, exactly?"

"I've never really had to think about it," I admit. "I've never really—"

And Elizabeth just takes that and says, "Okay. We'll go

slow." Like it's the easiest thing in the world.

She doesn't need to know what I think right away. She doesn't demand a quick, snappy answer. We can just sit here, in her car, and be unsure together.

The radio switches to a new song, and her fingers move under mine a little.

And for just a minute, I'm not thinking about Ivy at all.

I tell Elizabeth not to wait—I don't know how long this will be, and I'll just make Max bring me home—and as soon as I walk in the front door, I run into Niya. She's got her big faux-fur coat on and a cardboard box with her makeup bag and some outfits inside. She's older than most of our girls, but it doesn't matter. She has the it factor.

"I'm sorry, pumpkin," she says to me.

"At least weeknights. Something."

"I can't."

"You said we were like home."

"The tips aren't coming in, angel," she says. "People aren't coming here anymore."

"We're going to turn it around," I say. "But we need you. We can't do it without you."

Losing her means losing the club. It means losing my family's everything. I can't think about what that would do to my parents. My dad.

I don't even know what I would do.

She sighs and puts her hand on my cheek.

"I'm not a fairy godmother," she says. "You have to rescue yourself."

But I don't know how.

I never have, really.

I walk to the back office in a daze. I can hear Catherine and Max arguing before I've even reached the closed door.

"We're not changing the whole fucking spirit of this place," Catherine's saying.

"For this place to even have a spirit, it needs to exist, and at this rate—"

"I'm not working at some fucking Girl Dungeon knockoff! That is not what I signed up for! That's not what any of us signed up for!"

"Without Niya—"

"She's *one* girl!"

"It's not just—"

"Just because she's the one you were fucking doesn't mean she's God's gift to strippers, Max!"

Oh.

Whoa.

I can't make out words after that, just their quiet voices. They both sound pretty calm now. Max is being soothing, but Catherine doesn't sound like nearly what my romance novels have taught me is an appropriate amount of dramatic for these situations. I'm guessing Max sleeping with Niya is news only to me.

I watch the clock on my phone for three minutes before I knock. Catherine opens the door. She doesn't look like she's been crying. Her blonde hair is pulled back in a clip, and she's wearing a T-shirt with our logo on it. My grandmother designed it.

She says, "Honey, you're off tonight. Go home."

"I was out with Melody. Niya texted her."

Catherine sighs. "Yeah."

Max is sitting at the desk, his tie loose and his chin in his hand. "Hey, Andie."

I have no idea what to say to him. He's my brother, but I love Catherine. And I thought I loved Niya.

So I just say, "I want to take the books home. Try to figure out where we can make cuts to keep our doors open."

"That's not your responsibility," Max says.

"It's *our* responsibility. Gimme the books. I'll run my ideas past Dad."

He opens the top drawer of his desk. "And me."

"Fine."

I don't really want to wait for Max to bring me home anymore, so I walk to a coffee shop nearby and sit there and pore over the numbers for a while, doing calculations on my phone and writing notes on napkins. Once they start to close, I pack everything up and walk to the bus stop. The house is dark when I get home and set myself up at the kitchen table with some coffee and my laptop. My parents go to sleep early, and Ivy's either still out or already in bed.

Turns out it's the second one. At around one a.m., I hear footsteps coming down the stairs and into the kitchen. It's Dot, wearing one of Max's T-shirts and nothing else. "Hi," she says, pulling it lower on her legs.

I roll my eyes and turn back to the books.

"You know, at some point you're going to start liking me," she says. "You won't even notice it's happening and then poof."

I so don't have time for this right now. But I can't help myself. "Is that how it worked with Ivy?"

"Ivy always liked me."

It's extremely annoying that at this point I don't know

if I can argue with that. God, what is Ivy doing bringing her back here over and over? What the fuck kind of alternate dimension is this where a girl Ivy's slept with multiple times comes down the stairs in the middle of the night in my brother's clothes and I don't even find it surprising?

"What are you doing here?" I ask her.

"Hungry," she says, I guess assuming that I meant here in the kitchen. She crosses the room and opens the fridge like it's hers. "What about you?"

"Work."

"Wow. I hope they pay you overtime for this."

"Not really how it works."

"Hhhhhow come?"

How did I get roped into a conversation with this girl in the middle of the goddamn night? "It's the family business," I say. *Or it was*, my mind supplies darkly. Thanks. "It doesn't really have hours."

"Wow," Dot says again. "You're, like, a really good daughter."

"Mmm."

"Seriously. Your family's really lucky to have you. You're like my brothers. They really want to work our family business, which is awesome for my parents. And them. And me, since I don't want to."

"Not everyone gets to do the work they want to do," I say. "That's not life."

"Well, yeah, you have to do other stuff on the way, but that should be the goal, right? Like, I'm going to do makeup, Ivy's gonna do fashion merchandising, and you're going to keep the strip club going."

Does this girl honestly think it's my dream in life to run a failing strip club, or is she fucking with me? I think

I'd have more license to be offended if I had any idea what my dream in life *was*. So I just say, "Fashion merchandising wasn't even Ivy's dream. You have no idea what you're talking about."

"She says it's her dream," Dot says defensively.

"She wanted to be a designer, but she knew it was stupid, so she's doing merchandising instead. That's what grown-ups do. We compromise."

"Ooh, there's ice cream left," Dot says, and I roll my eyes and turn back to the books.

Dot's getting out a bowl when Ivy appears in the doorway to the kitchen, half asleep, with her hair an absolute mess. She yawns and says, "Where'd you go?" to Dot.

She holds up the ice cream carton. "Want some?" she says, and Ivy nods and drags herself to the kitchen table and slumps over it.

"Long night, dear?" I say.

"Mm-hmm."

"You know you were a complete asshole to Elizabeth, so thanks for that."

Ivy shrugs. "Trial by fire. Gotta see if she's good enough for my girl."

"Oh, that's what that was?"

She grins. "Can you prove it wasn't?"

I can't stay mad at her. "I hate you, you know that?"

"I know. So what'd she say about me?" Ivy turns around in her chair and says, "Spot, is there chocolate sauce?"

"I'll check," Dot says.

"She says you're protective of me."

"You're damn right," Ivy says, and she gnashes her teeth, and I smile even though I don't want to.

Dot comes to the table with ice cream and chocolate sauce. I didn't want any, but I'm still annoyed that she didn't at least ask me. Though I guess it's technically her ice cream.

"You never told me you used to want to be a fashion designer," she says to Ivy.

Ivy waves her hand carelessly. "I haven't told you all sorts of things."

"I remember one of your friends saying you almost went to RISD."

"Apparel design program," Ivy says. "And almost went is a stretch."

"Did you get in?" Dot says.

Ivy looks at her for a long second, then says, "Yes."

Hang on. "Wait," I say. "I thought you didn't apply."

Ivy shrugs and digs into her ice cream. "Didn't seem worth mentioning. They didn't offer money. Was never going to work."

"So you just don't design anymore?" Dot says.

"It's not like some policy. I'm just busy. School. Now this internship." She licks her spoon. "Sex."

"Yeah." Dot leans over and kisses her cheek. "I've noticed."

Ivy rolls her eyes. "Get off me."

Enough. Enough learning shit about my best friend because I overhear her telling some girl she barely knows. Enough of this. I gather up my shit. "I'm going to move this upstairs."

"We're leaving soon," Dot says. "Going to sleep."

"Or something like that," Ivy says.

Dot nudges her. "You have school in the morning."

"So do you."

I leave them to work out that little conundrum on their own and go up to my room and shut the door.

Why the hell didn't she tell me she applied to RISD?

Why the hell did she tell *Dot*?

I stare at the strip club financial records strewn over my bed and try to imagine someone thinking this is my passion. Try to imagine doing this forever.

There's only one thing I've ever thought about when I thought about forever, and she's downstairs making eyes at a high schooler who thinks everyone can be a fucking artist.

I know I should get back to work, but instead I open my laptop and go to YouTube. I type "Dot makeup" into the search bar and after a lot of weird polka-dot eyeliner tutorials, I finally scroll down enough to her. "Dot Does Makeup." How clever.

She has eight thousand subscribers, and some of her videos have more than a hundred thousand views. The most popular one is about doing a cat-eye when you don't have a lot of lid space. I have lids for days but still no idea how to do a cat-eye, so what the hell. I turn it on, making sure the volume is low as hell—the last thing I need is them coming upstairs and overhearing—and get my makeup from my desk and kneel down in front of my mirror.

Her lighting and camera look really nice. She's just filming in her room, but it still looks professional. She's bare-faced and smiley, her hair up in some intricate braided bun I could never do.

"Hi, hi, what's up; it's your girl Dot! So I wanted to make this video because I know a lot of people have trouble with cat-eyes if you have hooded eyelids or if you have monolids, so let's get right into this and before you know it, you'll have this down, okay?"

She goes through the products she's using, pulling each one out of a silver metal case, and I find some version of them in my stained makeup bag. She zooms in close to her eye and goes over the cat-eye step by step, lining her top lid nice and slowly.

I mess it up immediately, wipe my eye off, rewind the video, try again.

And again.

And again.

Dot beams at me from my screen, showing off her knife-sharp wings, and I throw my eyeliner across the floor.

November

On a very dreary Thursday, the second week of November, I'm trying to head home after a morning restocking a strip club that is blessedly still open and my fucking car won't start. God, this thing is such a piece of shit. My parents used to pick me up from kindergarten in it. I'm amazed it still has all its doors.

My mom's at work and my dad's at home, but since I have the only car, I call Ivy. "Where are you?"

"On my way home from school," she says. It's about a thirty-minute drive each way for her, but she doesn't have afternoon classes on Thursdays, so she usually comes home and marathons *Project Runway* on the couch. A model roommate.

"Can you pick me up? I'm at the club and this damn thing won't start."

"Which club?"

"It's three in the afternoon—what club do you think?"

"Okay, but I…" She sounds funny. Nervous.

"You what?"

"Nothing," she says. "I just have this thing I'm supposed to do."

"Pick me up first, I'm freezing my fucking tits off and if I go back inside, they're going to make me work the front desk."

She laughs. "Not with no tits, they're not."

"Get over here."

Ivy pulls up about ten minutes later, right before I'm about to give up and wait it out inside. I hurry into her passenger seat and blow on my hands. "Thank you. I love you."

"I know, I know." She still seems weird. She's flicking the windshield wipers on and off even though it's not raining, and she keeps checking the rearview mirror.

"Are we on the run?" I say.

She pulls out of the parking lot. "Yes, always."

"That's exciting."

"I just have an errand. It's not a big deal."

"Where is it?" I ask.

She doesn't answer me, just turns the music up louder. Whatever. She's probably just being antsy about bringing me to pick up some E or something. It's sweet. She plays the shit we used to rock out to when we were in high school, which is fun, but before I know it we're pulling up...at a high school.

No goddamn way.

"You're kidding me," I say.

Ivy puts on a pair of sunglasses. "Whatever."

It's a freaking Catholic school, all girls from the looks of it, and they're in these plaid uniforms, giggling and chatting on their way out of the building. I watch one girl drop all her books and lose a bunch of papers in the wind.

"I can't believe this," I say.

It hasn't escaped me that Ivy knew exactly how to get here and where to park. Which means this is not her first time here. I briefly allow myself the hope that this isn't Dot's school, and Ivy is just here trolling for a fresh seventeen-year-old. What a dire world where *that's* the nicer option.

I look at Ivy as she rakes her fingers through her hair to push it back. She's like a goddamn movie star in those sunglasses and her black T-shirt dress and leather jacket. She is not supposed to be picking anyone up at school. *Waiting* for someone. Ivy doesn't wait for people. People wait for Ivy.

At least we're not waiting very long. Dot comes up to the car with a giggly friend with blonde hair and freckles.

"Hi, Ivy," the girl says.

"Hey."

Dot opens the door to the back seat and climbs in. At least she didn't try to get me to move. "Text me those Lit notes, okay?" she says to her friend. "Hi, Andie."

"I told you I would," her friend says.

"You're the best." Dot leans to the front seat and smacks Ivy's cheek. "Hey, nerd."

"I'm not the one who wants Lit notes," Ivy says. "Can we get out of here, please? Catholics give me the willies."

"Maybe you should stop fucking one, then," Dot says, poking her in the shoulder.

"Maybe I should."

"Yes, please, let's get out of here," I say, and Ivy sticks her tongue out at me, blows a kiss to Dot's little friend, and starts the car.

"This is like the fucking Twilight Zone," I mumble to myself. Not quietly enough.

"Oh, relax," Ivy says. "She needed a ride. Some of us have functioning cars and have to give people rides. My burden to bear."

"Yeah, yeah, I get the point."

Dot leans forward between us and waves her phone at Ivy. "Did you see this?"

Ivy spares the phone a glance as she drives. "How many views?"

"Hundred and six thousand. I am so close to getting sponsorships." She puts her phone down and turns to me, all bouncy. Like always. "How's life? Did your car break down?"

Her backpack spills onto the floor and a bunch of watercolor paintings fall out, and I see a few as she slips them back in. Ballerinas, robots, a ship hitting an iceberg. They're…really good. I'm surprised and pissed. Suddenly her RISD dreams make a lot more sense, and I'd rather they stayed ridiculous, like everything else about her.

"Life's fine," I say.

"How's Elizabeth?"

Ivy says, "Ugh, are you still dating her?" before I can respond, even though she knows very well that I am. I showed her this funny meme Elizabeth texted me at dinner last night, and my mom was charmed because of her obsession with the mystique of Elizabeth or me having a love life, period, and Ivy thought it was amusing until she found out who'd sent it and then claimed she thought it was boring the whole time.

"Elizabeth is great," I say to Dot. "Thank you for asking."

"Quick question," Ivy says. "Is she still a nun?"

"Believing in monogamy does not make you a nun," I say.

She flicks on the turn signal. "You're right. It's worse than being a nun. It's being a heterosexual."

"Quick question," Dot says to her. "Do you ever get

tired of being a complete and total gay stereotype from the nineties?"

"The fuck do you know about the nineties?" Ivy grumbles, as if we know anything, either, while I perform an act of charity and shoot Dot a look that's hopefully conveying that you do *not* do that. It's just better for everyone not to argue with Ivy. She's never going to change her mind. Just don't give her any ammo and eventually she gets bored.

Dot doesn't catch on. "What's wrong with monogamy for people who want it?" she says. "I'm not saying it's for everyone, but you're really saying no one can make it work?"

Ivy adjusts the rearview mirror. "Exactly. No one can make it work. People make promises they can't keep and end up hurting each other. It's a bad situation. And queers don't need to put themselves into bad situations. We already have our families."

"I think people can make it work if it's what they really want," Dot says. "I mean, it's not for me, but follow your bliss or whatever."

"They all fucking cheat," Ivy says. "Look at my parents."

I glance at her.

"But look at Andie's parents," Dot counters.

"They've been together for, like, thirty years," Ivy says. "Trust me, one of them's cheated at some point."

I think about Max and Niya and don't say anything. How can I pretend I really know what's going on in anyone's relationship after that?

Dot sighs like a Disney princess. "I love your parents," she says to me.

"I'm aware." If she weren't so blatantly obsessed with

Ivy, I'd think she was only dating her to get to my parents.

Christ, *dating*? I try to picture Ivy's face if I'd accidentally said that out loud and nearly burst out laughing. They're sleeping together, not taking midnight walks along the river.

"Her mom was asking about you," Ivy says to her. At breakfast this morning. *So, Ivy, how's Dot?* My mom thinks annoying me is a sport.

"Oh my God, she was?"

"Wants to know how your psych test went."

"Well, then I'll have to give her all the exciting details. Are we going out tonight? I want to dance."

"I have homework," Ivy says, pulling to a stop at a red light. "You have homework." There's this amazing blue convertible next to us. The top's up, but I can picture myself in it anyway, hair down, beach-bound, Ivy riding shotgun. Singing to those same songs and this time not stopping.

"There will be more homework tomorrow," Dot says. "I'm not attached to this particular homework." She pokes me.

There is no Dot in the beach fantasy. "Ow."

"Let's go out."

I briefly imagine a night out, just Dot and me. It sounds like a sitcom episode. Luckily, "I can't," I say. "I promised my parents I'd help them make this shrimp thing."

"Oh no," Ivy groans.

"Oh my God, what shrimp thing?" Dot says. "Where did they get the shrimp from? You have fresh, right?"

"You can't mention shrimp around her," Ivy says. "She's like Bubba Gump incarnate."

"Bubba Gump was two people," Dot says.

"Yeah, well, you would know."

"What are they making?" Dot says to me. "I can help. I've been cooking shrimp since I was three."

"Shrimp fra diavolo."

"Ah! Yes. Delicious. I know a trick! Let me help."

"I thought we were bringing you home," I say with a sideways glance at Ivy, who just shrugs a little.

"Nooooo thank you," Dot says, collapsing back in her seat. "I cannot go home. I have this assignment that's just… staring at me. I can't."

"You still haven't started that Bio thing?" Ivy says.

"I don't even understand what the assignment is, and I think if I send the teacher one more email asking him, he's going to hire someone to murder me. My real AP Bio teacher is on maternity leave," she says to me. "And they replaced her with this guy who I think is trying to get us to fail the AP. I think it's like that guy in Willy Wonka who wanted the kids to take the jawbreaker thing."

"When is it due?" Ivy says.

"Monday. And now we need to stop talking about it, because if I think about it for another second, I'm going to have a nervous breakdown."

"Hmm," is all Ivy says.

We get home, and Ivy settles down on the couch while Dot grabs a banana from the kitchen. "When does your mom get home?" Ivy asks me.

"Eight. Why? It's not like she cares if you fuck her while she's in the house. I think proximity to queer shit is how she replenishes her energy."

"I was just wondering," Ivy says. "Is there a rule against wondering?" Her eyes follow Dot as she comes back into the living room.

"Wonder away," I say, then I head up to my room before they start making out.

Ivy has school the next morning, and I have work, so I barely see her until the next evening, when she throws my keys at me when I get home and says it's time to drink, so we head out to Mama's. Diana, Melody, and Alyssa are already there, amped up for the weekend, and after a few drinks, Alyssa asks if we're headed to Kinetic after this. "Is Dot meeting us?" she asks.

Ivy doesn't volunteer an answer, just picks up the drink menu like it might have changed sometime in the past two minutes, or in fact in the last three years, so I say, "I think she's working on this thing for school."

"God," Diana says. "You could not pay me to go back to high school."

"What subject?" Alyssa asks Ivy. She's one of the freaks who liked high school.

Ivy shrugs and says, "How the fuck should I know?" Which is weird, because I know that she knows. But she's acting strange tonight, checking her phone all the time, playing the disinterested act even harder than she usually does. She puts down the drink menu and heads to the bar.

The girls raise some eyebrows.

"I told you," Diana says to Melody. "Didn't I say this? You ask her something casual about Dot and she acts like you're trying to talk to her about china patterns for the wedding."

I roll my eyes. "They are so not in a relationship."

"Come on," Diana says. "They're not *not* in a relation-ship."

"You're ridiculous," I say.

Melody jumps in all peacekeeper and says, "They have been spending a lot of time together. Dot's here half the time we are, and half that time they go home together. Let's at least admit that they're friends, which is odd enough for Ivy."

I can't remember the last time Ivy made a friend. She has me and the friends she's met through me. She just doesn't need people.

"I don't think they do much talking," I say. "And why are we talking about Dot when we finally have a night without her? We could just sit and enjoy the quiet."

"Why are you so bitchy about her?" Diana says. "She's sweet."

Melody gives her a look.

"Ohhhh," Diana says. "That."

"She's annoying," I say.

"Yeah. Sure." Diana chuckles and drinks. "It's because she's annoying. That's definitely why you've got a bone to pick with Ivy's sex partner of choice."

"She's choosing plenty of other girls, too," I say.

"And I still think Ivy gives a shit about her," Diana says. "As much as Ivy's capable of giving a shit about anyone."

"Besides Andie," Alyssa says, and my stomach flip-flops.

"Well, of course," Diana says, like it's nothing. "Obviously besides Andie."

Ivy comes back with her drink, which she tosses back quickly before planting the glass upside down on the table. "Let's get out of here. I want to dance."

Now that we're done with the talking portion of the

evening, we pay our tab and head over to Kinetic, where we dance as a writhing group for a while, pushing and pulling off a horde of giggly gay guys who can't keep their hands off us, grinding on each other and screaming to the music and generally being us. Ivy gives me a short, sloppy kiss before she goes off with a Black girl in a gold dress, and we watch her hump her damn leg like no one named Dot has ever existed. So much for those feelings, hmm?

Ivy Harlowe is not your girlfriend, and she is never, ever going to care more about you than she cares about herself.

Unless, of course, you're me.

I spend the next day with my dad, taking the car to the shop and then going over ideas for the club, trying not to panic right along with him about how we're losing money like it's our goal, and the evening working and Sunday with Elizabeth.

We go to this little café we've been through a few times now that has this incredible pain au chocolat. She's always introducing me to shit like that. It's amazing. She kisses me under a lamppost and maybe it's that, or maybe it's the fact that my dad is visiting his brother and my mom has been in the basement the entire day working on some project with no sign of emerging, but I say, "Do you want to see my house?"

Maybe it's that it's been nine thousand years since I've had sex, but let's not be crude.

It's not until I have her up in my room, the muted music Ivy's listening to beating faintly through the walls — she's been quiet lately, holed up in there more often than not — that I remember all the fucking romance novels.

My room is sort of a shrine to them. I have two big bookshelves, and there are some textbooks and yearbooks and a bit of assigned reading from high school and framed photos and small stuffed animals and all the other random kind of shit that accumulates on bookshelves, but most of it is my meticulously organized romance novels, sorted by author and then by title. Nowadays I mostly do ebooks on my phone, but back in the day I used to love collecting the paperbacks, and I still love going over to the shelf and pulling out a favorite and curling up in bed. It makes me so, so happy.

And right now, so, so embarrassed, and I am hoping to God that Elizabeth at least doesn't remember me steadfastly denying reading them on our first date.

Elizabeth walks past them slowly, like they're a museum exhibit. "Wow," she says with a small laugh.

"Mmm. Yeah."

She smiles at me. "Romance fan?"

"Yeah, you know."

"It's a good guilty pleasure," she says. "You should see how many true-crime shows I have on my Netflix queue. Yours is much more wholesome."

I don't really know how I feel about calling my favorite thing in the world a guilty pleasure, but she's smiling at me, so I'm not really caring all that much. She really has such a beautiful smile.

And then she's coming toward me, resting her lips on my neck, and it's hard to think about anything else.

"You're sweet," she says softly between kisses. "You feel things."

I can still hear Ivy's music leaking through the walls. "Maybe too many," I whisper.

She shakes her head. "No such thing. I'll show you."

Her fingers travel under the hem of my shirt, and she kisses me, backing me up until my legs hit my bed, and I lay down and bring her with me. I toe my shoes off and snake one foot up her back, and we move in a hurry, undoing bra clasps, squirming out of jeans.

Her mouth finds my collarbone, and she blows cool air against my skin between bites, like she's soothing me. I put one hand in my hair and cover my eyes with the other.

Her fingers slip inside me.

Finally. Finally. I close my eyes and move to the music.

Elizabeth and I are still lying in bed together and my legs are still shaking a little and I'm still feeling floaty and giggly when I hear my mom's voice in the kitchen. Which is very much not the basement. I sit up. "Shit."

Elizabeth laughs a little. "Not ready for your mom to meet me?"

Eek. "No, I'm not ready for you to meet her. She's…a lot. I think you might like me. Let's not ruin that in five minutes. How are you with climbing out windows?"

She laughs like I'm joking, even though I'm not sure I am. "Not amazing, but I am good at sneaking away unnoticed. Come cover for me and I'll slip out."

"Ugh, it's no use; she's seen your car. She's probably

waiting downstairs to ambush us." I get up and start getting dressed, trying to mentally will my mom in advance to chill the hell out. My parents get way too excited when I bring someone home. They'll wait at the door like puppies. "Are you feeling brave?"

"Always," she says.

"Yeah, we'll see. My mother will probably ask you some wildly inappropriate question about your income or your sexual history."

"Prepared to answer either."

"And my dad will just sit there and laugh, because after all these years, he still thinks she's charming."

"That's just cute."

"There might be cake."

"Oh, I can be very brave for cake."

So we get dressed and take a deep breath and I hope to God this isn't the last moment I'll be able to look Elizabeth in the eye, and we head downstairs, but... there's no ambush. My mom doesn't even come out of the kitchen. Elizabeth and I shrug at each other at the front door and she gives me a quick kiss, and then she's gone, and I wander into the kitchen because I'm curious what body snatcher has replaced my mom. And if there's cake.

And there's my mom, washing some kind of craft goo off her hands, chatting away with...Dot. They stop and look at me when I come in.

"Uh, hi?" I say.

"Hi!" Dot says brightly.

"Hi..." I look at my mom. "Can I talk to you?"

Mom and Dot exchange looks like they're trying not to laugh, and yeah, that's not how this is going to work.

It's suddenly very important that I go to the garage

and get my laundry out of the dryer. I've barely started unloading it when my mom comes in, shutting the door behind her.

"You know, I just spent the last three hours trying to convince her you're not a monster," she says. "You could try assisting me with that."

"What the fuck is she doing here!"

"I've been helping her with her biology project," Mom says.

"You've been helping Ivy's little fling. In my house?"

"I'm sorry, do you pay the mortgage here?"

"Mom."

"The girl needed help. And she's sweet, Andrea."

"God! Why do you have to interfere in *everything*?"

She laughs and puts her hands on her hips. "Oh, trust me, if I was interfering in *everything*, you'd know."

"The fuck is that supposed to mean?"

"It means that I know exactly what you're upset about and it's not me interfering."

So I say, "You know, Ivy's not going to love this, either. You being all buddy-buddy with this girl. She's already pissed that people think she's in some kind of relationship. You're just causing drama she's going to hate."

"Oh yes, Ivy is definitely very low-key. That adds up."

I finish with the laundry and head upstairs with the basket, steadfastly avoiding the kitchen. And Mom follows me.

Ivy's door is open, and she's sitting on the edge of her bed, looking out into the hallway. She's in a pair of silk pajamas, no makeup, brushing out her hair, and God, she's like a princess. I can't even look at her. I go into my room to put the laundry away, but Mom stays in the hall, halfway between our doorways.

"The project's going well, by the way," my mother says. "We spent three hours making enzymes out of Model Magic. She's going to be fine."

"Well, that's great," I say, and honestly, at this point even I can't tell if I'm being sarcastic or not. It's not like I want Dot to fail Biology. I would just like her to not fail Biology somewhere other than where I live. But I come out of my room to give Ivy a dress that got mixed in with my stuff, just in time to see her mouth *thank you* to my mother.

And it all falls into place, and I feel simultaneously stupid and angry and…something else I can't identify, but it doesn't feel right.

I shoot my mom a look to tell her she better fucking follow me and go into my room. Thank God she listens to me this time.

"Ivy asked you to do it, didn't she," I say.

My mom crosses her arms.

I hate this, I hate this, I hate this. "Jesus Christ! She asked you to help Dot with her damn homework? She asked you? *Why?*"

"She thought I was the best person for the job. I don't know if you've noticed, but I'm a nurse."

"Not *that*," I say. "Why did she ask *anyone*?"

My mom shakes her head and says, "Andie," like she feels sorry for me. And I feel it like a punch in the stomach.

"God!" I say. "Fuck! Her?" This cannot be happening. "She's the one who's going to make Ivy feel something? *Her?*"

"Honey," my mother says gently. "Why not her?"

"Because she's annoying as hell! She's this airheaded,

intrusive kid; she has an ego that rivals *Ivy's*, because…
she's irritating, she's too young, she thinks she knows
everything, because—"

"Because she's not you?" Mom says.

I sit down on the edge of the bed where an hour ago
I was having sex with a completely unrelated girl. I am
maybe not a great person.

But it's not that I want Ivy and not Elizabeth. It's just…

This is not how the story is supposed to go.

That's that feeling I can't sort out. It's that something
is inherently *wrong* here, that things aren't happening the
way they're supposed to. That all of a sudden there are all
these people complicating what was supposed to be me
and Ivy's story, and it doesn't…it doesn't feel right.

Sex with Elizabeth felt great, but also like a
transgression. Like a betrayal to a relationship that doesn't
even exist.

And this, Ivy reaching out, this is like another level. Ivy
might be convinced sex isn't serious, but I don't think even
she could pretend *this* is meaningless.

"Can I go back now?" my mother says.

"Yeah, go."

She leaves, and I roll onto my back on my bed on
top of my unsorted laundry. I have a text from Elizabeth
telling me what a great time she had.

And Ivy Harlowe gives a shit about someone. Who
isn't me.

December

I'm trying to be a good person.

It's a little early for a New Year's resolution, but I figure it's overdue. I apologize to my mom. I hug my dad. I put in extra hours and I'm super sweet to Catherine and I don't slap Max for cheating on her, which is as close to a Christmas present as he's getting from me this year. I go over to Alyssa's house for Hanukkah and make nice with her parents who ship us really hard and it's always awkward, and Elizabeth and I invite her and Diana and Melody (Ivy has to work) to a game night at her place, and everyone gets along and it's really nice. Ivy's still living with us and saving up for her own place. Her internship's going well.

So everything's kind of chugging along okay, but I know things are going to get messy soon. They always do this time of year. Home is a careful dance of us all planning holiday events at the club and simultaneously avoiding mentioning Christmas in front of Ivy. We go all out at Dav's, replacing the palm trees with Christmas trees and dressing the girls up like elves.

But at home we're quiet. And so's Ivy.

Elizabeth and I get back from a date one night about a week before Christmas. We shake snow off our boots and head into the kitchen for some coffee, and after a little while, Ivy and Dot wander down from upstairs, about as sex-haired and half dressed as you'd expect. Elizabeth says hi to them both and pours the coffee and asks Dot how things are with school, and I just…admire her for a minute, how she remembers little details about people's lives.

"Getting better," she says. "All thanks to Andie's mom."

Yeah, so my mom's still helping Dot with a bunch of assignments. And, in the world's most bizarre twist, in the process of schlepping stuff back and forth between here and Dot's house, she's become friends with Dot's mom, Hai. She doesn't speak much English, but there is nothing in the world that can get between my mom and making a friend, once she's decided she's doing it. They go to Vietnamese church together, for God's sake.

I don't know how much Hai knows about Dot and Ivy's relationship, but according to my mom, Dot's parents say she's allowed over here as long as she's "always supervised." Obviously Mom is treating that mandate with all the strictness you'd expect from her, and now Ivy and Dot are always walking around freshly fucked, thanking my mom for keeping such a diligent watch. Dot's her perky self as always, flitting around my house like a sprite, and okay, if sleeping with Dot makes Ivy happy, I'm not really inclined to mess with that right now, so it's fine. Besides, I have a girlfriend.

"I still tell her I'm at my friend's house a lot instead," Dot says. "I think she knows exactly where I am and what I'm doing but is afraid that if she calls me out, I'll, like, run away or something."

"Ahh, the possibility of getting rid of you," Ivy says. "I know that optimism well."

"I'm sticky," Dot says. "Like bubble gum."

Elizabeth sips her coffee and looks around the kitchen. "You know, I would have expected this place to be all decked out for Christmas by now," she says to me. "Your mom isn't exactly the low-key type." She finally met them about a week ago, when I had her over for dinner. She was lovely and my parents sort of behaved themselves and my mom high-fived me after Elizabeth left.

Ivy shrinks into her shirt a little, and Dot stands on her toes to root through a cabinet and doesn't notice. "Is there any of that French vanilla stuff left?" Dot says, and Ivy goes into the living room and sits cross-legged on the couch.

I mouth *Ivy doesn't like Christmas* to Elizabeth, who shrugs and gives a little nod.

"Hey, where'd you go?" Dot says, and she brings her coffee into the living room, but Ivy shakes her head when Dot tries to sit down.

"I think it's time for you to go home," Ivy says.

"Yeah?"

"Your mom's waiting up. Go home."

Dot shrugs and goes to get dressed, and Ivy and I look at each other and don't say anything.

I vy wakes me up bright and early the next day. Well, "bright" might be an overstatement, both because the sun's barely up and it looks like it's going to be another day of snow and because Ivy herself is dark and stormy, with a glare on her face and a beer dangling from her hand.

I sit up and stretch. "Early start."

"Seize the day," she mutters.

You can never predict when exactly Ivy will go off the rails, and sometimes it happens for no good reason at all, or at least no reason she shares with me, but for the past three years there's always been a point in December where she cracks. She pulls herself back together, puts the mask back on, transforms back into her sexy, aloof alter ego that she wants so badly to be the real her, but for a day in December every year…I get to see her, and I hate that she has to be miserable for me to get that.

I stand up and give her a hug, and she hugs me back, the beer bottle cold against my back.

"Come on," she says, giving me a squeeze.

"Where are we going?"

"Christmas."

Okay. Christmas. I bundle up and get my keys and stuff some granola bars in my backpack while Ivy fills hers with more beer and a handle of whiskey, in case I had any questions about where her head is at. Thankfully, she walks right past the driveway and toward the bus stop, and on our way she hands me a beer.

"Catch up." She slings her arm over my neck. "It'll keep you warm."

It starts snowing while we're waiting for the bus, fat, sticky flakes, and Ivy turns her face up and lets them cling to her eyelashes. She's gorgeous, her lips and cheeks stung pink in the cold, her hair coming down in waves under her black hat.

The bus comes pretty quickly, and we board and slide into an empty seat.

"I wish I had some coke," Ivy says.

"It's eight in the morning."

"Okay, so I wish I had a *lot* of coke."

"Have you heard from your mom at all?" I say gently.

Ivy doesn't answer me, but a minute later she says, "Remember when we used to make plans in chemistry class to run away?"

"Yeah." We'd print out bus schedules to get out of town and draw up way-more-complicated-than-necessary escape plans. Money-making ideas. Packing lists. Dream houses.

"We should have done that," Ivy says. "Should have gotten the fuck out of here when we had the chance."

I don't know what made us have the chance when we were sixteen more than we do now, but it feels like I'm not supposed to question Ivy today, so I don't. She's here, and she's raw, and she's real. My job isn't to participate. I'm a witness.

We get off at College Hill and walk to this hole-in-the-wall place with really good crepes. It's a Tuesday, and Ivy's school has let off for break, but I guess Brown and RISD haven't yet, because there's a long table full of college kids laughing and talking over one another, backpacks and textbooks strewn around them.

It's weird that I automatically think they're older than I am, when for all I know they're freshmen. College still seems far away, sophisticated, even though I grew up right around the corner from the fucking Ivy League.

Maybe Ivy's thinking something similar, because after we order and we're sitting at the counter, she says abruptly, "College isn't what I thought it would be."

"No?"

She shrugs. "I used to dream about living in the dorm, going to parties. And then you realize that shit costs money

and you have a perfectly good shack with your deadbeat
mom, when it's not on fire. I just drive in and out every
day. Everyone else is living some big college experience
and I'm just doing high school with a longer commute."

"Well, I'm not," I say.

"You never wanted to go to college."

"Neither did you. The plan was to run away to Paris,
remember? You'd design and I'd write." All the pictures
I've had tucked away in my head come back. Ivy and me
at a café. Ivy and me at the Louvre. Ivy and me, holding
hands and looking up at the Eiffel Tower.

She nods vaguely. "In the villa."

"Yeah."

Our food comes, and she doesn't say anything more
for a while.

We walk College Hill even though it's freezing,
wandering Thayer Street and cutting through the
frozen quads on Brown's campus. All the buildings look
ancient and important, and the students brace themselves
against the wind. "Do you think we'll ever get out of here?"
Ivy says.

"You will," I say. "I won't." It's maybe the first time I've
said that out loud.

"Don't be stupid," Ivy says. "You're going wherever I
go."

I smile a little. "Okay."

Ivy's getting darker as the day goes on, though, and
while we're waiting for the bus, she sucks on her vape pen

for a while and then says, "Remember when my dad took us to that…what even was that. That thing on the campus here. That opera shit." Here it comes.

"Yeah." It wasn't her dad, actually; my parents suggested it to him as a fun outing for us when we were about twelve, but then he ended up doing something with his friends and my parents took us themselves. But that's not the point of the story that Ivy's in right now, so I don't correct her.

"What the fuck was that? Some pirate thing?"

"Gilbert and Sullivan." You don't get raised by theater people without knowing *Pirates of Penzance*. That was not my first time seeing it.

"God. And they had to project the lyrics up above the stage, 'cause otherwise how would you know what the fuck anyone was saying." She shakes her head and takes another pull on the vape. "Someone had to come up with that. That was someone's idea."

"I guess."

"That was a part of someone's life," she insists. "That's part of their story, coming up with those captions." She's starting to sound drunk. "And now it's part of our story, sitting there looking at them. Those stupid captions were part of my dad's story. Isn't that fucking pathetic?"

It's been years and I still never know what to say. "Um…"

"Thirty-eight years and part of it is sitting in that crappy auditorium, watching Gilbert and Sullivan."

So I say, "I don't think it was him. I think my parents ended up taking us." Because maybe it will help. Or maybe it will make her stop saying things I can't fix.

Ivy doesn't react for a minute; then she nods slowly.

"So I know even less about him than a minute ago," she says. "That's right. That seems right."

Ivy cracks another beer open on the bus and looks out the window for a while. We're passing by the railroad tracks now, and two men are loading cargo onto the back of a train.

"So," she says with that kind of sarcastic brightness. "How's your relationship going?"

I roll my eyes. "We don't have to talk about that." I feel like it'll break the only thing holding us together today—the magic of Ivy and Andie—to bring Elizabeth into it.

"Come on. I want to hear about the happy couple."

She's mocking me. "My relationship is good," I say. "How's yours?"

She scoffs. "I am not in a relationship."

"Oh, okay, so what do you call what you're doing?"

"What I'm doing with who?"

She's so exhausting. "Dot."

She waves her hand. "We're sleeping together."

"And that's all it is," I say. Interrogating. Hoping.

And she looks at me like I'm crazy. "You know me," she says. "I don't do relationships." She rests her head on my shoulder. "Except with you."

Her hair smells like peppermint, and I close my eyes for a minute and just get lost. God. I have to say something before it gets awkward. "Why don't you like her?" I say.

"I do like her."

"You do? You always talk shit about her."

Ivy laughs and sits up. "Elizabeth. I thought you meant Dot."

"To be fair, you talk shit about her, too."

"I do not. And I just don't like that all Elizabeth's opinions automatically become yours, too. You have your own opinions."

"You mean I have your opinions."

She looks at me, her eyes big and green and magnificent. "No, Andie. I don't." For just a second, she doesn't seem drunk at all, and I feel like I'm floating.

A minute later, she pushes the button for our stop, and I take a deep breath and get ready.

We always end up at either the gravesite or the road where it happened. This year it's the road. I follow Ivy off the bus at a stop outside the city without a word and walk the three blocks to the curve I know well now, that never feels as haunted as it should. It just feels like a road to me, but I'm not Ivy, and my father didn't die here.

I stand next to her, a little behind her, and when she speaks, finally, I can tell she's crying a little, and it hurts somewhere between my throat and my chest. My hands start shaking.

"I just want to know why," she says. "Was he on something? Was he changing the CD? Did he get a phone call? Was it important?"

"It doesn't matter, baby."

"Where was he going? Some girl he was sleeping with? Was he coming home? It was Christmas. We hadn't seen him in weeks. Was he even going to come home?"

This is the Ivy nobody but me gets to see.

And this, right here, this is the problem with Dot. This is why it isn't right. I want to go back in time and explain it to my mom. Ivy might have, God forbid, some kind of feelings for her, but Dot doesn't know the real Ivy. She knows sexy, fierce, razor-sharp Ivy. She doesn't know *this*, because Ivy will never let her see this. She's never let anyone see it but me.

"And now my mom's not even going to come home?" she says. "It's the fucking anniversary of when he died, she's not coming home?"

"I'm so sorry."

"I'm an orphan," she says. "That's what I am, I'm a fucking orphan." She breathes in unsteadily. "I swear to God if I ever see her again—"

I put my hand on her shoulder and she turns around and fits herself into my arms, shaking a little bit while she cries quietly, and it's cold, but she's so warm, and I would do absolutely anything in the world for this girl.

"Don't let go," she whispers.

"I won't. Not ever."

We get back to the house late, after I've force-fed Ivy some fast food to try to get something non-alcoholic going through her system. I sit her down on her bed and tug off her boots.

"I want to go out," she says.

"I know you do." Ivy, despite school and the internship and her not-girlfriend or whatever, still goes out all the time and still hooks up with everyone she wants to, but I've cut back from every weekend without fail to once in the past month. It's just not Elizabeth's thing.

"Find your keys; I can't drive. This is what you get for staying sober. I told you not to."

"We are not going out."

Ivy gets up and starts changing her clothes.

"We are not going out," I say again.

Yeah, I'm sure you can guess how this one ends. Fifteen minutes later, I'm in the car, driving Ivy to Kinetic while she screams along to ten-year-old pop songs on the radio.

God, I get so fucking sick of myself.

We walk into Kinetic and it could be any night in the past few years. Nothing ever changes, and maybe for the first time I feel the kind of desperation to get out of this town that I've been pretending I understood since chemistry class. It's the same fucking thing here all the time. I can't be thirty or forty or seventy-five and standing by the bar while Ivy picks up some new girl.

I just don't know what else there is for me to do.

Ivy makes a beeline for the dance floor as soon as we get in. At first I'm just grateful she's not drinking anymore, and then I see Dot on the dance floor, some young-looking girl wrapped around her. Dot, obviously, dislodges herself from her as soon as she sees Ivy, who leans into Dot's ear and says something and then rests her hand on her shoulder and leans in while Dot stands on her toes to meet their lips.

Everyone in the club keeps grinding and writhing, except for Ivy and Dot, slow-dancing with their foreheads together and their eyes closed, and except for me. Witnessing.

January

"So she has, like, a policy?" Alyssa says as we come through my front door. She's in town for the weekend, avoiding some sort of massive hetero extravaganza happening at BU, and we had cheap and amazing seafood and a few beers, and now we're coming home for a few of my mom's triple-chocolate brownies. Sometimes living at home has its perks.

"I don't know that it's a policy," I say. "She just, like… historically hasn't been involved with them. But she didn't ask me about it until tonight. And I don't think she would have broken up with me or something if I'd said yes."

"Said yes to what?" my mom asks. She's sitting on the couch, watching *British Bake Off* and icing her feet. She worked a double shift today, and nursing is a full-body workout.

"Don't worry about it," I say. The last thing I need is to ask my mother's opinion on queer culture. God knows I get enough of it already.

But of course Alyssa goes to the kitchen and gets a brownie and says, "Elizabeth doesn't date bisexuals." I smack her shoulder when she gets back.

"Mmm," my mother says, with a sage nod. "I've heard that's a common bias."

"What's wrong with bisexuals?" Ivy says lazily. She's at

the kitchen table with a stack of paper and a pen, reading something with her eyebrows furrowed.

"Nothing's wrong with them," I say. "I think she just worries about girls...experimenting."

"Biphobic," Ivy says.

"It's not biphobic. She's not saying they're not valid or they don't exist; she just doesn't want to date them. You don't have to date everyone. I don't date people who live out of state. Alyssa doesn't date girls who are shorter than she is."

Ivy crosses something out on the page. "Biphobic."

"What are you reading, anyway?" I ask Ivy. She waves me away.

Dot comes out of the bathroom, wiping her hands on her sweatpants. I'm not even surprised to see her nowadays.

Alyssa says, "Dot, you're bi."

"Yyyyes?"

"What would you call someone who doesn't date bisexuals?"

"Uh, unfortunate." She goes over to the kitchen table and looks over Ivy's shoulder. "How is it?"

Ivy nods without taking her eyes off the page she's reading. "Better. You're still a little wordy in the second support."

Dot sits down. "I know, but I have to meet the page count limit."

Ivy shrugs. "Make the periods bigger."

"That's a good trick," I say. "That got me through senior English."

"That's what this is for!" Dot says.

I groan. "God, I'm old."

"Watch your mouth," my mother says. She gets up and

smacks a kiss on my cheek on her way upstairs.

I think my dad's up there lying down; he was there when I left, and he's been going through a rough patch the past week or so. I don't think anything happened to trigger it, besides continued stress about the strip club continuing to go downhill. Bipolar disorder's just a bitch. My mom is so amazingly good at helping him deal with it after all these years. When I was a kid, I barely even noticed anything was up. Honestly, I rarely notice now. They're a well-oiled machine, those two.

"Well, I'm glad Elizabeth's impressed with your exclusive diet of cunt," Ivy says. After my mother's upstairs, because even Ivy has her limits.

"I live to please," I say.

Ivy hands the papers back to Dot. "Conclusion's good. Just make the changes on the second support and you should be ready to go."

Dot slumps back in her chair. "I can't do it. The ennui. It takes me."

"It takes you?" Ivy says.

"*Takes* me," she says miserably.

"Hmm. I've got a touch of that myself," Ivy says. "Ladies?"

"I could stand to have a little less ennui, yeah," I say.

"I know where this is heading, and I don't know if I feel like going out," Alyssa says. "It sounds hard."

Ivy sighs. "It does sound hard."

"Come oooon," Dot says. "Stop being old." Dot always, always wants to go out.

"Shut up, pip-squeak," Ivy says idly.

"I'd go out," I say. I'm already dressed kind of cute for dinner with Alyssa, and I haven't sat down yet, so I'm still in doing-shit-inertia mode.

Ivy glances at all of us like she's weighing her options, then finally turns to Dot for a long moment. She sighs. "I do have E."

Dot slaps her hands on the table. "I love you! I love you and I love E."

"So I've heard." Ivy stands up.

Ivy and Dot get changed—I think Dot brings club clothes with her every time she comes over here, just in case—and we head to Kinetic, where Alyssa abstains because E doesn't agree with her, but Ivy feeds me and then Dot each a tab off her tongue.

Half an hour later, Dot's making out with Melody—I don't even know when she got here—and with any boy in here who will have her, Ivy's twirling up a storm on the dance floor, and I'm just mesmerized by how beautiful all the lights look. And Ivy, the glow bouncing off her skin, her eyes closed and her chin pointed toward the ceiling.

Kinetic's packed tonight, some bachelorette party or something—they couldn't go to Dav's?—and there are dancers on the platforms and someone spills a drink on me and the whole thing is amazing, like I'm part of the same living, breathing animal as everyone else in here. Parts of a whole.

"Here." Alyssa nudges me. "Drink some water." Her eyes are sparkly. They're a really nice shade of brown.

"You're pretty," I say, and she blushes and looks away. I sip the water. "Elizabeth doesn't do drugs."

"That doesn't surprise me."

"She doesn't know I do. Do you think that's bad? I don't do them very much. I didn't even hook up with anyone tonight even though I wanted to, so I don't think I did anything wrong. Look at Ivy, wow." She's spinning so fast, I can't even believe it, her arms out like a child, and I can't stop watching the colorful squares of light from the disco balls dancing on her bare arms. Long and fragile like tree branches.

"She really likes you, huh?" Alyssa says.

"Ivy? I hope so."

"Elizabeth."

"Oh. I think so. But I don't know why."

"Who wouldn't like you?"

Dot comes bouncing over and wraps her hand around my wrist. "Dance with me!"

I almost say yes, because *dancing, life, glitter*, but then I remember everything and shake her off. "Ask Ivy."

"Dance with me *and* Ivy!" She throws her arms up in the air. "I love dancing. I love dancing so much. I want to die dancing."

"Or you could stay alive and keep dancing," Alyssa says.

Dot points at her. "Yes. Yes. Also an option. I guess we'll see! Where's Ivy?" she says, like she's just noticing she isn't with us.

I roll my eyes and point toward her, and Dot's off in a flash, running across the dance floor and leaping onto Ivy and wrapping her legs around her waist. Ivy staggers in her heels and says something to Dot, then chuckles at whatever Dot says back, and then they're both laughing and Ivy's spinning Dot around. Slowly now, like they're on a turntable.

"She's like a missile," I say.

Alyssa shrugs. "She's cute. Wish she'd make out with me instead of Melody."

"Yuck. She's a baby."

"She's not that much younger than we are. Two years."

"It's not just the age, it's… She's a baby." She's never done anything or experienced anything. She wants to be a makeup vlogger, and she's *succeeding* at it for God's sake. She doesn't have any responsibilities. Nothing's hard. She's in love with the first person she ever slept with. "She's brand-new," I say.

"Well, whatever it is about her, Ivy looks happy."

"Ivy's high."

"Yeah, so are you, grouchy. I'm just saying, whatever Dot has going on seems to work for Ivy. Are the two of them still sleeping with other people?"

"Yeah. Of course."

"Then I guess it's not that serious. Although Melody and Diana aren't monogamous and they're plenty serious."

I snort. "Ivy and Dot are not Melody and Diana. Melody and Diana are a couple. Try telling Ivy that she and Dot are a couple. She'd bite your head off."

"So they're, what, Ivy and a patron?"

"As usual." I sling my arm around Alyssa's neck. "Don't worry. You'll find a baby to fawn over you, too. The Alyssa…patron thing."

"Eh. I don't want a baby." She watches the happy couple on the dance floor, her head tilted to the side. "She is sort of exhausting."

I put my hands up. "That's all I'm saying."

"Did we used to have that much energy?"

"I don't think anyone else in the world has ever had that much energy."

Ivy and Dot come back a few songs later, sweating and panting, and Alyssa fills them both up with water. Dot kisses her cheek, which makes me laugh, and then I can't stop laughing. Ivy slaps me on the back like I'm coughing.

"Why don't we do E every day?" Dot asks.

"Money," Ivy says. "Brain integrity."

"Those sound very inconsequential," Dot says.

"To you they would, yes."

Dot spins around. "The world is so beautiful. I wish it were always this beautiful. Look at the sparkles in here!" She sits on a barstool. "The world is like Ivy."

"Maybe half a tab for you next time," Ivy says.

Dot points at her. "Don't you *dare*."

"Your boobs are lighting up."

"My *boobs* are—you're the one who needs half a tab—oh! My boobs are lighting up!" She reaches into her bra and pulls out her phone. "It's Trang!"

"Who the fuck is Trang?" Ivy says.

"He works for my parents!"

"Uh, maybe don't answer that right now," Alyssa says, but it's too late. Dot's already on the phone, yelling over the music in rapid Vietnamese. Ivy shrugs and leans across the bar to order a drink. Dot doesn't get off the phone until the glass is halfway drained.

She stuffs her phone back into her bra. "We need to go now," she says.

"Go where?" I say.

"Down to the docks."

"It's one in the morning."

"Shrimp waits for no clock!" she says.

Ivy rolls her eyes. "Spot, what's going on?"

"One of the nets is stuck and the boat can't come in!" Dot says. "They want me to come cut it!" She makes scissors with her hand, like we won't understand the concept of cutting without a visual.

"Why you?" I say. "I thought this was your brothers' and your parents' thing."

"They're out of town! Why do you think I've been at your house all the time?"

"You're always at my house all the time," I say.

Ivy says, "Okay, why can't the guy calling you cut it?"

"Because my parents will be mad! Those things are expensive. I'm not gonna cut it, I'm gonna save it! I have to go save the boat!"

"Honey," Alyssa says. "How are you going to save a boat?"

"I can do it!" Dot says, while some drunk guy plows into her and nearly knocks her over. She looks around like she's forgotten we're still in the club. I kind of had, too.

Alyssa says, "You're high out of your mind and it's forty degrees outside."

"I can do it," Dot insists. "I have to do it or all these people are going to be in trouble. They might get fired!"

"Maybe they should get fired," Ivy says. "It sounds like they fucked up."

Dot smacks her. "Heartless."

"Not news."

"I will save the net and I will save the boat and I will save my family's money and I will save the fishermen's jobs!"

Ivy finishes her drink and sets the glass down. "Okay, Oprah, fuck it. Let's go save the world."

. . .

Alyssa drives us down to the water while Dot rides shotgun and barks directions and Ivy and I exchange looks from the back seat. I used to come down here when I was a kid and watch the boats with my dad. It's weird to think I might have seen one of Dot's family's.

At half past one in the morning in January, there's no one here except a bunch of rather intimidating fishermen, one of whom Dot marches right up to the second we're out of the car. They start talking to each other in Vietnamese, and he points out into the water where there's a dimly lit, rickety-looking boat maybe fifty yards away from the dock. We get out of the car and bounce up and down a little to keep warm, but the drugs do a lot to help with that.

Dot comes back over to us, tottering a little in her heels.

"Fucking idiots, going out this early. Can't see for shit," she says to us before she turns around and yells something in Vietnamese to a few nearby guys, who all jump to attention and start getting another boat ready. Being fourth in line to a shrimp boat business probably doesn't impress much in the general world, but here she certainly seems to have some pull.

"What are you doing?" Ivy says.

"I told you, I'm saving the boat. Can I borrow your gloves?"

Ivy tugs them off with her teeth. "Right, but how exactly are you saving this boat?" she says with her mouth full of cotton.

"I don't know yet." Dot looks out onto the water. "I'll figure it out once I'm there."

"You're going to freeze to death," Ivy says.

"I have your gloves!" She kisses Ivy's cheek and

wobbles off, shouting more orders and swinging herself onto the rescue boat like it's the most comfortable thing in the world.

We go to the edge of the dock, shivering, and squint out after Dot as her boat takes her to the one stranded away from shore. They're small from back here, but we can see Dot and the fishermen with her climb from boat to boat and give the shipwrecked fishermen some blankets. Dot's voice cuts through the wind off the water, and she goes over to where the net's slung and does some sort of net triage, I don't know.

"If she gets in that fucking water," Ivy says.

"She's not going to get in the water," I say. "That's insane."

"Have you met her?" Ivy says.

We can hear faint arguing on the boat from where we're standing, and then the Dot-shaped blur on the deck steps out of her shoes and takes off her coat.

"Goddamn it," Ivy says. She takes her phone out and dials Dot and puts it on speaker. "What the fuck are you doing?"

Her voice is tinny and shrill. "I'm gonna see if I can unstuck it. Stick it."

"In that freezing goddamn water."

"I'm putting on a wet suit right now."

"It's polluted as shit. You're gonna end up with a lung full of pneumonia."

"Do you *honestly* think I've never done this before?"

"How do you even know how far down it is?" Ivy says.

"I don't. I'll see when I get in."

"I'm not telling your parents you fucking died."

"Oh, but you're the one they'd want to hear it from,

darling," Dot says, and Ivy snickers and hangs up the phone.

"Stupid fucking kid," she mutters.

"This so isn't safe," Alyssa says.

Ivy takes a long pull on her vape pen. "You can't stop her," she says when she lets her breath out. "She does what she wants."

I try to imagine diving into this water, picturing how it would freeze to your ribs, how pitch-black it would be while it throbbed all around you. Like an ice-cold Kinetic with the lights off, the bass beating in your ears. And without anyone there with you.

It's suddenly very, very important that this doesn't happen, and I don't know why. "She shouldn't go," I say. I feel like I'm too loud. "She shouldn't do this."

"She'll be okay," Ivy says, her eyes fixed on the boat, just as we see Dot dive. Ivy takes a sharp breath in.

"Jesus Christ," Alyssa says. I think about taking Ivy's hand, but she has her arms tightly crossed. She doesn't look scared, anyway. Just focused, like if she stares at Dot hard enough, it'll help.

"I didn't even know she knew how to do this kind of shit," I say. I've never really pictured her doing much outside following Ivy around.

"She was raised on these boats," Ivy says.

"I know, but—"

Ivy shakes her head without looking away from the boat. "You think she's a princess."

"I mean, she is an heiress."

It feels like forever, but it's probably less than a minute before Dot comes up for air. I hear her shout something at the fishermen.

"Is she giving up?" Alyssa says.

"No," Ivy says.

Sure enough, a few seconds later Dot sinks back under the water. The fishermen are all leaning over the side of the boat, watching her. I'm guessing they'd be in a lot more trouble for letting the boss's daughter die than for ripping the net. Or maybe, the uncynical part of me realizes, they've known Dot since she was a baby. Maybe these people care about her.

I look at Ivy and her narrowed eyes.

It's getting to be not so hard to believe.

The next time Dot comes up for air, the fishermen are immediately all over her, throwing something down to haul her back onto the boat, wrapping her up in blankets as soon as she's on deck. At first I think she's called it quits, but right after Dot, they're pulling up the net. The boat starts toward us. She did it.

Ivy takes off her coat and meets Dot at the end of the dock to put it around her shoulders. She says something to her that we can't hear that makes Dot laugh. Her mascara's all over her face and her teeth are chattering. She looks proud.

"Okay," I say quietly. To Alyssa. To myself. "Okay, she's kind of a badass."

Alyssa drops us off at home, and Dot runs immediately into the shower, and I head up to my room to change and crawl under the covers to try to get warm. I settle back into the book I've been reading, this seriously awesome one about a woman who keeps a lighthouse and this guy who may or may not be a ghost.

I'm planning just to read a little before I go to sleep, but I end up three chapters deep at quarter to three and really craving some hot chocolate, so I get up quietly and creep down the stairs. I'm almost at the entrance to the kitchen when I hear Dot and Ivy talking. It hadn't even occurred to me that they might still be awake. Or be out of bed, at least.

"I don't know what it is you think I'm going to say," Ivy says. She sounds serious, so I freeze, just out of sight.

"Jesus, I'm not trying to trap you or something," Dot says. "But is it seriously that ridiculous that I'm wondering about this? I'm a senior. Everywhere I turn it's like, *think about your future.*"

"They mean college. Not whether you're going to keep fucking the girl you're fucking."

Oh God. Is Dot trying to push Ivy into a relationship discussion? She couldn't just take the win from the shrimp boat and run with it. She's got to try to conquer Ivy, too.

"I just want to know your plans," Dot says. "Why is that so threatening to you? I'm not trying to tell you what they should be. I'm not even asking you for anything."

"Yes, you are."

"I'm asking you to talk, that's it. I'm not asking you to be sure or to make some kind of decision. I just want to know whether you...when you look into the future, next month, six months, a year, am I there?"

I'm not even mad, honestly; I'm just *embarrassed* for her. I don't really want to hear Ivy destroy this girl's dreams, but I can't get myself to move. It's like one of those cringe-comedy TV shows. You have to watch between your fingers.

"That's not how I think about things," Ivy says. "I can't keep myself going by relying on other people. How do you think that would have worked out for me?"

"I'm not talking about *people*. I'm talking about me."

"God, your ego needs to go on fucking keto or some shit."

"It's been five months," Dot says. "I don't think it's ridiculous for me to wonder this."

"*What's* been five months?" Ivy says. "Since I brought you home and fucked you? What are we measuring here?"

"Do you really have to put on a show right now? There's no one else here."

Whoops.

"We're never going to be some married couple," Ivy says. "We're not going to be Melody and Diana."

"Okay, I just had my tongue down Melody's throat, so I don't see how they're some scary example of the heterosexual agenda."

"This is what I'm saying," Ivy says. "This is it. You're trying to trap me." She sounds upset.

"That's bullshit. Why would I want to trap you? Why are you so sure that I *want* all that shit you're afraid that I want? When have I ever even indicated that?"

"When you try to get me to have a talk with you like we're in some kind of relationship."

"All I want is for you to give me an answer to a question that has to do with *me* and not whatever crap you're projecting on me. It's just me." Dot sounds older than I'm used to, and her voice is a little less high-pitched. She's composed, while Ivy's the one getting agitated.

There's a long pause, and finally Ivy speaks.

"I'm going to keep going where I'm going," she says,

and now she sounds calm, too. "And you can come with me for as long as you want. That's what I have to offer."

Holy shit.

Holy shit.

Ivy Harlowe just told a girl she could be with her for as long as she wants.

Oh God. Dot's not the one who needs to be embarrassed. I am. I'm the punch line.

And my feet still won't move.

I'm pretty sure I couldn't possibly be more stunned until Dot says, "That is such crap," and nope, turns out I was not at my threshold.

"What the fuck are you talking about?" Ivy says.

"Telling me oh, you can come if you want to," Dot says. "I'm not some kid tagging along."

"I never said you were," Ivy says firmly.

"I want to be *wanted*," Dot says. "Not tolerated."

"I don't tolerate very many people," Ivy says. "This is a big deal for me."

"Okay, well, it's not enough," Dot says. "I'm happy for you and everything but it's not enough for me."

After a few seconds of silence, Ivy says, "So what, are you ending this?"

I hold my breath.

But Dot just laughs a little. "I can't believe I just got you to admit there's something to end," she says. "And no, obviously I'm not fucking ending this. I'm going to keep doing what I've been doing since September."

"What part exactly."

"The part where I hang around until you realize you can't live without me."

I cannot imagine having that kind of confidence to say

that to anyone. Let alone to Ivy, who's always been just fine without anyone.

There's quiet after that, and at first I think Ivy's trying to figure out how the hell to respond to that, and then I hear soft kissing noises, so...what.

I think a part of me is giving up on trying to understand them, and on the one hand that's a relief.

On the other hand, it literally, physically hurts that Ivy just told someone else that they can come with her, and that I have once again made a complete fool out of myself, at least this time only in my own mind, by thinking I have any damn clue what's going on between Ivy and Dot.

And I just...

I have waited for God knows how many years for Ivy to be ready. I've crept up to her like she's some scared little woodland creature, because I knew she wasn't ready for a relationship; I knew she had all this baggage about it that Dot's calling her out on. And while I was being thoughtful and sensitive and patient, some cocky little shit is going to waltz in, right in the middle of my hard work, in all I've done making her comfortable with her life, and break through Ivy's walls with persistence and persistence alone?

Apparently yeah, and I hate that I'm starting to get what Ivy sees in her, that Dot is bold and fearless and yeah, a goddamn missile, and it feels like being squeezed.

What if all this time, all I had to do was say, *You have to give it a shot, I'm not backing down,* and she would have fallen in love with me?

Would it even matter? Am I the kind of person who can do that?

I think I'm not. I think I'm the kind of person who

reads love stories and doesn't live them.

Except oh my God, *I have a girlfriend.* Just throw me into the river without a wet suit.

I'm halfway up the stairs when there's a sudden and very insistent knocking at my front door.

"What the hell?" I hear Ivy say. "It's three in the goddamn morning." And because she's Ivy, instead of ignoring it or checking through the window or generally showing any caution whatsoever, she's immediately up and crossing through the living room to answer the door.

From where I am on the stairs, I can see Ivy's back but not the person at the door, but I don't need to see her to know that voice. Flinty, strong. Familiar and disorienting at once.

"Ivy Kaitlin. Can you tell me where our house is?"

Ivy's mom is back.

February

"Stay," Elizabeth says.

"I caaaaan't."

We're in the living room of her small apartment, sprawled out on the floor with a bunch of nail polish and a tray of fancy cheese. It's so warm here, and the cheese is good enough to be a meal, and Elizabeth is wearing this blue sweater that makes her eyes sparkle.

"Sure you can." She stretches, tangling her legs up with mine. "You don't have to go to this lunch."

"I promised Ivy I'd be there."

"She can't have lunch with her mom by herself?"

"They have a…complicated relationship."

It's the first day of February, and Ivy's mom has been back—and living in a motel—for the past three days. Ivy's been mostly dodging her, pleading class and internship, but she finally pinned her down for a lunch she can't get out of. Ivy is sure, 100 percent sure, that she's about to be hit up for money, and she's hoping that her mom won't ask if I'm there. Which seems like a lot of class to expect from Bette Harlowe, but hey, miracles happen.

"I don't think she's ever been gone for this long before," I say. "And she didn't come home for the holidays, which is when Ivy's dad died… It's a thing."

She sighs. "Why can't your parents just be everyone's parents?"

"They practically are," I say, but it feels weird to say, because my dad's in the hospital right now. I haven't told Elizabeth, because it's my dad's business and he's a private sort of guy, and also because I guess it would feel like a bigger deal if I said it to her, and really, it's manageable.

He went voluntarily and he's getting help and he'll be home in a few days, but outsiders can blow it up into this thing that it's not. They hear "psych ward" and think it's some cuckoo's nest shit. He's just sleeping and doing a lot of therapy and getting his meds adjusted. I miss him, though, and I know it makes Ivy anxious, having him not there. She made him some cookies, and Dot did this watercolor floral painting of the rose bushes we had blooming back when she first started coming around and gave it to me to bring to him. Dad loved it so much, he cried. It was my first time really seeing her art, and, I have to say, that impression I got quickly in Ivy's car that time was right. She's really damn good. And I know good; I was raised on Ivy's art, after all. She used to make my dad cards, too, back when she still drew, but she gave that up a long time ago.

We're missing visiting hours at the hospital today to do this lunch, which has Ivy in an even worse mood about the whole thing.

"She needs me," I say.

Elizabeth sighs. "Why did I have to fall in love with someone who's such a good friend?"

Hang on.

I sit up. "What did you just say?"

"What? You're a good friend."

"No, not... Did you just say you love me?"

I'm expecting this to be a big moment. Where she stutters and says she didn't mean to or else comes in with some huge declaration. I expect her to act like I've caught her in something.

But she just smiles a little. "Yeah, of course I do. You didn't know?"

"I, um..." Oh God. This has never happened before. I've forgotten how to human.

She leans forward and kisses me. "You don't have to say it back," she whispers, so low and sexy that in that moment, I think I'd say just about anything. "No pressure."

So I just whisper, "Okay," and she kisses me again.

In all honesty, though, sitting there on her floor, no one around but me and her, no complications and no bullshit and just me and her, I really think that I do love her. I really think I do.

But now I have to go to lunch.

Bette meets Ivy and me at this run-down diner close to the train station. The servers are all women and could be anywhere between twenty and sixty, and they're all wearing a pound of makeup and look sassy and tired. I wonder vaguely if any of them are looking for stripper work. We definitely pay better.

Bette's already in a booth when we get there, and she scoots out and half stands to give Ivy and me a hug at the same time, patting us on the back with the flats of her hands. She's skinny and tan and doesn't look anything like Ivy.

"So good to see you girls," she says. "What a cute top, Andie."

"Thanks. It's Ivy's."

"It is so sweet of your family to let her stay with you."

"I'm getting my own place soon," Ivy says. She wants to save up for something that's not a trash heap. My parents aren't exactly the type to push her out the door, and God knows I'm in no hurry for her to leave, so she's not really feeling any pressure to move out. She's started paying my parents some rent and she chips in for groceries, which is welcome right now when we're surviving on just what my mom makes from nursing.

We sit down, and Bette flags the waiter over and orders coffee instead of food. Ivy gets a Spanish omelet and I get a BLT. Ivy clicks her nails on the lacquered table.

"How was Costa Rica?" I ask.

"Mmm." Bette sets down her water glass. "Incredible. Transcendent. Getting to explore other cultures…it's such a blessing. And how are you, Andie, how's school?"

"I'm not actually in—"

"Oh, right, right, of course. I was never much for school, either. Don't know where Ivy gets those brains from! Are you seeing anyone? I asked Ivy if she has any boyfriends, but she never gives me a straight answer."

"Stacks on stacks on stacks," Ivy says dryly. "Like pancakes."

I'm not sure why Ivy's never come out to her mom. It's not like she'd have a problem with it. I think it's just a way Ivy keeps some power in their relationship. It's something about her that her mother can't touch.

"And how's your family, Andie?" Bette says. "How are your parents?"

"They're good," I say. "They're really good."

Ivy tangles her foot up with mine under the table. I put my other foot around it, too, protectively.

We're halfway through our food, eaten mostly in very awkward silence, when Bette claps her hands together and says, "I have something for you girls."

"What, a Christmas present?" Ivy says, and Bette gives her a look that lets me know she noticed the snark but isn't going to respond to it. Ivy chews her lip like she's been scolded.

Bette takes a small plastic bag out of the pocket of her leopard-print coat and opens it and drops one bracelet into Ivy's hand and one in mine. Ivy's is green and mine is purple. It's not my style, but it's pretty enough. The beads are swirly. Maybe I'll give it to my mom.

"Thank you," I say. "Are these from Costa Rica?" Mom will dig the back story.

"No, no, no," she says. "These were made by a friend of mine. She's got this whole venture making them out in California."

"Here we go," Ivy says under her breath.

Bette gives her another look, a little longer this time. "It's a genius idea, really. They look just like normal jewelry, right? But there's CBD oil in the beads—don't ask me how; I'm no scientist—and the warmth of your skin melts it into you and you get all those good CBD effects just from wearing a bracelet! People are going to go wild for these."

"For a tiny bit of CBD oil in a bracelet," Ivy says. "You know you can just buy the stuff."

"Oh, you know how people are," she says. "It's about the lifestyle. Or maybe this will ease people in who are worried about it! Possibilities are endless."

"Endless," Ivy says. "Okay. So let me guess. You're about to leave for California to help her with this."

"This is a great business," she says. "This isn't some scam like Costa Rica turned out to be."

"I thought Costa Rica was transcendent."

"And," Bette says, "you could come with me."

Ivy laughs. "Come with you. Move to California?"

"Aren't you sick of the weather here?" she says. "God knows I am, and I just got back. And you'd get on this business right at the start with me. We could do something together. Like we used to when you were little."

Ivy starts to speak, and I can tell whatever she's going to say isn't really diner-appropriate, and to be honest, there's just no point. There is no point in getting into it with Bette. She never learns. She's never going to.

So I just grab Ivy's hand and squeeze her fingers hard enough to hurt. "She'll think about it," I say to Bette, with my best customer-service smile.

On our way out of the diner, Ivy throws the bracelet away and slams the car door without a word.

I have to get to work, and Ivy comes in with me instead of dropping me off, like she does sometimes when she doesn't have class or her internship. She hangs out in the dressing room with the dancers while I go do inventory in the kitchen, and when I come back, she's sprawled in a chair, talking to Libby, one of my favorite girls who's been here forever. She's doing a bachelor party tonight, and

I settle in with the books in a free chair and start going through this month's numbers.

Libby says, "Andie, how's your dad?"

"He's doing a lot better, thanks," I say. "They're messing with his meds some and he says he can already feel a difference." We don't have secrets here.

"You're sending him our love?"

"Of course."

"Shit," Libby says. "Are either of you any good at contouring? My face just looks dirty. I need these tips tonight and this is not working." Libby's blonde and blue-eyed, like someone who could play Cinderella at Disney World.

"I barely know what contouring is," I say.

Ivy says, "My cheekbones are real, thank you." And incredible.

"God, shut up," Libby says.

"Be nice to me," Ivy says, pulling out her phone. "I'm calling in reinforcements." Any idiot can see where this is going, even me, and yeah, Dot's skipping through the dressing room doors in ten minutes.

"Hi hi hi!" she says. "I hear there's an emergency."

Libby laughs. "And who is this?"

"Ivy's foundling," I say, and Ivy kicks her shoe at me.

Dot sits on the counter and gets to work on Libby. She has this huge makeup bag with her and a mirror, like our walls aren't already covered in them. "Andie, this place is so cool," she says.

I look around at the peeling palm tree wallpaper and dented picture frames holding snapshots of the girls clowning around and the building, back in the day. There's not much to show off here, but hell, it makes me happy, too.

"You haven't been here before?" I say.

She shakes her head. "I dropped Ivy off once, but I've never been inside. Close your eyes, tilt your head a little — good." She runs a brush under Libby's eye.

"I just need the contouring fixed," Libby says.

"Oh, honey, no you do not," Dot says, and Ivy laughs.

"I'm glad someone thinks this place is cool," I say. "Maybe we should change our target demographic to seventeen-year-old queers. Might help save this place."

"You need saving?" Dot says.

"Yeah." I wave my hand and turn a page. "Don't get any ideas, Joan of Arc. No nets to clip here."

"Hmm," is all she says. She puts on Libby's lipstick and walks around to her other side to do something to her eyebrow. She nudges Ivy. "Hi."

"Hey."

It's been a big week for Dot. College acceptances are coming in, and she's gotten into all her safeties and yesterday got her RISD acceptance. She was surprised; Ivy was not, and once Ivy showed me pictures of the portfolio she'd submitted, I could see why. The girl can do a lot more than put on blush or make get well cards. I'd told Ivy that, meaning it as a compliment, and Ivy got all offended, though. "She likes makeup." That's what you get for trying to make nice with your best friend's... whatever she is.

It's kind of a big week for everyone, actually, with my dad recovering in the hospital and Ivy's mom and also her apartment-hunting. Melody and Diana just got back from vacation. Alyssa aced her physics exam up in Boston. And then there's, you know, me. Doing the books.

"Okay," Dot says. "Take a look."

Libby looks at herself in the mirror. "Girl. They should hire you."

Dot beams and goes over to a chair next to Ivy and flops herself down, pulling her hair down from a messy bun and starting a French braid instead. She looks over Ivy's shoulder to see her phone, and Ivy notices her and angles it toward her, and Dot giggles at something.

Ivy glances up at her and then back down, the tiniest bit of a smile on her face. Dot takes out her phone, too, and it's obvious from their reactions that they're texting each other, which is ridiculous, since they're sitting right next to each other, but hey, at least this way I don't have to listen to them flirt. I get back to work.

Just a few minutes later, though, just after Libby's left to get the bachelor party started, Dot says, "Oh my God."

"What?" Ivy says.

Dot says, "I…uh. I got into Columbia."

"Huh," Ivy says.

I say, "Wait. Like, Columbia Columbia? New York Columbia? Isn't that a really good school?"

Dot shrugs, looking at her phone.

"Who *are* you?" I say.

"She got a 1520 on her SAT," Ivy says. "Does Columbia even have an art program?"

"Of course," Dot says, still sounding a little dazed. "But I wouldn't… If I'm going to do art, I'm going to go to RISD."

"Then what's Columbia?" Ivy says.

"Pre-law. My parents, you know. That's what they want me to do."

Ivy's staring at Dot like she's talking about growing an extra arm. "You're an artist."

"So were you," Dot says vaguely, scrolling down on her phone.

Ivy's quiet, then says abruptly, "I might be moving to California with my mom," and I almost fall out of my chair.

I don't think she'll really do it," I say to Elizabeth a few days later, when I'm recounting the whole sordid tale as we walk back to her apartment from lunch. "I mean, she spends forty-eight hours with her mom and they both want to kill each other. Can't imagine how she'd last without my house five minutes away to run back to."

"So you're not worried about it?"

I shake my head. "But now I am sort of worried she's going to go off the rails if Dot leaves. We'd all just assumed she'd stay local, and it sounds like she's really considering this Columbia thing."

"I thought she was totally committed to being, you know, a YouTube celebrity."

"Yeah, so did I. I don't know. Maybe she's growing up. She's seemed different the last couple of months."

"Or maybe you're just getting used to her."

"I hate that you're probably right."

We're at her apartment building now, but Elizabeth stops and takes my hand instead of unlocking the door. "Listen," she says. "While we're on the subject of...all of this."

"Don't tell me you're moving to California with Ivy's mom."

She laughs a little. "Not California."

My chest feels cold. "Oh."

She squeezes my hands. "Sorry. I haven't decided yet or anything. But you know I'm graduating in May and I got this job offer in Boston that sounds really good."

"Boston." Okay. Boston's not that far.

"It's doable, right?" she says. "I know it would suck, but..."

"Yeah, it's just a train ride." I take a deep breath. "It's okay."

"Like I said, I haven't decided," she says.

"No, you should do it," I hear myself saying. "It's this big opportunity, and I don't want you to stay and resent me."

"I would never resent you," Elizabeth says. "And they don't need a decision from me until April. I just wanted to keep you in the loop."

"Yeah. Okay. Thanks."

I follow her up the stairs to her apartment and try to calm down. Because she's right; Boston is doable, and it's not the end of the world. But it's just...Ivy, and now Elizabeth, and fuck, even Dot, everyone's got these opportunities and these other places and these *futures*, and I'm what, exactly? Going to be living in my parents' house, running their strip club forever? Is that really all I have to offer the world? All the world has to offer *me*?

God, I think it might be.

It's been a long week for all of us, so we decide to just meet at Mama's and relax there instead of going to Kinetic. Dance Machine Dot is, of course, indignant, and leaves us at the table and hits the bar's tiny dance floor with a bunch of gay guys who fawn all over her. Being that good-looking is just a different world.

"So wait," Diana says. "Where in California?"

Dot flits over to our table for a sip of her drink, and Ivy kisses her before shoving her back to the dance floor. "Santa Monica," she says to Diana. "All beaches all the time."

"God, that sounds amazing."

"You're not actually going," I say.

Ivy ignores me and shows her phone to Diana. "That's where we'd be living."

"Holy shit," Diana says.

I say, "And where will you be living after the jewelry scammer goes to prison?"

Ivy throws her hair back. "I don't care about that. I'm not going out there to join some jewelry venture. I'll fake it until my mom gets bored, but it's a plane ticket and a change of scenery and a chance to be a buyer in Hollywood."

"What about school?" Melody says. "And your job?"

And us?

"I haven't decided anything yet," Ivy says. "It's just on the table, that's all." She nudges Diana. "How'd that German exam go?"

"Oh God, I forgot to tell you," Diana says, and she launches into a story about her German professor forgetting their exam date and showing up fifteen minutes late in his pajamas, and it's a pretty funny story, but Ivy isn't paying any attention. "Why do you even ask?" Diana asks her when she's finished entertaining the rest of us.

"Students at Columbia are *really* unhappy," Ivy says

without looking up from her phone. "I have statistics."

"And what are you going to do with those statistics?" Melody asks patiently.

Ivy's already typing. "Text them to Dot."

"How the hell does she put up with you?" I say.

Ivy laughs. "There's no one like me."

She's right, too. That's the problem.

We head home fairly early, much to Dot's dismay. I sit in the back seat while she and Ivy bicker over the music like they always do, but with a little more tension than usual. Dot's pissed because Ivy pulled her away from this girl she was hooking up with because she was ready to go home. Ivy's pissed because…who knows.

"Columbia's not even one of the good Ivies," she says. "If you're gonna go to one, go to Harvard or some shit—"

"Great advice, thank you," Dot says. It's weird seeing her cut Ivy off like that. I don't think I've ever seen her do it before. Honestly, I don't think I've ever seen *anyone* do it before. I always just let her go until she gets bored and moves on to something else.

"Stop pouting. That girl was too old for you anyway."

"Trust me, I know too old for me. And I am so not the one pouting!"

Dot's mom is at the kitchen table when we come in, laughing with my mom. Dot kisses both their cheeks and goes to the fridge for a bottle of water.

"I can't stay," she says to Ivy. "I have to go home and edit that video I recorded yesterday."

"The skin care one?"

"Yeah."

"Mmm," Ivy says. "Think you'll still be able to do videos when you're a law student?"

Dot sucks on her teeth. "I don't know."

"I'm just saying, all that homework, all the study groups, all the time spent convincing douchey frat guys you belong there—"

"Oh my God, Ivy, back the fuck off," Dot snaps.

We all kind of stop and stare—me, my mom, *Dot's* mom. Everyone except Ivy. "I know I'm right," she says simply with an overly casual shrug. "If you don't want to listen to me, that doesn't change. I still sleep like a baby."

"In California," Dot says.

Ivy holds eye contact with her. "Yeah. In California."

Dot leaves with her mom pretty soon after that, and my mom wipes down the kitchen table while I start the dishes and Ivy sorts recycling. "What was that about California?" she says.

"I'm thinking about moving," Ivy says. "My mom's headed out there. Would be a nice change of scenery."

Okay, here's the part where my mom tells her that's crazy, and that Ivy's mother is a disaster, and that she doesn't know anyone out in California, and anyway what about Andie? In three, two...

"I think that could be really great for you," my mother says.

I really should have seen that coming, since this whole month has been some sort of study in irony.

"You think?" Ivy says.

"You've been wanting something bigger for a long time, honey," my mom says. "And you've got some money saved up now. Maybe it's time to strike it out on your own, 'cause Lord knows that's how you always end up when you're with your mother."

"Yeah, I know."

My dad walks in from downstairs, his glasses on top of his head, and says, "We're talking about getting rid of Ivy? Finally."

Ivy kisses his cheek on the way to the trash can.

"Ivy's acting like she might move to California," I say to him.

"I like California," my dad says.

"Now you have an excuse to visit," Ivy says.

"Or to stay far, far away," Dad says.

Ivy considers this. "Definitely one of the two."

"Lord, I miss traveling," my mother says with a sigh. She kisses my dad. "Someday you'll win the lottery and we'll finally take Andrea to Italy."

"This is my responsibility?" Dad says.

"Mmm-hmm."

"What the fuck is going on here?" I burst. "Ivy's lived here since she was born. Her entire life is here. She has a job. She has school. And now one conversation about possibly moving to California and everyone's on board? Your mom's probably not even going to go! She's going to flake out and end up in Toledo or fucking West Virginia."

Ivy rolls her eyes and takes a bag of trash out the back door without a word. My parents are too busy exchanging looks with each other to be helpful, so I follow her out to the back porch.

I stick my hands under my arms to keep them warm while Ivy throws open the lid of the trash can. Tiny snowflakes glisten in the air, and they make everything sound muffled, fake.

"Are you really going to make me say it?" I say.

She doesn't look at me. "Say what."

God. God. "What about me?"

She sighs and closes the lid of the trash can. "What about you?"

"I thought this was just some hissy fit because your girlfriend was leaving."

"She's not my girlfriend," she says. "And she's not leaving."

"But now you're actually going to do it?"

"I don't know. Maybe."

"And I get that this is you, that you can just watch your literal fucking home burn down and think it's a good excuse for a fresh start, I get that, I know you, but I always thought…look, fuck school, fuck work, fuck the girls and fuck Dot and fuck everything that's familiar, but what about *me*?"

We were supposed to go to Paris.

Ivy comes toward me and cups my chin in her hand and kisses me, right here in the backyard with the trash. It's longer than our usual kisses, and I hold on to her hips and feel her so, so, so close to me. Like we're almost one person. We're *so* close.

"Come with me," she whispers.

Her lips are so soft. Her hand in my hair. Oh God. Oh God.

I imagine it. In that moment, I see all of it. How fucking beautiful it would be.

"No," I say.

"Come to California." She tucks my hair behind my

ears. "We could rent bicycles. Sell snow cones. Whatever the fuck."

I think about my dad just out of the hospital, and Max and the club, and how warm the sun must be from the Santa Monica pier. "I can't," I say. "My family needs me."

"Yeah." Ivy takes a step back and looks down at the ground. "Yeah, they do."

We're quiet for a minute, our breath fogging in the air.

Eventually Ivy turns her face up to the sky. "I have to get out of this town, Andrea."

"I know," I say, even though I don't want to.

"I've been just *stuck* for so goddamn long now. There has got to be more out there than this. This can't just be… this can't be it. There has to be more of a reason to fucking get up in the morning."

I thought we were enough. I thought I was enough.

"What about me?" I say again, when I can't not say it anymore.

She looks at me, then back up at the stars.

"There has to be more," she says softly.

We go back inside after that, and Ivy heads upstairs and to her room without saying anything. My mom's gone up to bed already and my dad's watching TV, and I stand in the kitchen and look around this tiny house I've lived in my entire life and feel like the walls are getting smaller and smaller.

The TV shuts off. "Andie?" my dad says. "Are you okay?"

I say, "Do you ever feel stuck?"

He watches me, his eyes sad. "I have. Used to a lot."

"Does anything help?"

"My dear," he says, "*everything* helps."

* * *

I'm back at the strip club the next day, figuring out the new bartender's schedule and mopping the floors and moping, basically. I'm also checking my phone every ten minutes, because Elizabeth's been texting me about the Boston job, and I'm pretty sure everyone in the state of Rhode Island is going to leave besides me. I must look about how I feel, because Max ruffles my hair as he walks by me. I bat him away.

I'm in the dressing room while Melody's getting ready, fixing her tits and dotting lipstick on her mouth. "What's with you?" she asks me.

"Do you want to leave Providence?"

"Ooh, let me guess who this is about."

"It's not just Ivy."

"Sure."

"It's not," I say. "It's Ivy, and it's Elizabeth, fuck, it's Dot. It's all these people who are going to move on and get these big new lives and just... Do you ever feel like you're trapped here?"

"What, like in the club?"

"No, just in your life. That you're supposed to be bigger or doing more or meaning more or something. Like there's something that you're supposed to be doing and you don't know what it is, but it's not *this*. It can't be this."

"Come here," Melody says.

She pulls me up out of my chair and over to the door that leads backstage. From here, we can just barely see Tara onstage, dancing for a crowd. She's wrapped around the pole, doing moves that, even after seeing them a thousand times, I will never figure out the physics for. She's stretched and shiny and beautiful, and glitter pours down on her and catches on the purple lights on the stage. The music blares. People cheer. Everything looks like what I picture when I imagine a galaxy.

"What's bigger than this?" Melody says, and right then I don't know. I squeeze Melody's hand and kiss her cheek and bask in the lights like they're on me.

My family made this.

I'm at home midday on Monday when Ivy comes home from class. She studies me. "You look forlorn."

"I was going for despondent."

She checks her phone. "I have to pick up the ward. Do you want to come?"

"Yeah." Might as well soak up as much time with her as I can.

We drive over to Dot's school, and I get out and climb into the back seat when Dot walks up by herself. "Where's Natalie?" Ivy says, which I guess is the name of that blonde girl who's usually with her.

"Out sick today, but I think she's just hung over."

"It's wild that your mom thinks I'm the bad influence," Ivy says. "You were a mess before I even got here."

"Eh, prove it."

We pull away from the school while Dot messes with the music.

"So," Ivy says in her fake-casual voice that she must still think fools *someone.* "Where's Natalie going to college?"

"Brown. She got in early."

"What's she studying?"

"She doesn't know yet."

"What's she good at?"

I see Dot shrug a little. "Flute."

"So why not music?"

"When did you become such a fucking idealist?"

"And when did you become a cynic?"

"Guess I've been hanging out with you too much," Dot says.

"Yeah, back atcha," Ivy says. I feel it would be in bad taste for me to chime in.

Dot puts her feet up on the dashboard. "I have done so fucking much to my parents," she says. "My mom has basically been forced to accept that I'm sleeping with girls in a matter of a few months and she's doing a damn good job of it, but it's *hard.* And my dad still barely talks to me. They fight about me all the time. Why is making you happy more important than making them happy?"

Ivy snorts. "This is not about making me happy," she says.

"Well, good to hear that, since it wouldn't make any fucking sense, since *you're leaving anyway.* What the hell do you care whether I stay local or not?"

"You think this is about what state you go to school in?" Ivy says. "I don't give a shit where you go. Go to SCAD. Go to Pratt. Go to the Art Institute, I don't *care,* but you cannot be a fucking lawyer. You're an artist. You *have* something. You can't give that up."

"You did."

"I didn't have what you have. Not even close."

"Don't bullshit me."

"Why would I bullshit you?" Ivy says. "I just know I've known you for six months and you've definitely never fucking mentioned your deep desire to be a lawyer, and you're not exactly *quiet*, so I'm pretty sure I would have heard about it by now, considering how many times you've told me that same fucking story about your aunt and the time, I swear to God, you listed off all the contents of your entire goddamn bedroom. Look, do whatever you want, I don't care, but do it because you want to, not because you think it'll make someone else happy. Because guess what, if you go and become a lawyer, you're gonna be a queer fucking lawyer. And your parents still won't be happy. And there is nothing you can do to change that, so stop trying."

Dot, for once in her life, doesn't say anything.

Her mom's there again when we get to my house, drinking tea and watching a movie on the couch with mine. Dot gives her a hug, then takes the remote and pauses the movie.

"What's wrong?" my mom says.

But Dot just looks right at hers. "Mom," she says. "I'm gonna go to RISD."

Ivy doesn't go to California.

"She just stopped talking about it completely," I tell Elizabeth while we're doing the dishes in her apartment after dinner. "And yesterday her mom left and it was, like, very anticlimactic."

"She probably realized it wasn't realistic," Elizabeth says.

"Yeah, maybe."

"Or." Elizabeth comes over and kisses my forehead. "There was someone here she couldn't bear to leave."

"Yeah," I say softly. "Maybe."

Elizabeth looks down and squeezes my hands.

"Oh," I say. "Oh. You're not going to Boston, are you?"

"No," she says. "I don't think I am." She looks up at me, her eyes warm.

She's staying for me. She's giving up a job because of me. She's choosing me over her future.

She's making *me* her future.

And she's amazing, and I think I love her, but I feel my stomach sinking like a stone.

March

Ivy moves out the second week of March. She gets an apartment in Warwick, about ten miles out of Providence and a little closer to school, in this old industrial building that's been turned residential. It has high ceilings and crossbeams and exposed brick. She's in love.

She disappears for a few days to get the place ready, then has me over to see it one afternoon. She pours champagne and tucks Dot under her arm, and she looks happier than I've seen her in a long time.

She's fucking radiant.

Meanwhile, my time's being taken up by Elizabeth. She wants to see me all the time. She drops one or two hints about me moving into her apartment. And I'm starting to notice that our dates always look the same. We go where she wants to go. We do it on her schedule. We eat at her favorite restaurants. We hang out with her friends. We go back to her place.

"I think I have made a mistake of gigantic proportions," I say.

Diana nudges her shot of tequila toward me. "Here. You need this."

We're at the bar at Kinetic on a Friday night. Elizabeth had a study group. Ivy ditched us as soon as we got here; Dot's been sick, so Ivy hasn't gotten laid in a few days and she's here on business. We've been inside for ten minutes and she's already wrapped around this blonde girl on the dance floor.

"I should have insisted she go to Boston," I say. "I ruined her life."

"She could still change her mind, right?" Diana says. "So it's not too late."

"I don't know," I say. "She might have already told them no. I don't want to *ask*." I take Diana's shot. It's my fourth. "And what if she goes to Boston and it turns out I miss her and *that's* the mistake of gigantic proportions?"

Melody orders another round and then turns to us and says, "I don't think this is really about Elizabeth at all."

I groan. "I know."

Diana says, "Andie, you really need to diversify your portfolio or whatever. Every problem cannot be about Ivy."

"And yet here we are," I say. "It's not my fault she's so…" I gesture to where she's dancing, her boots stretching up her thighs, the sparkles on her dress catching the light like water.

"Hot?" Melody says.

"I was going to say aggravating."

"Who's aggravating?" It's Dot, appearing as if from nowhere, like she always does. "Besides me, obviously." She has a lot of makeup on, but she still clearly has a bad cold. Her eyes are red and teary and her sinuses look a little swollen.

"I thought you were home sick," Melody says.

Dot shrugs. "Feeling better." She scans the room. "Where's Ivy?" She really must be sick if her Ivy-radar isn't functioning properly.

We point her out, and it must catch Ivy's eye because she notices Dot, says something to the girl she's dancing with, and comes over to us. "What the fuck are you doing here?" she says to Dot.

"Dancing strengthens the immune system."

"Go home," Ivy says. "I'm not here to babysit you."

"I don't need to be babysat. I'm good."

"Your voice is shot, you're sweating, you look like shit, and I am not peeling you off this dirty-ass floor if you faint. Go. Home."

"You're so mean."

"Old news."

Dot gives a stuffy sigh and a pout, but Ivy just raises an eyebrow and Dot actually listens—miracles do happen—and leaves. Ivy goes back to the blonde girl and immediately locks her mouth on hers, and Melody hands me another shot.

"Such a loving and concerned girlfriend, that Ivy," Diana says.

"Whatever," Melody says. "You want to know what I think?"

"I want to know what anyone who's not me thinks," I say. "I am so sick of being in my head."

"I think you're never going to be able to fully commit to Elizabeth until you get closure from Ivy. You're always going to be wondering *what if*. So you need to find out *what if*. It's time."

"I can't," I say. "She's with Dot."

"She's not with Dot," Melody says. "She just sent her home sick by herself, without even offering her a ride to her house, so that she could get back to her conquest of the night. That's not a relationship."

But it's the closest Ivy's ever come. Maybe that's enough for it to count. Ivy's never really been the caretaking type, not even for me, so it's not like I would expect her to fall all over herself to baby Dot and her cold. "She's never had a relationship," I say. "Not really."

"Right," Melody says. "And do you think maybe she was waiting for you?"

That's not what I was going for, but...God.

What kind of question is that? Of course I think maybe she's been waiting for me. I've thought it every single day for as long as I can remember. It's not that I think it's likely or anything, but it's *possible*. It's always been possible that Ivy is madly in love with me and too afraid of scaring me, of messing it up, of ruining what we have now to do anything about it.

I'm not saying it's likely. I'm just saying it's possible.

And usually that's felt like a security blanket, but tonight it feels like a ticking clock. I think it's the alcohol. I order two more shots.

"Lots of people were friends before they got together," Melody says. "Look at me and Di. We were best friends for years and we decided to give it a shot and...y'know. Fairy-tale shit."

Holy shit, I am getting much too close to actually considering this.

"You need an answer," Diana says.

"I need an answer. I need vodka."

I don't know why tonight is different. I guess I haven't been this drunk in a while. But for some reason, I reach a point where I know that the thing I've been desperately hiding is coming out tonight. And once I've made the decision, there's no going back. There's just drinking, running lines in my head, and getting brave.

It's happening. It's happening. Thank God, holy shit, it's happening.

Except by the time I'm enough drinks deep, Ivy's gone. I find the girl she was with, who's still sweaty and flushed from whatever Ivy did to her back on the couches, and she says she went home. Makes sense; she has work early in the morning, and she did say this was a business trip.

So I guess it's a false alarm, like every other time I thought I'd psyched myself up enough to tell Ivy how I feel. I go home—Diana drives my car for me—but I feel too electric to sleep. I pace my room over and over and look at my hoard of romance novels and then at myself in the mirror. My hair's a mess and my face seems somehow… unfamiliar. It's my eyes, I think. They look sure.

They've never looked like that before.

I'm not going to sit around and wait for life to happen anymore. I'm not going to be a supporting character in my own story.

"Fuck it," I say, and I get an Uber to Ivy's apartment.

I hit the buzzer for 3B over and over and over again.

"Ivy," I say into the box, even though she hasn't picked up. "Ivy. Ivy. Ivy."

Finally there's a crackle and her voice comes through the line. "What the fuck?" she says.

"Ivyyyyyy."

"Jesus Christ," she says and buzzes me up.

She's standing at her open front door by the time I make it up the stairs. She's wearing sweats and her hair is up in a messy bun on top of her head. She's beautiful. She has her arms spread wide across the doorway like an action villain, but when she sees me, she softens.

"God, you are wasted," she says.

"Lemme in."

She laughs once. "No. I'm getting you an Uber."

"I just had an Uber."

"Well, that's good to hear."

"Let me *in*. I need to talk to you."

"How about tomorrow? You know, when there's daylight?"

"No. No daylight. This is important."

She studies me, then sighs. "We can talk outside. Let me get my fucking coat, God." She steps away from the door and goes inside, and I hold on to the doorframe and wait. Her living room is messy. At first I think it's my fault, but then I remember I haven't been inside and I figure I'm just drunk.

Ivy comes back and locks the door and leads me outside, holding on to my arm so I don't tip over. "You realize it's a *weeknight*, right?" she says to me as we step outside the building. The air is cold, but it doesn't feel cold. It feels alive. Like a wave. Pushing me. "Even I don't get hammered on weeknights."

"Yeah."

"What happened, did what's her name break up with

you or something?"

"No."

She furrows her brow. "Is everything okay with your parents, I—"

"They're fine, they're fine, they're fine. Everything's okay. I just needed to be brave."

She watches me, her arms crossed, her eyes glittering in the moonlight. I wonder if I woke her up. I couldn't have. Nobody looks that good when they just woke up.

That's stupid. *She* does. I know she does. I've seen her wake up a thousand times. I know everything about her.

"I'm in love with you," I say.

Oh.

I actually said it.

All these years and I actually just said it.

The clock in my head stops ticking. Time stops moving altogether.

She stares at me and uncrosses her arms. I hear everything, a car alarm a block away, the streetlight buzzing over our heads. Her breathing.

Everything is so, so still.

"I think I always have been," I say. "I think I was in love with you before I knew what that even meant. And I don't even know why I'm telling you this, because I'm with Elizabeth and it feels like that's getting really serious, but I needed you to know before it does. I just wanted you to know that I've always been here and I guess I have to know if you even noticed. I need something to happen to me."

This is coming out all wrong.

And Ivy is just standing there, not running into my arms, not melting. She just looks…scared.

"You're drunk," she says eventually.

"That doesn't matter."

She presses her hand to her forehead and breathes out.

"I think we could be really good together," I say. "And I know, because I've thought about it a lot. I could be really easy. We could go slow. I can be really, really patient."

She still hasn't said anything else and I *cannot stop talking*.

"I know all about you, so you don't have to worry about me finding anything out," I say. "I already know everything. You can't surprise me. And you can't scare me off. You don't have to worry. You'd never have to worry about anything."

She isn't looking at me anymore.

"Am I hurting you?" I say. "You look like I'm hurting you."

She closes her eyes.

"Please say something," I say. "You have to say something."

"I…" she starts, and she looks like she's struggling for a very long time. "I don't understand why you're telling me this."

I feel so small. "I just wanted you to know."

"Jesus Christ, Andie, you think I didn't know?" she says, and then she winces and pushes her fingers into her eyes and…God.

Small and cold.

The car alarm stops.

"How long have you known?" I say, and she sighs and looks at me. "Oh," I say.

And I finally get why she looks scared. Because I'm breaking open this fragile thing we've both been carrying, this bit of willful ignorance that has let us keep this friendship alive.

There was always a chance she didn't know.

For both of us, there was always that tiny, tiny chance that she didn't know how I really felt.

"You don't love me," I say.

"Of course I love you."

"But not like that."

She pulls her bottom lip in between her teeth.

I would give everything I have ever had in my life for her to argue with me right now. To engage. Something.

To say it isn't true.

This is happening too fast. "You just…" I say. "You can give me a chance. You've never seen me like that, I get it, but you could try it. It happens all the time. It happened with Melody and Diana."

"Andie."

"You could *try*," I say.

"Do you *honestly* think I haven't tried?" she bursts.

I catch my breath. "What?"

She paces. "Do you think I don't know how much easier everything would be if I could just…just fucking do it, be your little wife like you want? I could get enough sleep and come out to my mom and we could adopt a Hungarian orphan or something and we'd live this pretty little life and—do you know how exhausting it has been being the reason for all the problems in your life? Every single time something is wrong with you, I think, *well, you could make her happy if you really wanted to*. But I don't. I don't want to. Not like that. I have *tried* to want it, but I don't, okay?"

Oh God.

Oh God.

But I can save this. I can turn it around. "That's not about me; that's about settling down," I say. "I'm not asking for that. That's not what I'm saying. You're not understanding me."

"It's not," she says, and she sounds so tired and sorry. "It's not about settling down."

"I wouldn't make you do that."

"It doesn't matter," she says.

"I told you that I know you," I say. "Come on. You're Ivy Harlowe. You're not anyone's wife."

"Well, everyone knows that," she says, and we laugh just a little, somehow.

We're quiet for a minute.

"You could still sleep with other people," I say, and I hate myself.

It's mutual. I can tell by her face. "Andie. Stop. Please."

I can count on one hand the number of times Ivy has said "please" to me. This has got to be in the bad love confession hall of fame. Who the fuck begs you to stop?

I pinch the bridge of my nose. For a long time neither one of us says anything. I mean, what is there to say at this point? How are we ever going to talk to each other again?

Maybe she's thinking the same thing, because eventually she says, "What did you think was going to happen here?"

I clear my throat and shake my head hard enough that everything goes spotty for a minute. "I don't know. This, probably. But…maybe it wouldn't. You know?"

"Yeah," she says.

I want to touch her so badly. "Do you hate me?"

"Of course not."

"You hate me."

"God, you are so drunk," she says. "I do not hate you."

"You wouldn't even let me inside."

She snorts and rolls her eyes. "I just didn't want you to wake up Dot. She had a fever earlier."

What? "Dot's here?"

"Yeah."

"But…" I feel like I've been punched in the stomach. "You sent her away. You told her to go home."

Ivy shrugs one shoulder.

And suddenly it comes together. The messy living room with the tissues everywhere and the DVDs pulled out and the blanket crumpled up on the couch. She's been over there while she's been sick. When Ivy told her to go home, she didn't mean Dot's house.

"You hate sick people," I say. "When I'm sick you treat me like a fucking biohazard, you don't… God. It's not settling down you don't want. It's *me*."

"Andie," she says.

"You'll do all that shit, just with someone else."

"Well, I'm not running out to adopt the Hungarian orphan."

"All this time I thought you were the problem," I say. "I thought you were just scared and broken and too fucked up for a relationship and it was *me*." I might throw up. "I'm the problem. I'm too boring and selfish and I'm this, like, embodiment of staying in Providence, which you fucking hate, I'm just this fucking stupid basic bitch townie and—"

"It's not you," Ivy says.

"It's me."

"It's not."

"Then *what*? Why can you do this with someone else

and not me?"

"It's…" Ivy sighs and looks away. "I don't know what it is."

God. She can't even come up with anything else. It's me.

"I'm sorry," I say. "I didn't mean to be in love with you."

She quirks up half of a smile. "You're not the first to be in that position."

"Shut up."

Her smile fades. "Okay."

"I just…" I have to say it. I can't not say it anymore. "I just don't know why you can't do this, whatever you want to call what you're doing, I don't care, just, with me. All I want is what you have with her. You don't have to do anything else. I just want…I want you to be as happy as you are with her but with me instead." I swallow. "And preferably somehow you do it without hurting her, because she's starting to grow on me."

Ivy just looks at me and then says, "No."

And I swear to God, I feel myself physically sink into the ground.

"I know," I say. "I know. I'm gonna go."

"It's the middle of the night."

"I'll get an Uber."

"No," she says. "Come on. Just…try to be quiet."

Getting home sounds really, really hard, and my head is pounding and I just want to lay down, and I also sort of feel like if I don't go with her right now we'll both disappear into how goddamn awkward this is and avoid each other for the rest of our lives.

So I follow her up the stairs of her building. I don't even feel like I'm walking. Moving is just something that's happening to me. I don't want to follow her. I don't want to be in the same space as her. It's too close. It's not close enough.

Ivy unlocks the door and opens it quietly, then sweeps stuff off the couch to make room. "I'll get you a pillow and another blanket," she says.

"Yeah. Thanks."

She goes to her room, and I hear her open up the closet and root around and a second later, Dot's voice. "What's going on?"

"Shh. Everything's okay."

"Is Andie here?"

"Yeah. Take your temperature again. You feel warm."

I bury my face in the couch cushions and bite down as hard as I can.

"Andie? Andie."

I blink and watch everything swim until Dot's face evens out over me. Mother of fuck, my head hurts. Why is light so bright? Who decided that?

"Hey," I croak.

She smiles. "Hey. How are you feeling?"

I sit up slowly. "I think I'm supposed to be asking you that."

"Better," she says. And she looks it this time. She's wearing sweatpants and a URI tank top and she has a little bit of makeup on. "Do you want some water?"

"Ugh. I don't know." Last night is coming back to me, piece by intolerable piece. "Where's Ivy?"

"At work."

I stretch my neck until it pops. "Right."

I'm not sure I've ever been alone with Dot before.

She looks so comfortable standing here in this apartment. That Ivy left her in while she went to work.

God, I wonder if she has a key.

I drag myself out of my colloid of self-loathing and self-pity long enough to notice Dot watching me with her head tilted to the side, a thoughtful look on her face. Her eyeliner wings are tiny and perfect.

"What?" I say.

"There's a café next door," she says.

"I know."

"So do you want to get breakfast?"

"What, you and me?" I'm not the most tactful when I'm hungover. Or ever, really.

But she says, "Come on. My treat."

I've walked past this café on my way up to Ivy's apartment but never actually been inside. It's small, just three booths and two tables, and a lot of the walking space is taken up with newspaper stands and displays of Korean snack foods. Dot smiles at a server behind the counter, who clearly goddamn recognizes her, and we slide into a booth.

"Ivy's, like, obsessed with the French toast here," she says.

"Yeah, Ivy loves French toast."

"It's so easy to make," Dot says. "I'm always telling her

not to waste money on it."

A server comes by and gives us coffee, which I gulp down like I'm dying of dehydration, which I guess I probably am. Dot sips hers and watches me over the rim.

"Ivy told you everything," I say. No one looks that smug unless they know what's going on.

She sets the mug down and blots her lipstick on her napkin with a shrug.

"God," I say. "Can we skip the speech where you tell me to back off if I promise that right now I dread even looking at her ever again?"

She laughs. "That's not what this is. I just wanted to see if you were okay."

Hang on.

What?

I blink at her.

"What's wrong?" she says.

"What's wrong is I just tried to steal your girlfriend away from you and you're wondering if *I'm* okay? I'm the bad guy here."

"She's not the Hope Diamond," Dot says. "She's not locked up."

"So you either really trust her or you're *that* confident that you're her first choice."

She smiles a little. "Why not both?"

I groan and slump back in the booth. There's a group of friends at the booth next to us that has way, way too much energy for this early. Don't they have jobs? I guess Dot called out sick from school. Her mom probably thinks she's at her cousin's.

The server comes by to take our order, and Dot gets an omelet; I get the French toast, mostly because I forgot to look at the menu. Dot hands them back to the server with a dazzling smile and sits back in the booth and looks at me.

"How did you do it?" I say. "How did you fucking... get her."

"I didn't do anything," Dot says.

"Come on." I'm ready to peek in the back of the book for the answers now. I've already lost. At least let me find out how I could have won.

"I'm serious," she says. "It's not like I tamed her or something. I just kept being around until she decided she didn't really mind. Became a habit, I guess."

That can't be it. "She doesn't mind me around, either."

"No, she doesn't," Dot says. "And I hope this doesn't change that. I'd kill to have a best friend like you guys have."

"Want to trade?"

She smiles demurely. "Maybe not."

"You must have done something," I say. "Even if you don't know what it is. People don't just change for no reason. You did that smile of yours and cracked her open or something."

"She didn't change," Dot insists. "We're just in each other's orbits now or whatever." She shrugs. "I don't know. Neither of us has anywhere else to be."

"She talks to you," I say. "She tells you things."

Dot sips her coffee.

"She doesn't do that," I say. "It's, like, impossible to get her to talk to me about anything real."

"You just have to keep trying."

"I don't want to push her away," I say. "She's more fragile than you think."

"I don't think she is, actually."

And she says it like it's nothing. Like I'm supposed to stop trying to fix the person I've been trying to fix since I first realized there was something broken about her.

"Do you know about her dad?" I say. I hate that it's my trump card, but it is. Ivy doesn't talk about it.

But Dot just nods. Fuck.

And my mind goes crazy trying to imagine how Ivy told her. If Dot found a picture and asked. If they were driving and Ivy mentioned her dad liked a song that was playing and tried to drop in casually that he'd died. If it was the middle of the night and Ivy was crying and she woke up Dot for comfort.

I know it's not my business, but it's Ivy, so it kind of is.

"I let her do whatever she wants," I say. "I let her get away with anything."

"Yeah. I would imagine that gets pretty boring for both of you."

I take a minute, making lines in my napkin with my fork. Dot straightens a poster on the wall and checks her phone.

"You're really not threatened by me at all," I say.

"I guess not. Sorry."

I groan. "After last night, I can't imagine why you would be. I have been very, very rejected. Picture me begging and her looking at me like I'm a sea slug. So very rejected."

She scrunches her nose up in sympathy. "Never fun."

"How would you know? Has anything bad ever happened to you?"

"I had a fish that died," she says.

"I really wish I hated you."

"And I have a phenomenal imagination."

I roll my eyes. "Can I ask you something?"

"Yeah."

"Does she, like… When you're alone. Does she call you her girlfriend? Does she tell you she loves you?"

Dot laughs softly. "Why, should she?"

"I mean, most people do. And I would want that," I say. "If I were with her, I'd want that."

Dot reaches across the table and squeezes my hand. Her hands are so soft.

"I know you would," she says, and that's it, and something maybe clicks into place.

The server comes with our food and we eat in silence. It's a little awkward, but not as much as it should be. Dot checks her phone and laughs every once in a while. She glances up at me at one point, right before Ivy texts me a heart.

"We'll be fine," I tell her. "Stop worrying. You're not the biggest problem we've ever dealt with."

Dot chuckles. "That's the spirit."

And when Dot asks me, when I'm paying—I don't let her do it—if I'm okay, I say, "Yeah," and I think I mean it. At least a little bit. At least for a second.

April

So, what do you do when you have to completely shift gears on your entire life?

Me, I spend most of the beginning of April working extra hours, trying to keep the club afloat, reading, and avoiding crying as much as physically possible. I lose myself in books.

Ivy and I aggressively evade talking about anything deeper than what our plans are for the weekend. We go out with the girls and Ivy continues to hook up with anything that moves, besides me. The weather gets warm and wet and Dot's sneezing all the time from the pollen and Ivy makes fun of her. I go to College Hill on my day off and walk around Thayer Street and pretend I'm some out-of-town college kid, coming here for a fresh start.

I just…recalibrate.

I really thought we were going to end up together someday. I don't think I knew how much I really thought that until the door shut on it. I thought Ivy still had a lot she needed to get out of her system, but when she was ready to settle down, when she was going to flirt with someone in diner booths and drag someone home by the collar afterward, it would be me.

And it's not. Because Ivy doesn't love me. Ivy doesn't love who I am. Something about me just isn't good enough.

And as much as that sucks, well, something about me is good enough for Elizabeth, so I focus on being the best girlfriend ever to make up for being the absolute, categorical worst in ways that she doesn't even know. I buy her things. I hang out with her vet friends. I cook her dinner.

I'm coming up with a grocery list one day at the strip club when Ivy makes her announcement. She's here to pick up Dot, who's been coming semi-regularly to do the dancers' makeup, since they now won't shut up unless they get her. Dot's been busy with finals but continues to be nice to me in a way that reminds me how much she pities me, and she and Ivy blow straw wrappers at each other and use hand signals across the room and get half naked on Kinetic's dance floor, moving faster than the music.

Ivy looks over Dot's shoulder to check out the cut crease she's forming and then turns to me and says, "I'm throwing you a birthday party."

I cough out a laugh. "You're what?"

"I'm throwing you a birthday party," she says. "Next week. Unless your wife already has you tied up."

"We're just doing a little dinner," I say. "I told her I didn't want anything special."

"Wow. Nothing special for your birthday. Your *twentieth* birthday. The end of your teenage years."

"Very old," Dot says, and I stick my tongue out at her. She beams.

"I don't need a party," I say.

Ivy waves that away. "I haven't had people over since I got the apartment. It's all decorated now."

"Oh, so this is about you."

"Obviously."

"I could use a nice party," Dot says. "My friends' parties are getting very edgy."

"Russian roulette?" I say.

Dot blots Abby's lipstick. "I wouldn't be surprised if that's next."

"Catholic school," Ivy says with a shudder. "They're into weird shit."

"Why is Dot invited to my birthday party?" I say, just because it's a bit at this point.

Dot pretends to pout. "You love me, really."

"Make sure to invite Elizabeth," Ivy says. "Even though she hates all of us."

"She doesn't hate all of you," I say. "She hates you specifically."

"Good to know I can still inspire strong emotions in people in my old age."

"Hey, you're not the one turning twenty."

"And thank God for that." She spins around in her chair. "It'll be fun. We haven't had a party in forever."

I hate parties, but whatever. That conversation was the most natural interaction Ivy and I have had in weeks. "It'll be something," I say.

Dot comes over on my birthday, before I meet Elizabeth for our pre-party dinner, to do my makeup. She begged, and I figured today was as good a day as any to finally let her. It's my good deed of the month. "Hold still," she says. "No wonder you can't do eyeliner. You're so twitchy."

"I'm not twitchy when I'm the one approaching my eyes with a sharp object."

"It is so not sharp." She stabs it against her hands a few times. "See? Now hold still."

I close my eyes and take a deep breath and try not to flinch when I feel the pencil against my lash line. "Did you get that PR package yet?" I say to distract myself.

"Yep, came in yesterday. I'm using their blush on you, so tell me how you like it."

"Okay." She's been getting a lot more free stuff from brands as her channel keeps growing. Ivy has this blank wall with great light that she's been using as her backdrop, and it makes her videos look a lot more professional than they used to. Yeah, sue me, I've watched one or two. The kid's good at what she does.

"Excited for tonight?" she asks.

"Uh, anxious. It's an Ivy party, so I'm thinking sex swings and whips."

Dot laughs. "She's not that wild really. I'm the one who's always talking her into shit."

"I so don't need to hear that."

"Open," she says and starts tracing my lower lash line.

"Are any of your friends coming?" I say. I have all of four friends, so we're going to need more bodies to fill the space.

But she says, "Nah. Ivy doesn't like them. She thinks they're a bad influence."

I laugh and probably make Dot screw something up. "I'm sorry—Ivy thinks someone else is a bad influence?"

"I know. It's the end of the world."

"You really must talk her into things."

"I'm saying."

"What did you tell your parents you're doing?"

"Staying with my cousin," she says. "Same as always. My aunt's the rebel of the family, so she covers for me."

"I think you're probably the rebel of the family," I say.

"Hmm." Dot looks at herself in the mirror, considering this. "Maybe. I was always just the disappointment."

"And now you're getting PR deals."

She smiles.

Elizabeth takes me back to Clair de Lune, where we had our first date. I remember how uncomfortable I was here back then. I hadn't been to any of the places I have now, the tiny, fancy cafés that Elizabeth loves, the ballet, the opera. I'm some kind of culture kid now.

I don't read romance novels as much anymore; I read the books Elizabeth recommends, the ones that are heavy and serious and usually about men and make me think a lot about what it means to be human. I don't really understand all of them and I really don't understand why most of them aren't shorter, but I like hearing what she thinks about them.

We're meeting for an early dinner before we head over to Ivy's for the party. Elizabeth gets us three courses and keeps the wine flowing and talks to me about this documentary she wants me to watch. At dessert, she pulls out a tiny gift bag and hands it to me. Honestly, I'd thought the dinner itself was my gift, though I guess Elizabeth paying for our dates isn't out of the ordinary.

"You didn't have to," I say. "Seriously. I know people

say that but, like…seriously."

She laughs. "It's your birthday. We should celebrate."

I take a small white box out of the bag and lift the lid. It's a bracelet, silver with blue stones. It winks in the candlelight on our table. It is definitely the prettiest thing I've ever seen.

"Those are sapphires," Elizabeth says.

"This is really nice, holy shit."

"Here," Elizabeth says, and I hold out my arm and let her put it on me. She kisses my hand after she's finished with the clasp.

"It's really beautiful," I say. "Thank you."

"You should have nice things," she says, and she smiles at me.

And a part of me isn't grateful. A part of me is looking at my life and thinking, *I thought I already did.*

But it's a really nice bracelet.

Ivy's apartment is full by the time I get there, crammed with blue lights, alcohol, and people. She clearly had the same realization that I don't know enough people to crowd her bathroom, let alone the apartment, and she invited her friends from school and casual acquaintances from around the old neighborhood and whatever lesbians she happens to have saved in her phone, so it's basically Kinetic relocated.

Dot hands Elizabeth and me drinks the second we walk in and then immediately runs off to refill a chip bowl or something, and I find Alyssa camped out on a couch and give her a hug. "Happy birthday, squirt," she says. Alyssa's the oldest of all of us, already almost twenty-one.

"Teach me how to be an adult, please."

She kisses my cheek. "With my eyes closed."

Elizabeth sees someone she went to college with and goes to catch up, and the second she walks away, Alyssa tugs me down to the arm of the couch and says, "Did you really deliver a drunken love confession to Ivy?"

"Please tell me you didn't hear this straight from Ivy. Or Dot. I have to convince myself that they've developed selective amnesia and forgotten all about it. It's my birthday. Lie if you have to."

She laughs. "Melody told me."

"It was the most supremely embarrassing moment of my life. I'm serious about the amnesia thing. I wish I had it."

"It could have been a lot worse," she says. "You guys are still friends. You still have Elizabeth."

"She does not know, obviously."

"I figured." Alyssa shakes her head a little. "I don't get it."

"Well, I'm an idiot, so that was most of it there."

"No. Turning you down. I don't get it."

I shrug and look around the room kind of absently, but of course my eyes land on Ivy; they always do. She's laughing with a few girls, but she puts her arm out without looking, and a few seconds later, Dot materializes under it. Ivy knocks her head to the side and keeps talking.

"She's happy," I say.

"Well, how about you?"

"I'm working on it," I say, but I don't look away from Dot and Ivy.

Pretty soon, Ivy pulls me up to dance with her and Alyssa and the girls, and I tug in Elizabeth to join us. She's not much of a dancer, but hey, it's my birthday.

Ivy lets me go after a few songs and gives my hair a ruffle when we collapse on her floor pillows. "Not too shabby, huh?" she says.

"I'm amazed this many people came."

"Everyone comes when I call." She picks up her beer and frowns. "Spot?"

She appears, of course. "Hi. I put out more toilet paper."

"How much toilet paper do these people need? Someone here needs to see a doctor." She holds up the beer. "Can you grab me another?"

"Say please," Dot says, and Ivy pulls her down and swallows her whole instead.

They're kind of like that the whole evening. They bicker over which dip to put out and Dot gives someone directions to the bus stop while Ivy fixes one of the string light strips when it falls. Dot separates recycling. Ivy pours drinks.

They are making sense.

Who the fuck could have seen this one coming?

And who the fuck could have anticipated that it sort of wouldn't kill me?

"You're staring," Elizabeth says to me.

"No, I'm not."

I'm drinking for the first time since the night that shall not be named, and everyone's telling me "happy birthday" and pulling me up to dance and it's...kind of amazing. I really thought I didn't want a party, but it's sort of fun to be the center of attention every once in a while.

"Not too shabby," Ivy says again, surveying her land.

"I still think we should have gotten strippers," Dot says.

"I see strippers every day," I say. "It'd be like going to work."

"That's what I told her," Ivy says. She flicks Dot's cheek. "We'll do strippers for your birthday."

Dot considers this. "That's not for four months. Won't you be sick of me by then?"

"God, one can only hope," Ivy says.

The crowd starts to clear out around midnight, and once there's some breathing room, Ivy turns the music down, claps her hands together once, and says, "Presents."

"I don't need presents," I say. "I'm a grown woman. I'm old." I'm currently collapsed on the couch with my head on Elizabeth's leg.

"All the more reason," Ivy says. "Retirement gifts."

I get a cute dress from Sloan's from Diana and Melody, an eye shadow palette from Dot, and this leather-bound journal from Alyssa that I'll probably never use because it's too pretty. Ivy hands me a small, wrapped present, and I break through the tape and pull out Ella Gennesy's *Electric Touch*, the very first novel from one of my favorite romance writers. I have a copy at home, but mine's totally falling apart from how many times I've read it, and I'm scared to even open it nowadays in case it completely goes to pieces.

"Open it," Ivy says. "Open it, open it."

It's signed. *To Andie. Your love story is coming. —EG*

Holy shit.

I look up at Ivy, who's smiling, looking a little nervous, running her hand absentmindedly up and down Dot's back.

Why is she nervous? Was there any chance this wouldn't be the best thing I've ever owned?

I spring up and throw myself around her neck. It's our first hug since The Incident, but she hugs back right away, and it feels easy, feels right.

"You are so fucking amazing," I whisper to her.

"I know," she whispers back with a squeeze.

"This is... Holy shit." I let go of Ivy and grab the book off the couch. "She actually touched this exact book. Like, with her fingers. How the fuck did you get her to do this? She never signs stuff."

"I wrote her a billion emails about my poor best friend who's obsessed with her books until she finally couldn't ignore me anymore."

"The Dot method," Alyssa says, and Ivy kicks her, but Dot laughs.

And just for a minute, everything feels so right. All the strangers have cleared out, and it's just me and my people, in my best friend's apartment, with the best present I've ever gotten.

I'm leafing through the book, thinking about how the hands that typed this actual story are the same ones that wrote my name, when I feel a hand on my shoulder. It's Elizabeth.

"Hey," I say. "Sorry, I'm kind of in a trance."

She smiles a little. "I'm going to head out," she says. "Can you get a ride home?"

"What? I mean, yeah, but...what?"

"We'll talk tomorrow, okay?" she says. "Happy birthday." She starts toward the door, and I feel panic rise up in my throat.

"Wait, hang on." I get up and stop her, my hand on her

arm. "Don't go," I say. "Come on, let's dance or something."

"Really, it's okay."

"Elizabeth," I say. "What's going on?"

She sighs and glances around the room. "Let's talk outside, okay?"

That didn't really work out well for me last time with Ivy, but at least this time we stop in the hallway by the stairs instead of going all the way outside.

Elizabeth sighs and scuffs her feet on the floor and doesn't look like herself, and it's not that I don't know what is probably happening here, it's just that…she just got me this bracelet. It doesn't feel real. I feel detached, like somehow I've already lived this and now I'm watching a recording of it.

She says, "I think I'm going to take that job in Boston."

I'm not surprised, but I feel cold, colder than I would have expected. "Oh."

She shrugs and looks away.

"Um…why?" I say.

It's just a train ride, I tell myself. *You went over how it was just a train ride.*

Maybe this isn't over.

She says, "I am never going to make you light up like she does."

Oh.

She just got me this bracelet, which I didn't love nearly as much as a five-dollar paperback.

God, I deserve this, but that doesn't mean I want it. Suddenly it's so, so important that I not get rejected for the second time in two months. Something needs to hold together.

Damage control. "Okay," I say. "I know I was a bad

girlfriend tonight."

She looks at me.

"And a lot of other nights, too," I say.

"It's okay."

"It's not okay. I'll do better. I'm working on it. I really am."

"You're in love with Ivy," she says. It hits like a hammer, and I hear the tears in the back of her throat.

"I'm working on that," I say quietly.

Her eyes are shining. "And you're not in love with me."

"I..."

But it doesn't matter what I say now. As soon as I paused, I lost her.

I'm working on that, too?

I'm trying so hard to turn into you?

I wish I were a bratty seventeen-year-old who gets everything she wants, but I'm a fuck-up of a twenty-year-old who doesn't know if she wants you to stay or go?

But it doesn't matter what I want anymore. I know that.

"I wish you hadn't led me on," she says. "But it's not like I didn't let you. I guess I can't be too angry about it."

"You can be," I say quietly.

She shrugs. She's angry about it, biting down on her bottom lip, averting her eyes from me, but she wants to be the kind of person who isn't. Her whole persona is about being the kind of person who would be graceful in situations like this.

For the first time in our entire relationship, I'm being the honest one.

"I don't want to be in love with her," I say.

"I know," she says. "Why would you?"

"Yeah." I breathe out. "Yeah, exactly." I shake my head

a little. "You should take the bracelet back."

"No, no. It's yours. Listen, I'm going to go, okay?"

"Okay."

"I'll see you around. Happy birthday."

"Yeah. Thanks."

She turns and goes down the stairs. Her shoulders are beautiful under her tank top straps. Her hair's freshly shaved in the back. She tried to look good for my party. It worked, and I can still feel her skin underneath mine.

I might never see her again, and that feels like regret, but it also feels like relief, and that makes me just furious at myself.

At Ivy, and that suddenly rushes through me like a train.

I stay there frozen for half a minute, waiting for it to dissipate like it always does when I'm angry at Ivy—push it down, push it down—but it just stays, gathering speed inside me, and before I can think, I turn and go back into the party. Ivy's leaning against her kitchen island, watching with an eyebrow raised while Melody tries to balance bottles on top of Dot's head, but I take her by the wrist and pull her into the bathroom.

"Uh, ow," she says. "What's with you?"

"Elizabeth just broke up with me," I say.

Ivy blinks. "All right. Are you okay?"

"Why the fuck did you give me that book?" I say. "Why did you have to do it in front of her? *Your love story is coming*? When she's sitting right there? What the fuck is she supposed to think about that?"

"I didn't care what she thought about it," Ivy says. "I cared what you thought about it."

"Stop it," I say. I point at her. "You don't get to do that."

"Do what?"

"Come in here and be all fucking dreamy and thoughtful like you're my fucking girlfriend. You're not my girlfriend."

"If I recall, I was *pulled* in here—"

"Why do you do this?" I say. "You spent the entire time I was with her sneering and making snarky remarks about how much she sucked. Why the fuck do you do that if you don't even want to be with me?"

"Because she—wait for it—*sucks*. She's pretentious and she steamrolls you and she was trying to turn you into some mini version of her and she made you feel like all the stuff about you that wasn't about her didn't matter."

I know that that's true. But I also know that it's not the whole truth.

"You liked having me in love with you," I say. "Maybe liked having me there on the back burner in case you ever decided you wanted me, or maybe you just liked the goddamn attention, but don't give me any more shit about what a curse it's been to have me wanting you when your whole fucking life is so carefully constructed to have everyone fall in love with you, without you having to ever find out what loving someone might feel like."

Her eyes narrow, and she takes a step toward me.

"This blaming me for all the shit in your life is really fun and everything," Ivy says. "But maybe it's about time you take some responsibility for your goddamn self. You knew I didn't want you and you lusted over me for how long, exactly?"

I can't breathe.

"How long did you hold on to this thing you knew would never happen just because you like being victimized?" Ivy says. She takes another step toward me. "And guess what? I didn't make you fuck up your relationship with Elizabeth. You were a *phenomenally* shitty girlfriend all on your own." She shakes her head. "Now let me out of my fucking bathroom."

I do. The music swells and then quiets as she shuts the door behind her.

I hear the party inside. I hear my heart beating.

I don't have Elizabeth.

I'm not going to have Ivy.

My breath catches in my throat.

I'm free.

M y parents are at the kitchen table with my brother when I get home, a half-eaten coffee cake between them, my brother's tie loose around his neck.

"Hey!" my mother says. "Did you have fun?" The windows are open and everything smells like violets from my dad's garden outside.

"Um…I think so." Honestly, I think I'm going to be processing all of that for the next year of my life, but around all the embarrassment and shame, there's this floaty feeling in my stomach that I can't shake. I hang up my jacket and say, "Max, what are you doing here?"

"Good to see you, too. Happy birthday."

"Thanks." They all seem serious, and I know I walked into something. I just don't know what I could walk into that they wouldn't tell me. Maybe Catherine kicked him out?

My mom gives me kind of a long look and then says,

"Come here," and leads me up to her bedroom.

"What's going on?" I say.

She roots around her dresser drawer. "Now where the fuck... I swear I just..."

"Mom."

"What?"

"What are Dad and Max talking about?"

"Nothing you need to worry about," she says firmly.

"Is Catherine okay?"

"Catherine's fine." She takes an envelope out of the drawer and hands it to me.

"Mom," I say.

"Oh, will you just open it? It's your damn birthday."

I sigh and open the envelope while my mom mumbles about me being an ungrateful brat. Inside is a brochure. And a flight confirmation for the end of May.

I've never been on a plane before.

"What is this?" I say.

"Look at the brochure," she says.

So I do. It's this program for people my age, two-week trips to different parts of the world to learn about various things at each one: architecture in Hong Kong, theater in London, food in Spain. There's a page dog-eared. Italian literature.

"Italy?" I say.

"You know I always meant to take you there. And they'll take you to Lucca, see, that's where your great-grandmother was from."

"But I don't...I can't read Italian."

"Oh, it's in English. Trust me, I made sure!"

"Mom." I close the brochure. "This is too expensive."

"It's done," she says firmly. "The reservation is booked,

your name is on a list, you're going." She puts her hands on my shoulders. "You need to get out of this town for a little bit, huh?"

And just like that, I'm crying, and I nod really hard, and my mom hugs me. And she doesn't know what's been going on with me—God, she probably does; she figures out everything—but it's enough. Just feeling her around me and holding the promise of something bigger than this, even if it's a month away, even if it's just for two weeks— I'm going to see the goddamn world.

"Thank you," I say, and she kisses my cheek. She sighs and pulls back a little, tucking my hair behind my ears like she used to when I was a kid.

"And now we need to go talk to your dad, okay?" she says.

"Yeah. Okay."

We go back downstairs. Max and Dad have moved to the couch. Max has a beer, and Dad looks like he could use one.

"Okay, what's going on?" I say.

They look at each other.

And Dad says, "We have to close the club."

May

"I could sell the tickets," I say.

"I could beat you with this coat hanger," my mother says. "Are we listing stupid ideas?"

We're at Sloan's, and she's helping me spend my birthday money I got from my grandmother on clothes for Italy before I leave in two weeks. Normally this would be a job for the dynamic duo, obviously, but…well. I guess we're not really much of a duo these days, dynamic or otherwise. I haven't seen Ivy since my party, except for once at a distance at Kinetic, and we've barely even texted. It's been like having a stomachache for half a month. It hurts and sometimes you can forget it's there.

"It just feels extravagant," I say. "Considering."

"Selling a pair of plane tickets is not going to save the club," she says.

"I know, but jeez, let a girl dream."

Mom leafs through some sundresses. "You need this," she says. "You broke up with Elizabeth; you're going through whatever the hell's going on with you and Ivy."

"They're just not… Neither of them is the one," I say. "And I thought at least one would be."

"Okay. So they're not the one. So you pick up, you keep going, you travel to Italy. Maybe you meet the one there."

"You don't want me falling in love with someone who

lives in Italy."

"No, I suppose that would get expensive. But how romantic."

"I just wish I could get some kind of, like, fast forward," I say. "Like, just for a *minute*. I could come right back here, but if I could just see whether or not things were going to be okay."

"You really think you've invented a new and exciting problem here, huh?" she says. She pats my cheek. "Everyone would like that."

"Right, but I *need* it."

She holds up a pair of pants. "These would be cute."

"Sure, on Ivy." I groan. "What are you even supposed to do when it turns out nothing is what you thought it was and everything you'd been planning is totally for nothing? How do you just keep starting over?"

"Because what's the alternative?" she says. "Sometimes you're going to have to call it quits and keep going with something else. Look at your father and me now."

"What are you going to do?" I say.

She sighs and hangs a shirt over her arm. "I don't know. I'll go back to full-time. He's always talked about doing translation work. Maybe he'll try that."

"I can't believe we're going to close. I really don't believe it."

"I wish people could see what you see," she says. "What makes it so special. How we treat our girls, how happy they are. But the people who care about that kind of thing, they're not the ones who are going to strip clubs. They don't care if the girls are happy. They care about the show."

I stop, a ratty sweatshirt in my hands, thinking.

"What?" my mom says.

"So they aren't the ones," I say. "The customers. It's just like Ivy and Elizabeth. They're not the ones."

"Okay?"

"I like your metaphor about giving things up and moving on and everything," I say. "But put that on hold for a sec, because I have an idea and I think maybe I can save the club." I take out my phone, type I need your help and send it to one Dot Nguyen.

Dot adjusts some kind of setting on her camera. "Weird to be filming someone else," she says. "All my camera strategies are specifically designed to make me look good."

"Well, now you just make Libby look good," I say. I'm fluffing up Libby's hair and getting her ready to be filmed. She's wearing her street clothes, and Dot put just enough makeup on her to bring out her features on camera but not like she's going onstage. She looks like a civilian, which is the point.

I step out of the frame and say, "Okay," and nod to Dot, and she presses a button on her camera and gives me a thumbs-up. "Why do you like working at Davina's?" I say.

Libby stretches and looks a little sheepish. "Dav's isn't like other places I've worked at," she says. "You walk in and immediately, the atmosphere is different. It's bright. It's happy. And that's not just surface stuff; we get paid really well, so we're not competitive about tips, and management makes sure the customers treat us well. There's never been any pressure to do things we don't want to do, and I got five months of paid maternity leave when I had my daughter. It's a family-owned business and you can tell, because they treat all of us like family, too."

Dot lowers the camera and I say, "That was awesome."

"Yeah?" Libby says.

"Definitely. Exactly what we were looking for."

"Plus you looked hot," Dot says. "And that's what's most important in any situation."

"Do you think this'll work?" Libby says.

"I have no idea," I say. "But we've got to try something."

"This place can't shut down," Libby says. "Never say die, right?"

"Maybe sometimes say die," I say, going to Dot to look over her shoulder at the footage. "Just not right now."

We film ten different dancers giving their iteration of the same thing—why Dav's is different, and why it absolutely shouldn't close, and why people who never thought of themselves as strip club patrons should come give it a look. They're feminist and personality-filled and make our dancers seem like actual people. We're leaning into the pink walls and the palm trees. We're playing for a different audience.

Dot edits it all together into a two-minute video and we upload it to Instagram and Facebook and whatever else Dot suggests and basically cross our fingers it'll go viral.

"It got picked up by some tiny paper I'd never heard of," I update my mom while we're doing dishes the Saturday night before I leave for Italy. "But it got a bunch more shares on Facebook from it."

"Is it translating to customers?" Mom says.

"Not…yet," I say. "But this is the first weekend since it's been out. People had plans. Next weekend we'll see."

"Next weekend you won't be here," she reminds me.

"I know, I know." I'm so excited and so nervous.

My mom starts to say something, probably nagging me once again about packing, but upstairs there's a muffled crash and my dad yelling, *"Fuck!"*

My mom and I exchange looks. He's been having a rough week.

"Can you finish up down here?" she asks me.

"Yeah, of course."

She goes upstairs to calm him down, and I take a deep breath and dive into the rest of the dishes. When they're done and I head back to my room, I can hear my mom talking quietly and my dad crying, and I feel that sick combination of worried and awkward that I always do when he's not doing well, and I pick up my phone to distract myself.

Normally I'd text Ivy. Tell her I need to get out of the house.

And nowadays, she'd probably tell me that she's busy.

Melody's working and Alyssa's up at school this weekend, so I text Diana. She'll meet me at Mama's in twenty.

"I'm honored to be your backup plan," Diana says to me. She's still dressed biz cas from work and looks so put together with her hair up in a clip and her eye makeup just so. Why can everyone in my life but me do eye makeup?

I say, "Shut up, I love you."

She laughs and sips her beer. "So what's going on with you and Ivy anyway? You're just nothing now?"

"I don't know. We had a fight on my birthday." I don't know if it was actually a fight, but I don't know how else to describe it.

"You two have had fights before."

"Yeah. I don't know. I'm sure we'll be fine. Or something. We'll be something." We're always something.

"But, uh...not that happily-ever-after thing."

"No," I say. "No, it's looking like the door's very much closed on that one."

She wrinkles her perfect little nose. "I gave you bad advice."

"In your defense, if this were a romance novel, it would have worked out great. We fall into each other's arms, the end. And instead life is just...still going. I don't know what to do with that."

"Well, the good news is, you know what they say about God closing doors."

"It proves his corporeal existence?"

"His what now?" Diana shakes her head and sets her drink down. "You have to figure out what's next."

"Okay."

"I know, like, six girls you would be adorable with. Girls looking for something serious. Get someone to U-Haul their way right into your heart."

I trace the rim of my glass. "I don't think I'm ready."

"Honey. You're more than ready."

I shake my head. "All of this with Elizabeth and Ivy... I think I need a break from looking for my one true love or whatever."

"Okay, that's even easier. Do something casual. Fuck around for a while. Now I know, like, sixty girls to recommend."

I laugh. "I've never really done the sleeping around thing."

"There's no time like the present." A new song comes on, this country thing my mom used to sing to me when I was little.

"I don't think it's me," I say. "I think I need to figure out how to be by myself for a little while." Channeling Ivy still, but different.

"Okay, but if I find out you didn't sleep your way through Italy, I'm going to be extremely disappointed."

"It's so weird that I'm leaving," I say. "When I get home, Dav's might be closed. Elizabeth will be on her way to Boston. And I'll just be…me."

Diana shrugs. "So you need a plan for the future. If your job's gone, your girlfriend's gone, okay. A fresh start. So then if it's not girls, what's it gonna be?"

"I'm thinking about going back to school." I didn't really realize I was serious about that until I said it.

"Yeah? What do you want to study?"

I laugh a little. "I have no idea."

"Well, what do you like?"

Ivy. My answer has always been Ivy. "Love stories, I guess." The kind that end when they're supposed to.

She throws her arms up. She's a little drunk. She gets drunk so fast. Diana's great at her medical receptionist job and aces her community college classes and would be a great person to come to for advice if she could stay sober for more than half of happy hour. "So write a love story!

You can be an author!"

"I have no idea how to write a book."

"Well, that's why you go to school."

"I'm about to spend two weeks studying Italian literature, so I guess I'm on the right track." My phone starts buzzing, so I shift in my seat to pull it out of my back pocket. "That's weird," I say.

"Who is it?"

"Ivy." We don't really call each other anyway—that's why so-and-so invented texting—and obviously not right now. "Should I answer it? I should answer it." It can't be good that she's calling me. Hopefully she's just drunk. Or maybe it's a butt-dial. That'd be ideal.

"I think you should answer it," Diana says.

I nod and take a few steps away from the table, as if that will make it any quieter in here. "Hey?"

"Hey," she says. She sounds out of breath. "Is your mom there?"

"No, I'm out. Why? What's wrong?"

"Can you call her?"

"She's taking care of a thing with my dad."

"Shit. Okay. All right."

"Ivy," I say. "What's going on? Are you hurt?" It wouldn't be the first time Ivy's called my mom for medical advice.

"It's—no, it's not me," she says. She takes a deep breath. "Dot took something and she's freaking out."

"What did she take?"

"I don't know. Hang on." I hear her speak away from the phone and something that sounds like crying. Then to me again, "Can you come here? I need help."

I swallow. "Yeah. Yeah, okay."

• • •

Ivy buzzes me up the second I hit the doorbell, and the door's unlocked when I get to the top of the stairs.

"What the hell's going on?" I say as I go inside, but there's no one here. The living room's in shambles; there are empty bottles and plastic red cups everywhere and broken streamers on the floor. And I can hear someone vomiting in the bathroom.

Ivy's kneeling on the floor next to Dot, her hand on her back, and Dot's shaking so hard that I'm afraid she's going to fall into the toilet. Ivy looks up at me, her eyes big.

"What the fuck did she take?" I say.

"I told you, I don't know. One of her friends gave her something."

"Her friends were here?"

Ivy turns back to Dot. "I threw her a graduation party."

"You *what*?"

Dot flails and pushes herself away, her dress snagging on the tile floor. She's crying. Her makeup's all over her face.

"It's okay," Ivy tells her. "It's going to be okay."

"Don't *fucking* touch me!" Dot screams. "Everybody get the fuck away from me!"

"It's just Andie and me," Ivy says. "There's no one here."

Dot gets up, her legs quivering underneath her. We both hover, but she charges past us and out of the bathroom. "It's getting hard to breathe," she says. "I can't breathe."

"Sit down," Ivy says, and to my surprise, Dot listens and

sits down on the couch. She covers her face with her hands and sobs, and Ivy bites down on her finger. "It's okay," she says. "You're okay."

I catch Dot's wrist to get her pulse. It's like a hummingbird, and her skin is clammy and hot. "Ivy, she's burning up."

"I know."

"Her heart's going so — "

"I know."

"You really don't know what she took?"

"I don't know! She likes E."

"This is not E."

"I fucking know it's not E!"

"I want to go home," Dot sobs. "I don't know what the fuck... I can't breathe."

I pull Ivy aside. "We need to take her to the hospital."

"No."

"Ivy."

"She's not eighteen. Her parents will find out." Her eyes are wild. "They will send her away."

"Okay, but that's better than dead."

"She won't be allowed to go to school in the fall, she won't be allowed to see her friends, or make videos, or do *anything* but stay in that house and work on those fucking boats. She would *rather* die than have her whole fucking life taken away. And she's not going to die. She's not going to die."

"I know she's not going to die, but — "

"You are going to be *fine*," Ivy says. She crouches down in front of Dot. "Spot, look at me. You're in my apartment, you're okay. It's going to stop."

"Ivy," I say.

Ivy doesn't look away from Dot. "Remember when you smoked all that pot after getting your blood drawn and freaked out?" she says to me. Tenth grade. Movie theater. Bad time. Not like this.

"This is not that," I say.

"It's that."

"I can't breathe," Dot says.

"I could *breathe*," I say.

"She's just panicking. She's upset. She's *fine*." Ivy takes Dot's hands, her fingernails digging into Dot's skin. "You are fine."

"I'm gonna throw up again," Dot says.

"Okay. Come on."

"Don't *touch* me! You can't fucking— I know what's going on, I'm watching you!"

I take my cell phone out and step into Ivy's bedroom, because Dot's sobbing so loudly, I'm not sure I'd be able to hear over it if I stayed in here or followed them to the bathroom. I call home and close my eyes.

"Andie?" Mom says.

"I think Dot's overdosing. I don't know what to do."

"What did she take?"

"We don't know."

"Where are you?"

"Ivy's apartment."

"You need to call 911," my mom says, obviously. "Is she conscious? You need to try to find out what she took so the paramedics know how to help her."

"She is, but she's not being cooperative. She's really upset. Ivy doesn't want to call 911; can you just help? Can you tell me what to do?"

"Honey, what you do is you call 911. Ivy needs to think

about Dot right now and not herself. And you need to think about what needs to be done instead of what Ivy wants to do."

I don't know how to answer her, don't know how to tell her that Ivy *is* thinking about Dot, that this whole fucking night happened because Ivy was trying to do something for Dot, to throw her a goddamn graduation party, and I don't know what to do, and then Ivy's voice rips through the apartment.

"Andie!"

"I have to go," I tell my mom.

They're back in the bathroom. Dot's on the ground, her body shaking violently, and Ivy's holding her on her side and saying, "Okay okay okay it's okay you're okay Dot. Oh my God."

"I'm calling 911."

Ivy nods. "Now. Do it now."

She's still seizing. Holy shit. Ivy lowers her forehead to Dot's hip, holding on.

I call 911. I tell them my friend took something and we don't know what and she's having a seizure. I give them the address. I don't tell them her name. Dot stops seizing, and they have me stay on the line to watch her breathing and take her pulse. It's so, so fast, and her heart's skipping around like crazy. She doesn't really wake up after the seizure, just takes these shocky breaths in and gags white foam onto Ivy's bathroom floor, and the overwhelming thought I keep having is, *I shouldn't be here.* I do not know how to handle these things. I do not know what I'm doing. This is not my life.

"Are they coming?" Ivy keeps asking me. "They need to come, are they coming?"

"I think so, I don't know, I don't know what's taking so long." But I check my phone, and I've only been on the call for two and a half minutes.

The paramedics show up, and I don't know how they get in without being buzzed up, but they do, and I can't keep track of everything they're doing. They don't really talk to us. They attach monitors and machines to Dot, and I can't figure out why it's taking them so long to get her out of here. They use words I don't understand.

"What's her name?" one of them asks Ivy when they're trying to get Dot to wake up, but Ivy just shakes her head.

The other one pulls Dot's wallet out of her pocket. "Dorothy Nguyen."

"Dot," Ivy and I both say automatically, and Ivy curses and drives her palm into her forehead.

"Dot," the paramedic says. "Can you tell us what you took? Can you wake up for me? Stay with us, honey."

"She said she couldn't breathe," Ivy says.

"You two need to clear out of here," the other one says to us. "Give us some space. You can meet us at Kent, okay? We'll probably beat you there."

"We just leave her here?" I say.

"We're about to take her. I don't have time to explain this to you. Your friend's in serious danger."

I'm surprised that he snaps at us, and then I realize that they probably think this is our fault.

I realize that Ivy probably thinks this is her fault.

I take Ivy's wrist and lead her out of the building and to my car, and she follows me like she's in a trance. It's not until I have my phone telling me where to go, there's rain beating down on my windshield, and we're driving to the hospital to meet someone who isn't even there yet, someone who we just left unconscious on the floor, that Ivy starts to break down. She stares out the windshield and starts crying, these big, shuddering sobs that start in her stomach and shake her all the way to her shoulders.

"She's going to be fine, okay?" I say. "She'll be okay."

"Sh-she graduated," Ivy says. "She just graduated. I was just fucking trying to do something nice for once in my fucking—"

"I know."

"What the fuck, what the fuck, an hour ago she was fine, she was here and she was *fine*." She gasps in a breath in fits and starts. "This stupid fucking kid, thinks she's invincible, this absolutely goddamn idiot kid, oh my God. Oh my fucking God, she broke. I broke her."

"Ivy," I say, but she doesn't say anything for the rest of the drive. She just sits forward and pants, tears coming down her face and dripping onto her lap.

An hour ago, we were fine.

An hour ago, Dot was the annoying girl who could do no wrong and I had no idea how much Ivy cared about her.

We get to the hospital, and I give them Dot's name and ask if she's here yet. She's not in the system, so the nurse behind the counter turns to the other and asks if she knows about her ambulance coming in.

"Is that the teenager on the way with the heart attack?" the other one says, and everything gets really, really real right then.

A fucking heart attack?

Ivy sinks to a crouch on the floor, her head in her hands.

I say, "We didn't know that," because I don't know what the fuck else to say.

"You should sit down," the first nurse says to me gently.

"We'll let you know when we have any news."

I walk over to a bench on autopilot, leaving Ivy on the damn floor, but a minute later she sits down next to me. She's not crying anymore. She just looks haunted. By a ghost of someone who isn't dead.

Yet.

I take her hand.

She blinks slowly and says, "I should have known this would happen."

I have absolutely no idea what to say. I feel like someone took my voice away. "How?" I finally croak, and it sounds like it comes from somewhere outside of me.

"What the fuck am I going to do?" Her breath catches. "Who… She's the one who knows what to do in these kinds of situations, she's the one who talks, I don't…"

"Ivy."

She shakes herself off. "I should pray."

"You what?"

She makes this desperate noise in the back of her throat. "She's Catholic. She'd want me to pray. I don't know how."

"I can do it," I say. "I'm Catholic, I'll do it, okay?"

"Yeah. Yeah, okay." She looks up and past me at the ER entrance. "Oh, fuck."

I turn around. It's Dot's mom and a man who I assume is her father. She's crying and he looks furious, like my dad does when he doesn't want to look scared.

"I should talk to them," Ivy says, and before I can say anything, she gets up and intercepts them on the way to the front desk. She starts talking to them, slowly and awkwardly. In Vietnamese.

God.

God. I close my eyes and clasp my hands together in front of me.

Come on, God.

Come on, Dot. Be okay.

I hear Dot's mom wail and Ivy's voice break while she says, "I'm sorry; I'm so sorry. I'm so sorry."

You have to be okay.

June

Italy is everything I'd imagined and read about and seen in movies, except it's actually real and happening to me. There are cobblestones under my feet. There are Vespas trying to run me over. There's food I can't even believe the taste of in my mouth.

I would say that real life feels so far away, but this *is* real life. This is really, actually happening to me, and it's not a fantasy and it's not a story and it's not somebody else's.

It's mine, all mine, and I try so hard to stay in the present and not think about home, to push it away, gently, like I push away my wineglass when I've drained it at dinner and I'm full of olive oil and gnocchi and hope.

There's a day in Milan where I'm in the middle of a street fair, sitting on a fountain with a beat-up paperback I borrowed from one of the other girls by an author I'd never heard of. There's music everywhere, and dancers, and I have an ice cream bar melting down my arm.

There's a minute to breathe.

I think it makes me a terrible person, but it is such a relief, just for a moment, to not think about people left behind.

And then Jenna, one of the girls in my group, says, "To being here," when we toast on our last night, and it hits like a brick that everything has changed and that *being here* isn't the kind of guarantee it used to be.

To being here. As long as you can be.

I get home from Italy on June fourteenth. My mom meets me at the airport with a sign that says ANDREA, like I wouldn't recognize her otherwise. It's the kind of silly thing I missed so, so much. I drop my bags and wrap my arms around her.

"Look how tan you are!" she says. She smells like lime and lavender and home.

I squeeze her. "*Grazie.*" It's about the only Italian I picked up.

"That's my girl. Come tell me all about it."

So I do. We get in the car, and I tell her about the trains to the hill towns, and the sunlight on the alabaster buildings, and the drafty churches, and the college kids who (mostly) didn't treat me like shit, and the books, the books, the books. But the closer we get to home, the farther away it all feels, and by the time Mom pulls into the driveway, I'm sort of questioning if any of it actually happened, just like I was afraid I would. But seriously, I jetted off to Italy for two weeks? That doesn't sound like me. It barely sounds like anyone, considering what I left behind.

But the trip was nonrefundable. What was I supposed to do?

Maybe I should pretend I had a bad time.

Maybe I should have had a bad time.

I take a deep breath. "So how are you? How's Dad?"

Mom turns to me with a small smile. "We're good, sweetie."

Here we go. "Ivy never answered any of my calls." I tried almost daily, from sketchy internet cafés in whatever city we were in that day. My parents always picked up, obviously, but they would never tell me anything; they'd say that everything was fine and that I shouldn't let it ruin my trip, this was once in a lifetime, everything could wait until I got home, and now I don't feel great about the fact that I listened. After the past few months, it was too tempting to just turn away from it all for two weeks.

Mom nods a little.

"Have you seen her?" I say.

"We dropped off food a few times," Mom says. "She's lost some weight. I'm not sure she's eating much. Drinking plenty, from the look of her. I tried calling her mom, but I couldn't reach her."

Figures. "If I text her now, is she going to answer?"

"I don't know, honey. It's worth a try. If she'd respond to anyone, it's you."

"Yeah."

She puts her fingers around my wrist and squeezes. "I have a little surprise for you."

"Is it cake?"

It is, along with Melody and Diana, who jump up and down in my kitchen and hug me like they haven't seen me in years. We eat cake and I tell them about Italy and they come upstairs with me to unpack and tell me about Alyssa breaking up with her girlfriend in Boston, and Melody making a fortune in tips the other night, and Diana finally sleeping with Hot Yoga.

"Have you seen Ivy?" I ask them eventually, when I can't pretend I'm capable of thinking about anything else for any longer.

Melody nods, looking guarded. "She comes out sometimes. Drinks and snorts shit and hooks up with anyone she hasn't had before."

"Business as usual," Diana says.

This isn't adding up. None of it is. "Where the fuck is Dot?" I say. "She's not making Ivy wait on her hand and foot?"

Melody turns back from the closet, where she's lusting over some of my band tees. "In the hospital."

"What? Still? I thought she'd be home by now."

"Yeah, I don't know," Melody says. "But we sent flowers yesterday and they said she got them, so she's definitely still there."

"Have you been to see her?"

"She hasn't answered any of our texts," Diana says. "We figured we shouldn't show up uninvited. When my mom was in labor with my sister, she about bit the head off anyone who came in unexpected."

"She's not in labor," I say. They don't understand. They weren't there. Nobody fucking gets how scary this was besides Ivy and me. "Ivy's been to see her, right?"

They don't say anything.

I say, "Tell me Ivy's been to the hospital since that night that we sat there for six hours waiting to hear if Dot was going to live or die."

I don't know which I hate more: that she's doing this or that I'm not even surprised that she's doing it.

"If she has, she hasn't said anything about it to us," Diana says.

Melody snorts. "Say anything about visiting her? She's too busy fucking her way through Providence to mention Dot's name. It's like she never existed."

"Like I said." Diana takes a shirt out of my suitcase and folds it dramatically. "Business as usual."

I can't really concentrate on holding a conversation after that, because I'm so confused and annoyed and just plain goddamn angry. She's not visiting the hospital; she's just staying home and drinking and not eating? Why does everything have to be so fucking dramatic? Dot overdosed. She's alive. Why the fuck can't Ivy button up her shit, stop performing this off-the-rails-partner routine, and be an adult about one thing, ever?

Anyway, I'm not great company, and unpacking isn't all that thrilling, so they leave before too long. I'm antsy, so I go downstairs to where my mom's watching *Bake Off*. "Where's Dad?" I say.

"At the club," she says. "It's been busy lately."

I feel a swell of pride, but it turns into something else when I remember who's really responsible for saving the club. Still, I manage to say, "I like to hear that."

"Mmmmmm-hmm."

I sit down next to her on the couch, and I must look serious, because she pauses her show, which she only does on very dire occasions.

"What's wrong, Duck?" she says.

I don't even know where to start. "What's going on with Dot?" I say. "Why is she still in the hospital?"

She sighs and turns to me.

"There's something you're not telling me," I say. "Melody and Diana don't know it, either."

"No, I don't imagine they do."

"You kept telling me everything was fine," I say. "I'd ask how she was and you said she was doing better and she was okay."

"She is okay. She is doing better."

"Then why isn't she home?"

She adjusts herself on the couch. "The heart attack caused a lot of damage. She needed surgery to have a pacemaker put in."

"Okay. Okay, that doesn't sound so bad."

"And they've diagnosed her with early-stage heart failure," my mom says.

I feel cold. "Her heart's failing?"

"Early stage. It's starting to."

"Well…well, what the fuck happens when it's not early stage anymore? Is she going to die?" *You can't live without a heart*, my brain reminds me helpfully.

"It means eventually she's going to need a heart transplant."

Or else she'll die. "When is eventually?"

"Probably within the next three years."

I slump back on the couch.

"She's seventeen," I say.

"I know."

"So by the time she's my age, she'll probably have had to get a fucking heart transplant. And then what? They don't last forever, right?"

"About ten years, and then she'd need another."

"And in between, she's going to be sick. She's going to be sick for the rest of her life. Because of one fucking night. This is…this is not real." We should have been more careful. We should have taught her better. We should have known better. "It's not like… She's not some regular drug user," I say. Hell, I do more than she does. "This shouldn't have happened."

"It only takes bad luck one time. That's what I'm always telling you."

"I know, I know." I rub my forehead. My thoughts are coming all slow and tangled up. "She's starting college in the fall. She was so excited."

"She can still have a life, honey."

"But it's going to be different. Because of one stupid mistake." I take a deep breath. "When does she get to come home?"

"Soon," my mom says. "They needed to keep a closer eye on her for longer because of the amount of damage."

"How is she? Have you seen her?"

She nods. "She's quiet. She's got a lot of anxiety from what happened." She pauses. "And she'd really like to know where the hell Ivy is."

Fuck. I'd forgotten about that whole aspect of our sordid tale. "She really hasn't been to see her?"

My mom shakes her head.

"Why?"

"Maybe it reminds her too much of her dad. Maybe she's trying to protect herself. Maybe she feels guilty and thinks Dot is better off without her." She shrugs. "Maybe she's a heartless shit."

"Yeah, seriously."

"The only person who can answer that is Ivy," she says. "But Dot's going to be out of the hospital soon. Ivy can't hide forever."

"Yeah, the hiding stops now," I say.

...

Ivy doesn't answer my texts, and she doesn't pick up when I call, so after I've gotten a few hours of sleep, I resort to driving to her apartment and hitting the buzzer until she finally lets me up, like I did all those months ago. Except nothing like I did all those months ago.

Her apartment door is still closed when I get up the stairs, and it takes a while of pounding on that before she opens up. My mom was right; she's definitely lost weight. Her hair's a mess, and she's wearing sweatpants and a ratty tank top with no bra. She is still, obviously, beautiful.

"Look, it's the conquering hero," she says, and I can tell right away that she's drunk. "All hail."

"I didn't exactly conquer anything."

"Well, the night is young." She turns and heads back into the apartment, and I follow and close the door behind me.

"How are you?" I say.

She raises her arms like she's proud. "I'm fabulous."

"Yeah, you look it."

She sits on the couch for about half a second before she springs back up and says, "You want to go out? Let's go out."

"That's what you have to say?" She doesn't want to talk, or cry, or *go to the hospital*?

"I didn't ask enough questions about Spain?"

"Italy, and you didn't ask any, but that's not—"

"I just need to change my clothes, okay?" she says. "Let me change my clothes and we'll go out. I want to go dancing. There's this new bartender I've been trying to fuck for a week now." She bounces on her toes, her thumbnail in her mouth.

And I say what I always say to Ivy. "Yeah, okay."

She claps me on the shoulder on the way to the bedroom. "Good, man."

A t least one thing's established quickly in this whole grand mystery: Ivy Harlowe is not okay.

She snorts something, drowns herself in alcohol, and shouts questions over the music, stuff like who did you fuck in Italy (no one) and did you go to any nude beaches (no) and why are you not drinking more, hurry up, hurry up. I mention Alyssa breaking up with her girlfriend and she sarcastically pretends to give a shit. I ask her what she's been up to. She tells me same old, same old.

"You don't look good," I tell her.

"I look beautiful."

I don't mention Dot. There's this danger in her eyes, like she knows I'm thinking about it, like she's daring me to try it. Like she's waiting to see if I'll make her completely fall to pieces. Or make her pretend not to care. Or both at the same time, somehow, because she's Ivy.

She isn't dead, I want to say. *You know she's not dead, right? She's ten minutes away.*

And I can't stop wondering what Ivy would be doing if it were me in the hospital instead of Dot. In both directions: Would she fall apart like this? Would she abandon me?

I think she'd be kind of fine.

There's always been something so exotic and intriguing

about how damaged Ivy is, and I don't really feel bad about saying that, because I know it's what she wants people to think. Ivy wears her trauma like it's a sexy dress. She puts up walls to make you desperate to break them down and turn her into that girl she was on the street around Christmas, and then she makes you feel like you're special for noticing them when they were so goddamn obvious in the first place. The fact that Melody and Diana didn't see what a mess she is, that's part of it. Ivy can fake normal a lot better than she is right now if she wants to. But she was saving this mess for me. It's a show. All of it is a show, when she could just fucking go visit her girlfriend and put everything to rest.

I guess when I said I was getting over Ivy, I really meant I was getting over Ivy.

Except for the fact that I'm standing right here, watching her shotgun whiskey, and I'm not saying Dot's name. I'm letting her pull her same shit because I don't know how else to deal with her.

And that's part of it, too. She knew she could self-destruct right in front of me and I'd be too chickenshit to say anything. I'd just let her burn up like a Roman candle and that's exactly the way she wants it.

I wonder if she's even actually worried about Dot or if she just likes the attention of playing the bereaved non-widow.

She puts down her glass and points across the room. "See that girl?"

"I thought you were after the bartender."

"I'm flexible." She stretches, one arm behind her head. "That girl's going to come home with me tonight."

I think about the state of her living room, all empty

bottles and dirty laundry. The streamers from Dot's party ragged on the floor. "Cool."

She shoves her phone and her wallet at me, just like old times, before she charges across the dance floor in pursuit of whatever girl I pretended to see. I order another drink, then mumble, "Fuck it," because we gave each other our passwords years ago, and unlock her phone.

Because she must at least be talking to Dot, right?

There are a bunch of unread texts from me, a few from Melody and Diana. A reminder from Duolingo that she hasn't practiced her Vietnamese in seventeen days.

But not a word to or from Dot.

She cried in that hospital like she loved her.

Or maybe like someone who'd temporarily lost the only thing she's ever really loved: control.

I look at Ivy across the room, already lip-locked with some tall blonde, and in that moment, I hate my best friend.

I spend the next day sleeping off my jet lag, working a half shift, and basically trying to adjust to the fact that my life isn't an Italian fantasy anymore. God, it was so incredible. I would stay awake in the hostel for hours and write about what we'd done that day. I'd go to discussion groups with college kids and I could keep up, most of the time. Turns out reading as much as I have provided some damn good education, even if they weren't the books Elizabeth would have me believe are important.

But now we're back to real life, and once I'm done

with work, I figure it's probably time for me to visit Dot.

The hospital looks so different when you're not there for an emergency. Everything's quiet and echoey, and it reminds me of going to the museum for field trips when you're a kid. I ask about Dot at the front desk, and they give me a visitor's badge and a room number. I thought about stopping at CVS and getting her a stuffed animal or some candy or something, but I don't know what she likes. I don't really know much about her at all, really. Except that she loves makeup, and painting, and dancing, and shrimp, and Ivy.

I take the elevator to the fifth floor, where there's another front desk blocking off the waiting room from the rest of the floor. A nurse asks if she can help me.

"Dot Nguyen?" I say. "Or Dorothy, I guess. She's in 409."

I expect her to type something, but instead she just sighs heavily, like my being here is a very tedious thing for her. "Are you on the list?" she says.

"I signed in downstairs."

"No," she says. "There's a list of people who can visit Dot; it's…here." She points to a piece of paper on a bulletin board behind her. "What's your name?"

"Uh…" This is super weird. "Andie DiStefano?"

She shakes her head. "I have a Karen DiStefano."

"That's my mom."

"Well, your mom is one of five people who are allowed to visit," she says. "Dot's parents were very clear. I'm sorry."

"They can do that?"

She looks sad now, and I think about how many times Dot must have begged for her friends. How fucking convincing she is. "She's under eighteen," the nurse says.

"They're allowed to ban anyone they want."

Well, that's fucked up.

And then it all starts to come together in my head. I feel like I can't stay standing. "Is Ivy Harlowe allowed to visit?" I say, already knowing the answer.

She sighs again and says, "No. And you can tell her that no matter how many times she shows up here, that's not going to change."

She's tried.

She tried.

It's me. I'm the heartless shit.

Oh, Ivy.

66 Jesus Christ," Alyssa says. She's finally home from college, and I've just filled her in on the whole situation while we're rocking back and forth on my porch swing. It's a gorgeous day outside, and there are bees buzzing around my dad's rosebushes and venturing over here every so often to bother us. "Did you tell Melody and Diana?"

"Yeah. And now we all feel like the worst people in the world. I swear to God, I thought she'd just abandoned Dot. Why did I think that?"

"Because it kind of sounds like something Ivy would do?"

"Not with Dot," I say. "She's never been mean to Dot. Not since the very beginning." I've been thinking about this all day. Anytime I've ever tried to apply how Ivy is with other people to how she'll be with Dot, I've been wrong. And yet I never stop trying. Never stop trying to rationalize this thing that won't be rationalized.

Alyssa gives the swing a push with her feet. "So what's the plan?" she says. "You must have something."

I laugh. "Me?"

She smiles at me. "You always have something."

Okay, well, I kind of do. "Dot's got to be out of the hospital soon," I say. "I looked up how long people usually stay after a pacemaker and she's already been there longer than usual, and my mom said she was doing better last time she was there, walking around and stuff. So until then, I guess we just keep Ivy together. And we hope that Dot doesn't hate her for not coming."

"She'll understand when someone explains it to her."

"When has Dot ever given anyone a chance to explain anything?" I say. "Plus, I imagine if her parents have her on lockdown now, that's not going to stop just because she's out of the hospital. At least she'll get her phone back, I assume."

Alyssa laughs a little. "Who would have thought you'd be the one trying to save Dot and Ivy's relationship?"

"Yeah, seriously. Not how I saw this one going," I say.

"So we're taking Ivy out tonight?"

"Or going over there, at least. I don't think she should be alone. Even if she wants to be."

We decide I'll head over there alone to take the pulse of the situation first, so I show up at Ivy's unannounced at around six. She doesn't really seem to care one way or the other that I'm there. The apartment looks the same as it has, and she's drunk again.

"I'm going out," she tells me.

"Let's go to Mama's," I say, because at least we can talk a little better there than at Kinetic.

"I don't want to."

"Come on, Kinetic's getting stale."

"You just got back from your triumphant adventure. How can it be stale?" She hops into a pair of jeans.

"You can dance at Mama's."

She sighs. "Is the brigade coming?"

I consider lying, but what good would that do when they show up? "I think so."

She rolls her eyes and peels off her T-shirt. "Fine."

I see everything about her with such different eyes now, and I hate myself for thinking this was a performance the other night. When really, it's like I told Alyssa; Ivy's never performed anything when it comes to Dot. She's never pretended not to want her around. She's never pretended they were going to get married. They've just been—like Dot said—in each other's orbits, and it was natural and it was easy and it was unspoken and now it can't be any of those. Now they can't even see each other.

Ivy's not really orbiting anything at the moment.

She's a lot lower energy tonight. The girls fuss over her and hug her and I think she knows we've figured out the situation, because she kind of just gives up and slumps over her drink at our table. I give the girls a look to leave us alone and they get up to dance, and I nurse my beer and wait for Ivy to talk.

"I think I'm going to get out of here," she says.

"We can go home. Watch movies or something. Talk."

"No, I mean here. Providence."

"Technically you don't live in Providence anymore."

"You know what I mean."

I do, probably more than she thinks I do. "Where do you want to go?"

"I don't even care," she says. "Somewhere new." She rolls the edge of a coaster across the table.

"Running away won't fix anything."

"You did it."

"Yeah, for two weeks," I say.

"And what a two weeks they were." It's the closest she's come to mentioning Dot since it happened.

I chew on my lip.

"I should have been here for you," I say.

"Whaaat for."

"Right, because you're fine, right?"

She shrugs and looks out onto the dance floor. Her eyes are focused straight ahead and narrowed slightly, and her eyeliner is smudged and uneven on one side. It's maybe the least perfect I've ever seen her, because it's not like when she was a mess in her apartment. She's trying to look flawless here and she isn't.

She's not the Hope Diamond.

I love her so much.

I take a minute to build up the courage, then say, "I went to see Dot."

She doesn't react at all at first, and I think maybe she didn't hear me over the music changing. But then she turns back around to the table, drains her drink, and says, "Well," softly, almost to herself, and I just ache for her.

"They didn't let me see her," I say gently.

"Mm." And I think that's going to be all I get, and honestly, if she's not getting up and walking away from me, I'm ready to call it a win, but then she says abruptly, "There's a night nurse who will tell you how she's doing," without looking up from the table.

"She doesn't have her phone, I'm guessing?"

"How should I know?" She gets up, wobbling a little. "I need another drink."

"I think you've had enough, baby."

"Let's dance, then." She looks at me with those big eyes. "Please."

What the fuck am I supposed to do? I'm here for her. "Yeah," I say. "Come on."

She of course gets another drink on our way to the dance floor, and after two songs and another, and another, she's a wild flurry of movement, grabbing whoever comes near her, boy or girl, and giving them a frantic touch of the Ivy magic before she moves on to someone else. She's never still. She reminds me of a weather event. She reminds me of Dot.

"Take her home," Alyssa says to me. "She's plastered."

As if on cue, Ivy stumbles and ends up on the floor. Diana and I get under her elbows and pull her up, and she wavers and clings to my shirt.

"I want to go home," she says in the direction of my face.

"Great idea. Come on."

I help her out to the car, her arm over my shoulders. I start to load her into the passenger seat, but she says she wants to lie down, so I get her settled in the back seat, where she flails around half asleep the whole way back to her place. It reminds me of when we first started going out, our senior year of high school, and Ivy had no idea what her limits were. She's been careful since then, methodical. Everything's always so planned.

"None of this was supposed to happen," she slurs in the elevator.

"I know."

"Why am I so sad?"

"Because she's sick. And you fell in love with her."

She pulls back like I stung her. "*She* fell in love," she says. "Not me. She's the one who did this."

"Okay. Okay."

"I didn't do anything."

I help her unlock the door to her apartment, and she sits down heavily on the couch.

"I didn't do anything," she says again.

"I know."

She puts her head in her hands. "She sat right here and told me she couldn't breathe and I didn't do anything."

"No, I..." I feel my chin shaking. "You saved her life, Ives."

She flops down on her side and pulls a blanket on top of her. Red with black zigzags. Dot loved that blanket.

"We should get you to bed," I say.

"No."

"Ivy."

"I want to sleep here," she says, and before I can argue any more, she's snoring.

I straighten the blanket over her and get to work cleaning up this place, because I don't think there's any other way I can help her. I'm not who she needs.

I rinse bottles and put them in the recycling and pick the streamers off the floor. I'm in the middle of cleaning out the fridge when her buzzer goes off. I check the oven clock, mumble, "What the fuck," and figure it's one of her neighbors coming home drunk who forgot their key. I buzz them up and have just about forgotten about it by the time there's a knock at the door.

I open it, and there's Dot.

She's lost weight, too. Her hair is loose and curly down her back, and she doesn't have makeup on. She's wearing a tank top, and there's a small row of stitches peeking out of the neckline.

"Hi," she says.

My stomach does this swooping thing, and I grab her and hug her so tight. She stiffens, but after a few seconds, she hugs me back.

"I know I should have called first," she says. Her voice sounds shaky, not like hers.

"She's asleep. It's okay." I let her go.

Dot looks around the place, taking in what remains of the wreckage. I hear Ivy stir on the couch, and when I turn around, she's staring at Dot.

"Am I sleeping?" she says.

Dot doesn't say anything. She slowly toes off her shoes and goes to the couch and lays down next to Ivy. Ivy rolls toward her, pulling her carefully close like she's worried she's going to break her, and buries her nose in the back of her neck.

Dot closes her eyes and I stay right where I am, afraid to breathe.

July

"I thought heart failure was, like, an emergency," Melody says.

We're at our usual table at Mama's. It's the first time we've all been able to get together in a few weeks, between Melody and me working extra shifts at the club as the customer count picks up, Alyssa working a summer internship, and Ivy…well. Ivy's had other stuff on her plate.

It's a Thursday night, but the place is surprisingly crowded considering most of the college kids are shuttled back to where they came from. They're playing Top 40 and it's mixing with the street noise outside, thrumming like a pulse.

"My mom says you can be in it for years before you even need a new heart," I say. "I didn't know anything about it, either."

"So she's just going to get sicker and sicker until they decide she's ready for a transplant?" Melody says.

"I think the pacemaker's supposed to keep her okay for a while. But yeah, eventually…I think in some number of years, stuff is kind of gonna go downhill."

"How's she doing now?" Diana says, and after I shrug—I've only seen her once or twice in the two weeks since she's been out of the hospital—Alyssa flags down

Ivy, who's over at the bar. She's talking up some older girl I've seen around here a few times. She cut her hair to her shoulders last week and it's hot as hell. She's drinking soda tonight.

She excuses herself from the girl and comes over and slides onto a stool. "What's up?"

"How's Dot doing?" Alyssa says.

If she's pissed at being interrupted for this, she doesn't show it. "Mostly she's just tired. A little jumpy." Ivy's helped Dot sneak out of her house a few times, but I don't think they've seen all that much of each other thanks to the intense surveillance Dot's under. Then again, when have I ever had an accurate guess of how much time Ivy and Dot spend together? "She doesn't remember what happened, but she has nightmares."

"Is she going to get better?" Melody says. "Like, is she still recovering?"

"We're not sure," Ivy says.

"Is she still starting at RISD in the fall?" Diana asks.

"She hasn't worked that out, either."

"So it's all just wait and see," I say.

Ivy shrugs. "I'm just going where she's going right now." Her phone buzzes on the table, and she picks it up and reads something. And smiles.

"How's our girl doing?" Libby asks me at the club the next day.

"I haven't really seen her," I say. "Ivy says she's okay."

"She better be coming back soon." Libby examines

herself in the mirror. "With these new crowds, I need to be looking my best. God knows I can't get my wings as sharp as she can. And I miss that laugh of hers."

"I miss her videos," Kayla says.

"She's still working on getting her stamina back," I say. "I'm sure she'll be back here as soon as she can. She loves this place more than we do."

"Tell her that thanks to her, there's gonna be a place to come home to," Libby says.

"Spin around and spit," I say.

Once I'm done making the rounds and checking the books—we're not making money yet, but we almost are, and Libby's right, talk of closing the place has been a lot quieter lately—I take my spot at the reception desk, since Hailey has once again called out.

It's too late for the lunch crowd and too early for the after-work crowd, so it's pretty quiet, and I read some and look at pictures from Italy for the millionth time and eventually work up the courage to check the OkCupid profile I made last week. Ivy would tease me forever if she saw it—I flat-out say that I'm looking for my big love story—but she's been a little busy.

I have three messages. God.

As always happens when any girl shows any interest in me whatsoever, my first instinct is to delete my entire existence and run screaming into the woods, but I force myself to open them. One looks like spam, one's just "Hi," but one's actually a sweet message from someone asking about my trip to Italy. Her name's Gretchen. She has a picture of a cat in her photos and brown curly hair. She's twenty and she goes to Johnson & Wales. She has a beautiful smile.

I draft a message back, and by the end of my shift, we have a date set for next week.

"We're trying again!" I announce to Ivy. "We are reentering society! Lesbian seeks partner!"

"That's the gayest sentence I've ever heard," Ivy says. She's spinning around in her desk chair, her legs slung over the armrest. Dot's here, was here when I arrived, and now she's on the couch, drinking tea and curled up small. Both her parents had to work today and her brothers weren't available to stand guard, so Dot promised she'd stay in the house, so of course she's here. She hasn't talked much since I got here, and when I give Ivy a look about it, she just shrugs and mouths, *She's tired.*

I've called Dot a lot of things, but quiet has never been one of them.

"You should be proud of me," I say. "I'm endeavoring to not waste my *entire* life hung up on you."

Can't relate, Dot would say here, but she just sips the tea Ivy made for her.

"So is she another pretentious paleontologist?" Ivy says.

"Veterinarian."

"Ah, but mine was alliterative."

"She's just a student," I say. "Seems sweet. She's never been to Italy." Her profile has a picture of her with a tray of cookies, so she seems wholesome and nice, and also like she might make me cookies.

"Oh God, please tell me you've found someone who

wants to hear about Italy," Ivy says. "I can't smile and nod anymore."

"Hey! It was a life-changing experience!"

"Oh my God, I know."

Dot says, "Where are you going for the date?"

I cover my face with my hands. "This café Elizabeth showed me." The one with the pain au chocolat.

"I changed my mind," Ivy says. "*That's* the gayest sentence I've ever heard."

"It's a good café!" I say. "It has nothing to do with Elizabeth. All the cool places I know are from you or her."

"So take her to one of mine," Ivy says. "Make sure this one doesn't hate Kinetic before you take your pants off."

"She already mentioned Kinetic," I say. "She likes it."

"Well, then I've probably slept with her," Ivy says.

"Probably."

"What do you think?" Ivy says to Dot.

"Yes, you've probably slept with her."

"Not that, brat."

I get what Ivy's doing, and I get that it's okay for her to needle Dot and not for me, but I still want to tell Ivy to leave her alone. She's clearly exhausted just from sitting here and listening to us. God, this sucks.

"I don't know." Dot squirms on the couch. "She sounds nice." She sets the mug down. Her hand is shaking.

Ivy notices, too. "You need a beta blocker?"

"No."

"You sure?"

"They make me dizzy."

"You're dizzy anyway."

Dot shrugs.

Ivy spins in the chair. "Then how aboooout you share

your opinions with the class?"

"I don't have opinions," Dot says. She settles back on the couch, playing with the scar on her chest.

"That's a new one. You want to sleep some?" Ivy says.

"I've been sleeping all day."

The dishwasher beeps, and Ivy goes to the kitchen and starts unloading it. She seems kind of stressed, and I know Dot notices, too, because she chews on her thumbnail and turns around on the couch to watch her.

Dot closes her eyes like she's steeling herself and then says, "I want to go out."

"You just got here," Ivy says, examining one of her glasses.

"Not home, out. I haven't seen everyone since I got out of the hospital."

Ivy doesn't look up from the glass. "Nah."

"Please?"

"There's a new fashion documentary on Netflix, did you see?"

"Ivy."

Ivy doesn't say anything, and at first I think she's giving Dot the classic Ivy Harlowe Silence of Finality, but then she sets down the glass and says, "Mama's, not Kinetic. For an hour. Okay?"

"Okay," Dot says, and after Ivy leaves to get dressed, she slowly stretches and sits up. She starts to braid her hair, but after a few twists says, "Fuck," softly and shakes out her arms.

"You sure you're up to this?" I say.

"It's just sitting somewhere else instead of here."

"You seem to have forgotten how exhausting our friends are."

Dot shrugs, then says after a moment, "I don't want to overwhelm her," quietly.

"I think your stalking days proved that's not really possible."

"That was different," she says. "I just...I want to be as easy to love as possible."

I don't really know how to respond. I want to say she shouldn't have to worry about that, but I also know Ivy, and I know how much smaller I've made myself to try to be what she wanted.

It never worked, though. Shrinking into Ivy's shadow never made her love me more. And Dot, physical size aside, has never been small.

"You're still you," I say eventually.

She gets up slowly and slings her bag over her shoulder. "I don't know if I am, really."

Diana and Alyssa are available, and they already have a table reserved when we get there. Ivy parks as close as we can get and lets Dot grip her hand on her way in. Dot seems nervous, and Ivy has that fierce focused face she puts on when she's trying not to seem nervous.

The girls exclaim and hug her and Dot flinches a little, but she smiles and takes her seat. Ivy drums her fingers on the table and goes to order drinks while Alyssa and Diana keep fawning over Dot, telling her how good she looks.

"I look like a corpse," Dot says. It's awkward.

It gets better when Ivy comes back with drinks. Alyssa asks Dot a lot of questions, how she's feeling, what the hospital stay was like, what happens next, until Ivy gets fed up and says, "What is this, an episode of *ER*? There must be something else to talk about that's more exciting than heart failure."

There's a long pause where we try to think of literally anything more exciting than that. "Um," Alyssa says. "I can talk about my internship?"

"Yes, good, that," Ivy says, and Dot squeezes her hand and mouths, *Thank you*, when she thinks no one is watching.

So we talk about Alyssa's internship, and Gretchen from OkCupid, and Diana's mom's new job, and Ivy laughs in the right places while Dot looks wistfully at the dance floor.

It's all going okay until a guy walks by and runs into Dot's chair. She jumps, he apologizes, Ivy glares at the guy and says, "It's okay, shake it off," to Dot. She'd mentioned to me that Dot startles easily now, and I've tried to be careful about loud noises and sudden movements and touching her when she's not expecting it. All of which this sort of was.

A minute later, Dot puts her hands on her chest and says, "I can't breathe," and I think my own heart just about stops. All of a sudden, I'm right back there, Ivy's apartment, the looks on their faces, the sirens approaching too slowly.

So Alyssa and Diana and I are panicking right away, but Ivy says, "Stop," and scoots in closer to Dot. "Slow it down," she says. "In through your nose, out through your mouth."

"I can't," Dot gasps.

"Yes, you can. Close your eyes, block it out."

I say, "Do we need to call someone?" Her mom. A

doctor. An ambulance.

Ivy shakes her head, keeping her eyes on Dot. "She's okay."

Yeah, I've heard that one before. "Ivy."

"It's a panic attack," Ivy snaps. "I know what I'm doing."

"What if it's a heart attack?" Dot says.

Ivy puts her hand on the back of Dot's head. "Then you'd feel your pacemaker go off."

"What if it's broken?"

"It's not broken. You felt it an hour ago."

"I can't breathe."

"I hear you breathing. You're okay. You're just scared. It's okay."

Dot bites down on her fist, tears spilling out of her eyes, and Ivy rubs her back.

I say, "Ivy, maybe just to be safe—"

"Quiet," she says.

Dot shakes. "My chest hurts."

Ivy strokes her hair. "Yeah, 'cause you're freaking out. It'll stop soon. Remember yesterday? Over before you know it. Breathe along with me."

Dot squeezes her eyes shut.

"Dot," Ivy says firmly. "I need you to listen to me. Breathe when I am, come on."

"Everyone's staring at me."

"No one's staring at you," Ivy says with a death glare at us. "No one's even noticing you with how busy this place is. That's what's freaking you out. But you're safe. If something bad were happening, people would notice. We'd do something."

Dot sobs. "What if you missed it?"

"I won't miss it."

"I'm scared."

"I know. Everything's okay."

Dot grapples for Ivy's hand.

"There you go," Ivy says. She laces her fingers through Dot's and puts her other hand on hers. "You're doing fine. You're going to be just fine."

I don't know how the fuck Ivy stays so calm when Dot is crying and panting and saying the same things she said the night of, but gradually she calms Dot down. Dot wipes her face and takes a few deep breaths. Alyssa says, "Welcome back," and Dot gives her a weak smile.

"Diana's going to come with you to the bathroom to get you cleaned up, okay?" Ivy says, and Diana nods and stands up.

"Okay," Dot says. Ivy kisses her cheek and helps her stand up, and as soon as Dot and Diana are around the corner, she leaves the bar.

Alyssa and I exchange looks.

"She's not…leaving her here, right?" Alyssa says.

"No, she wouldn't do that." I mean, she would, but not to Dot. I hope. "I'm gonna follow her."

"Yeah, do that."

I don't have to go far. Ivy's outside, under the awning, her arms around her waist, her body folded in half. She's crying so hard, I don't know how she's staying on her feet. And I think I feel my heart break.

I've only ever seen her cry this hard once.

"Baby," I say.

She shakes her head fast, and I put my hand on her arm. "I'm fine, I'm fine, I'm fine. I can't breathe."

I try to channel how she was a minute ago, how smoothly she talked Dot down. "She's okay. You were right, it was just a panic attack. You did great. I couldn't even tell you were scared."

She shakes. "I don't want her to worry. God fucking shit, they look just like heart attacks."

"Come inside and you can see her."

"No. No. I don't want to be trouble for her."

"Ivy, you're not."

"My chest hurts," Ivy says, and she cries and cries.

Somehow I end up relaying this whole story to Gretchen on our first date. She asks me about my friends, and all of it just kind of...comes out.

"And then Ivy pulled herself together and went back into the bar and got Dot home," I finish. "Like everything was totally fine. They're both so scared that the other one can't handle what they're going through. I'd say they need to have a conversation, but I'm still not sure they've ever had an actual conversation with each other in their entire relationship. Well, one. I overheard one once. I guess statistically it's not likely that the one conversation they've ever had is the one I happened to overhear, huh?"

"Probably not," Gretchen says, cutting into her chicken. She has curly dirty-blonde hair and she isn't wearing much makeup, but her cheeks are pink and friendly.

"Sorry," I say. "I know I'm talking too much."

"You've got a lot going on right now."

"Yeah," I say. "It's just, um...it's weird. I didn't really internalize how much Dot's squirmed her way into our lives, and now she's sick and everything just feels like it's on pause, waiting for her."

"Except she's not going to get better," Gretchen says.

"Yeah. I don't know what to do with that."

"It can be a lot to deal with," she says. "My sister has lupus, and it's hard to let go of the hope that someday she's going to magically wake up and be okay. But I try not to let her know that. She doesn't need to carry my stupid hope around."

"What's weird is I don't even like Dot that much," I say.

Gretchen laughs.

"I'm serious. She's my best friend's girlfriend, but she's always kind of driven me crazy."

"Well, don't start liking her just because she's sick," Gretchen says. "That's not fair to anyone."

I think about Dot on that dock that night in January, ready to dive into freezing-cold water to save some fishermen's jobs.

"I think I started liking her a while ago," I say. "I just didn't want to believe I did."

"A big part of adjusting to my sister's new life was getting used to the idea that the, like, ultimate goal in life doesn't have to be as capable as possible. Maybe the goal is to see the goodness in other people. You know? You can get angsty about needing help, or you can look at the fact that people are helping you and think, God, humans are so good. People's capacity to care for one another is, like...completely amazing, and Lucy sees that every day. Like we're both so in awe of my mom and how well she handles it."

"Ivy's never really been the caretaking type," I say. "I don't think she's ever helped anyone realize the goodness of humanity." Except maybe mid-climax.

"Do you think she can do it?"

"I don't know. I hope so." And then I think about how fucking weird it is that I hope so. There's really not a part of me that wants them to break up? All it takes is a medical emergency for me to get over all my shit? I'm all well-adjusted now?

"Well, I hope if she can't, she figures it out sooner rather than later, for both their sakes," Gretchen says, and then she pivots to talking about some friends of hers who broke up recently and I find out exactly how *not* well-adjusted I am, because I nod and try to listen, but I just want to talk about Dot and Ivy some more. I'm either interjecting with "oh, that reminds me" or desperately trying to make myself *shut up* and stop interjecting with "oh, that reminds me."

I don't know why I'm like this. I've always been the type to lose myself in a movie or a TV show at the exclusion of actual life. A book. A person.

I think this is how I participate in life. I watch.

Can that count?

Please?

Is it okay to just want to watch?

So needless to say, I'm having an existential crisis and I'm not the best date. I'm not entirely surprised when I ask Gretchen outside the café if I'm going to see her again and she hesitates.

"Can I ask you something?" she says.

"Eek. Yes."

"Are you in love with Dot?"

I laugh. I can't help it. "With *Dot*? She's a fetus."

"Okay, Ivy, then."

I stop laughing, but I still say, "No," and it feels…not

quite like the truth but something adjacent to it. That's interesting.

She doesn't buy it, and I don't know how to tell her that I'm definitely obsessed with *something*, but I don't think that it's Ivy anymore. I don't really know what it is.

So I say, "I just think they're kind of fascinating."

She nods a little.

"Maybe you have to have been there since the beginning to really get it," I say.

"Maybe."

"I just…I really want them to have some happily-ever-after."

"But what about you?" she says.

What about me?

I say, "I don't think I'm at the end yet."

I'm still contemplating all of that when I get home, which is probably why I enter quietly enough that no one seems to notice me. My mom is on the couch, watching something with the volume on low, and my dad is at the kitchen table. With Ivy, who's writing in a notebook while he talks.

Sue me, I'm curious. I get close enough to hear.

"I think when it comes down to it, it's just about reassurance," my dad says. They have two mugs on the table between them and an almost-empty plate of cookies. "That you're not getting tired of her. That you're not bothered. But don't say it unless you mean it. We can tell."

Oh.

"I don't know why the fuck I would be bothered," Ivy says. "She's not even asking me to do anything for her."

"When you're sick all the time, just existing feels like a burden to other people," he says. "That's what you're trained to believe. And especially since she's just getting used to it, she's just figuring out this new life right alongside you. It feels overwhelming to her, so she expects it to be overwhelming to you. And right now, she's probably afraid of scaring you off. Once she gets more comfortable, she might start testing the waters. Asking more from you. Expecting more."

She's listening. She's taking notes.

"Okay, so…" Ivy bites her lip. "What if I can't do it? What happens if I do get overwhelmed?"

"Then you communicate that. It's just about honesty. Trust. If she can't trust you to tell her when it's too much, she won't trust you when you say that it's not."

"I just…" Ivy makes a frustrated line in her notebook. "I want her to feel better," she says eventually, in a rush.

"She might not," my dad says firmly. "And you need to somehow get to the point where you can live with that. Because she has to."

"I get that, like, philosophically," she says. "But she's right in front of me and she's having a panic attack because she feels so terrible. How do I not wish that that would go away?"

He shakes his head a little. "I don't know."

She sighs.

"I haven't been on that side of it," he says. "I know it's hard for both people."

"I'm not trying to, like, compare it. I know she's got the short end of the stick here."

"It's not a contest."

"Her heart's failing, John." She takes in a shaky breath. "I do not know how to get used to saying that."

He gives her a second, then says, "What always helps me when I feel guilty…maybe this will help you. It's remembering that other people do this, too. Someone has been sick before her. Someone has been healthy before you. This is not the first relationship where one person is healthy and one person is not. You don't have to invent anything. It is possible."

"Yeah," she says softly.

"Other people are doing this as we speak. Other people are happy."

Ivy sits back in her chair and thinks about this for a while, and she must see me out of the corner of her eye. I expect her to be pissed at me for eavesdropping, but she just says, "Hey."

"Hi. How's Dot?"

"Alive."

"You know, I'm pretty sure he used the word 'relationship,'" I say.

She rolls her eyes. "Shut up."

"Mmm-hmm."

She sighs and checks her phone. "I should go. I'm supposed to break in and watch this hideous reality show about boat wives or something. I suppose I should be grateful for her interest in terrible white women." She reaches across the table and gives my dad's hand a squeeze. "Thank you."

"You're going to do fine," he tells her. "Just be you."

"Me is kind of an asshole."

"Maybe," he grants. "But it's the asshole she wanted."

"Kinky," Ivy says. She stands and packs up her shit, and she's just about to leave when there's a knock on the door. "Christ, did she sneak out again?"

But it's not Dot. It is, ironically, her mother.

"Oh, fuck," Ivy says. "Oh God. Something's wrong."

My mother meets her at the door. "What's the matter?" she says to her. "Is something wrong with Dot?"

Ivy grabs my hand.

"Dot is… She's okay," Hai says. It's the first time I've ever heard her speak English. She sits down on the couch with my mom and does a bit of a double take when she sees Ivy.

"I should go," Ivy says, but then Hai starts crying, and Ivy freezes.

"I don't know what to do," Hai says. "She leaves the house. She cries all night. She is so upset. So many doctors…"

God, this is so awkward. I so should not be here. This has nothing to do with me.

My mom holds Hai's hand between hers. "She's still recovering."

"She is going to get hurt again," Hai says. "I have to work; I can't see her all the time. She won't…she won't stay."

Ivy pulls her lip into her mouth.

"I don't know what to do," Hai says. "I can't help. I don't know."

And then I have the first good idea I've had in God knows how long.

"What if Dot moves in here?" I say.

Everyone looks at me, but no one immediately shuts me down and tells me I'm an idiot, so I keep going.

"She'd be living with a nurse," I say. "Dad's here most of the time to keep an eye on her. And she wouldn't...I mean. She wouldn't have to sneak out if she were here." For obvious reasons.

Hai looks at my mom.

"Hai, of course Dot is more than welcome here," she says. "You know that. I'll take care of her like she's mine."

My dad puts his arm around my shoulders.

"I will need to talk to her father," Hai says.

"Of course," Mom says.

Ivy squeezes my hand so tight. And after they've worked out some details, just as Hai's getting ready to go, she stops and puts her hand on Ivy's shoulder.

I see Ivy holding her breath.

"Dot tells me that it was not your fault," she says, and Ivy covers her face with her hands.

August

Dot moves into our house on August first.

Mom swears up and down to her parents that she'll keep a close eye on her. After they've had their tearful goodbye, Mom pulls Ivy and me to the side while we're bringing boxes upstairs. "This isn't like when you were living here," she says. "She's sick and she needs her rest and her parents are trusting me. I'm not letting anything else happen to that girl."

Ivy looks down and then up. "Me neither," she says.

Dot spends most of her time in Max's room, listening to music and watching YouTube videos. She emerges for meals and doctor's appointments and to see Ivy, but that's about it. She comes out with us sometimes if we go to Mama's, but we take Kinetic trips without her. Ivy's still fucking everything that moves. She seems happy.

But Dot withdraws more and more with each panic attack, even though they're getting fewer and farther between. My mom notices, too.

"Take her to work with you today," she tells me one morning, when we're cleaning up after breakfast and Dot's already retreated back to safety.

"You think?"

"She needs to get her sea legs back. The longer she keeps herself out of real life, the harder it's going to be to get herself back in. Back on the horse."

"I thought it was sea legs."

"Seahorse, then."

"I'll see if she wants to," I say. "I'm not gonna force her. That's Ivy's job."

Dot's back in bed, lying on her stomach on top of the covers with earbuds in, watching something on her laptop. She's decorated some in here, put up a few posters over my brother's hockey ones and taped up some pictures of her family and her and Ivy. Her bedside table is covered in orange prescription bottles. She looks up when I come in. "Hi."

"Hey. I'm going to Dav's now."

"Okay."

"Do you want to come? I can wait for you to get ready. You can see the fruits of your labor."

"I just held a camera," she says.

"You edited the whole thing together."

She squirms a little, thinking. "Do I have to stay all day?"

"No. I can run you back here if you get tired."

She hesitates, then nods. "Okay, yeah," she says. "Let's do it."

Dot's swarmed the second we get into the club, and Melody and I have to play bodyguard a little bit to keep her from getting overwhelmed. But she seems pretty okay, and I see one of the rare flashes of old Dot in the way she basks in the attention. She dodges their questions about her health but eats up compliments on her outfit.

Once the dressing room clears out a bit and things start to calm down, Madison says, "Dot, can you do my makeup?"

Dot nods and comes over to her to see what she has to work with. I keep half an eye on her—it only takes a few minutes before this is the longest I've seen her on her feet at one time—and the other on our DJ's contract I'm going over.

"Your skin's looking really good," Dot says.

"I got that soap you told me about!"

Dot laughs a little. "Cleanser."

"Right. Cleanser. Cost me a whole day's tips."

"It's worth it."

"It really is. I'm softer than my baby."

They keep talking about skin-care stuff, and I zone out because my skin care routine consists of splashing my face with water, if it's lucky, and I don't pay much more attention to them until I hear something clatter to the ground.

"Fuck," Dot says, and when I look over, she's cleaning pink powder off the floor.

"It's okay, sweetie," Madison says.

"No, I broke it."

"It doesn't matter. Are you okay?"

I get up and put my hand on her shoulder. "I'll get the broom; it's fine. Sit."

She makes a frustrated noise, but she listens. I sweep up the blush, and Madison finishes the rest of her makeup by herself. She gives Dot a kiss on the cheek before she goes out onstage, which, by the looks of her, Dot finds just as patronizing as I do.

"You okay?" I say to her.

"My arms go numb if I have them up for too long."

I have no idea what to say. "Well, that sucks."

"Yeah." She sighs. "Yeah, it does." She slumps in her chair. "It is just...it is so frustrating to not be able to do things. To see them right in front of you but then you can't do them."

"You need anything?"

"I'm just so tired." She won't look at me.

At least I can help with that. "Come on," I say. "I'll take you home."

I run into Catherine in the office after I get back.

"Sorry," I say. "I had to bring Dot home."

"How's our little underage mascot doing these days?" she asks me.

"Barely underage anymore. Her birthday's coming up."

"Speaking of things to celebrate." She beckons me over to the computer and shows me a spreadsheet. "Broke even last month."

"Seriously?"

"Seriously."

"God. Thank God." For the first time since I've been back from Italy—God, since before that—it feels like maybe something is going to be okay. Something really big.

"Yeah, you and the mascot did some damn good work." She pushes back in her chair. "Hey, how are you doing?"

"Me? I'm fine."

"Max told me you and Elizabeth broke up. I was sorry

to hear that. She seemed nice."

"Oh. Um…yeah. She was. I think." There's no non-awkward way to say that it turns out you haven't really been thinking about your ex-girlfriend because you're a little busy with someone else's love life. And because obsessing over other people's love lives is my specialty, I think back to her and Max in the club last fall and what I overheard. "Can I ask you something?" I say.

"Of course."

"How do people stay in relationships with each other long-term without being miserable? Like, how does that happen? I mean, can it? Can it even happen?"

"Of course," she says. "Look at your parents. Look at Max and me."

I don't say anything, but she tilts her head to the side as she reads my face.

"There are always going to be issues," she says. "There's always going to be shit about the other person that's hard. Every relationship is going to have bullshit, whether that's heart failure or your brother sleeping with a stripper."

"Heh." I guess it's not really a secret after all.

"You just have to decide what bullshit is important to you and what isn't," Catherine says. "Everyone's got their own opinions on what's not actually a deal breaker for them. And sometimes you don't know until it happens. You'd be really surprised what you can handle, when you're with the right person."

"So you don't care about Max sleeping with Niya."

"Not particularly. It's a good trump card to pull out when someone has to do the dishes and I don't feel like it."

"I feel like I'm never going to find anyone," I say. "Like there isn't anyone who wants my particular brand of bullshit. And I don't exactly blame them."

"Of course you will," Catherine says. "You're twenty. You have plenty of time. And you have a big romance coming. I just know it."

I used to know it, too. Now I'm not so sure. All my romance novels always made it seem like the hardest part was *getting* together, but my parents met at a strip club and that was that, and Ivy and Dot just crashed into each other and kept going. That wasn't hard. But this part? Can I even do what all the people around me are doing?

Because I wouldn't put up with my wife sleeping with a stripper. And I wouldn't want my girlfriend out sleeping with other girls at Kinetic while I was home sick. But I wouldn't want a girlfriend who was too sick to go out, either, and I feel like a horrible person for that, but there it is.

It's hard to believe I thought I could handle a relationship with *Ivy*, of all people. That I thought either of us would really be what the other one wanted.

But I think what I figured out that night on her sidewalk is true. It's not her. Dot's managing her just fine, heart failure and all. It's me.

Maybe it all really is doable when you find the right person.

But what if *I'm* not the right person for anyone?

I vy brings Dot home from the cardiologist a few days later and tacks a list up on the refrigerator while Dot wanders into the living room and turns on the TV.

"New med schedule," Ivy says. "She needs to get it tattooed on her. Kid can't remember shit."

My dad comes down the stairs and says, "Dot home?" and Ivy and I point to the living room. He has a piece of paper in his hand, which he brings over to where she's flopped on the couch. "See what you think of that," he says.

My first thought is he's taken up drawing again and he wants her opinion, but when Ivy and I come in to check what's going on, I see it's some kind of flyer. "A support group?" Dot says.

"At the community center, where I have my group," Dad says. "They have all sorts of them, but this one's for teenagers with chronic illnesses."

Dot hands the flyer back. "I'm not really the group type," she says.

"Tell that to your basketball team," Ivy says. "Or that couple at Kinetic the night we—" she continues, until Dot throws a pillow at her.

"Just think about it," Dad says. "I've found mine incredibly helpful."

Ivy and Dot go up to Dot's room for a while after that—I'm not sure what Dot is capable of sex-wise right now, and I'm slightly too tactful to ask, though I can't say I'm not curious—and then Ivy leaves to go out and I go back to work for the late shift. The house is dark and quiet when I fall into bed and then dark and not quiet when Dot wakes me up screaming in the middle of the night.

My parents almost definitely can't hear her over my dad's CPAP, and I've bolted out of bed in surprise before I'm even fully awake anyway. I pad down the hallway to Dot's room. She's twisted in her covers, whimpering more than screaming now, but she's crying and sweating and shaking.

Ivy had promised me nightmares, but this is the first one she's had since she moved in. Or at least the first one I've woken up for.

I perch on the edge of the bed and put my hand on her arm. "Dot. Hey."

She draws in a sharp breath and shivers.

"Wake up," I say. "Just a dream, come on."

Slowly, Dot sits up and scoots herself to the edge of the bed. She wraps her arms around herself like she's cold, so I pull the sweaty blanket off the bed and wrap it around her shoulders.

She chokes out a sob. "Fuck. God."

"Do you want to talk about it?"

She shakes her head hard.

"Do you want to call Ivy?"

She hesitates. "What time is it?" Her voice is so small.

I crane to see Max's old football clock on her bedside table. "A little after two."

"Okay. No. She needs to sleep."

"She'll go right back to sleep. You know her."

"I… No. She does so much."

"She doesn't mind."

"She doesn't understand this," Dot says. "She can't. I don't even understand this. Damn it!" She draws in a shaky breath. "Can you just sit with me for a little?"

I'm so, so tired, but…you know. Of course I can. "Yeah. Come here."

I put my arm around her shoulders and pull her in close, and we stay like that until the tears dry up. Once I feel her relax, I say softly, "Dot?"

"Yeah."

"Maybe that support group wouldn't be the worst idea."

There's a long pause before Dot takes a shaky breath in. "Yeah. Maybe not."

I feel, for the first time in God knows how long, that I did a good job at something.

Ivy catches a cold, which means she has to keep her distance from Dot for a few days, and my parents are both doing stuff, so I end up picking Dot up from her first support group meeting. I park in front of the community center, and she comes out a few minutes later. She gets into the car and buckles her seat belt without saying anything.

"How was it?" I say. Her eyes are pink and a little swollen. Maybe just allergies, but probably not.

She says, "Fine," and doesn't talk the rest of the ride home, and I think about when I used to wish that she would shut up. When I was in the passenger seat of Ivy's car and Dot was in the back babbling about school and her friends and my parents. It's so hard to believe that's the same girl next to me.

And that I'm the same girl, too, really.

But maybe she just needed time to process, because when my parents ask her the same question at dinner a few hours later, she pauses and says, "I think it was good. Most of the people there have been sick for a really long time, so I kind of feel like I'm...invading, I guess?"

"I'm sure no one but you is thinking that," my mother says.

"I know. It's just…I think it's really hitting me that this isn't going to go away."

"What were the people like?" my dad says gently.

"They were nice. Most of them seem like they're pretty well-adjusted with all of this. I guess that makes sense, since they've been doing it for a while. But then I don't know why they're going to a support group for it."

"Maybe to find people like you," my dad says.

Dot smiles, just a little, like it sneaked up on her. "Yeah. Maybe."

Mom, of course, made a big batch of chicken soup for Ivy, so I bring that over afterward. She's not too sick, but she seems antsy. "How'd she do?" she asks me.

"No panic attacks or anything, I don't think."

Ivy nods shortly. "Did she like it?"

"I think maybe, yeah. Sounds like she might make some friends there."

Ivy doesn't say anything, and she doesn't really relax.

"What's up?" I say.

"Nothing. It's good. It's good that she's going."

"Yeah, it is. Right?"

"I said it was good," Ivy snaps, and we don't talk about it anymore.

D ot's eyes are red again when Ivy brings her home after her next support group meeting, but she's grinning and talking Ivy's ear off about something funny Damon or Damien or something said at the meeting.

"He showed us this meme making fun of how healthy

people talk to sick people and it was just...so funny," Dot says. "It was so true. *Oh, my aunt's cousin's cat has that. Have you tried yoga?*" Ivy smiles blankly and nods along and otherwise just acts very distant, and as soon as they sit down at the kitchen table and Dot pulls out her phone — "I just want to send Susie this thing I told her about" — Ivy says something about how she needs to take out the trash and steps onto the back porch.

I can see right through that, obviously, so I follow her. "You don't even live here anymore," I say. "Also you didn't bring the trash with you."

She grips the railing on the porch and looks out onto our tiny backyard. "Shut up."

I don't know how I ended up playing marriage counselor for these girls, but I may as well commit to it. "Look, I don't know what your issue is, but whatever it is, just talk to her."

"I can't."

"Why do you have an issue with this?"

"I don't. It's great."

"Ivy."

"It is," she says, but then she thinks for a minute and shakes her head, like she's disagreeing with some silent conversation.

"Just talk to her," I say again. "Maybe it'll help."

"Maybe she'll think I'm a controlling jerk."

"She seems to be into that."

"God, anything to stop this conversation," Ivy says and leads the way back into the kitchen. Ha. She leans against the counter and chews on her thumbnail while she watches Dot.

Dot, who is also not oblivious, says, "So you gonna tell

me, or…?"

Ivy groans. "I'm going to say this once and that's it, so you better fucking pay attention."

"Okay."

"You're going on about your new friends and how much they understand you and how it's not like having to deal with healthy people and that's great and all except…" She shrugs. "We're healthy people."

She means *I*, not *we*, but I figure she can have this one. Besides, Dot knows. Of course she knows.

"I don't hate healthy people," Dot says. "It's just different. In group we talk about what it's like to be sick, but they don't want to talk about, like, the details of my heart failure. They think it's boring. Do you know what a relief it is to be boring when you're used to being treated like a science experiment?"

"I don't treat you like a science experiment," Ivy says firmly, and Dot tilts her head to the side.

"Of course you don't," she says. "You treat me like I'm amazing. I need that, too."

Ivy looks away, and Dot gets up and stands next to her at the counter.

Eventually Ivy says, "We've been so worried that you won't be able to keep up," in her smallest voice. "That you wouldn't fit back into your old life. But now it turns out you've got this new life and it can be all big and incredible and sick and…what if it's me; what if I can't keep up with this?"

I would have no idea how to respond to that, but Dot doesn't even hesitate. "You are more than what you do for me," she says. "That is not why I want you around."

Ivy watches her.

"It's not big and incredible if it doesn't have you," Dot says.

It's too much. It's the kind of thing I've never said to Ivy because I've been so afraid of scaring her away. It's the kind of thing I've wanted to say a million times, and I'd always blamed my hesitation on her.

But Ivy pulls Dot in and under her arm without looking at her, and they stay like that for a little while. I know I should leave, but I can't.

"Who says I think you're amazing, anyway?" Ivy says with a growl, and Dot shoves her.

We have this big dinner the next night. Me and my parents, obviously, and Max and Catherine, and Dot and her mom, and Ivy. I thought going to Kinetic alone with Dot would be a sitcom episode, but this could be a whole movie. Ivy buzzes around while we're cooking and criticizes everything and otherwise radiates nervousness about sitting down with Dot's mother, and Dot's not feeling well, so she just curls up in the armchair and looks very, very amused.

We make shrimp scampi, obviously at Dot's request, with garlic bread and sautéed spinach and my mom's signature lemon Bundt for dessert. Dot gives her mom a big hug when she arrives and lets her triage her, smiling patiently. Ivy half ducks behind me like a fucking coward, but when Hai gives her a hesitant wave, Ivy speaks a little bit of Vietnamese and Hai nods.

So we dig in, the weirdest little family ever, and it's

surprisingly nice. Hai gets lost during the conversation a lot, but Dot's always there to step in to translate, and honestly I think she follows more than she's letting on. She laughs when Dot spills sauce on Ivy and Ivy grouches about the amount of money Dot costs her, and Dot glares at both of them.

There's a lot to talk about. Catherine and Max are thinking about having a baby, so everyone's excited about that, and I mention casually how I'm thinking of going back to school in the spring, which makes everyone all amped, and then that flows into a conversation about RISD.

"You're going to have to decide soon," Ivy says to Dot. They've given her some kind of special accommodation given the circumstances, where she can decide at the last minute if she's going or if she'll take a year off. But the last minute is rapidly approaching. School starts at the end of August.

"I know, I know," Dot says, grabbing a bite off her mom's plate.

"You're still recovering," my mom says. "What's the harm in waiting a year?"

"I don't know if it's going to get any better than this," Dot says. "So I might just be wasting a year for nothing."

"So go," Ivy says.

"But I don't know if I can do it. I'd need to take all these breaks and ask for accommodations and—"

"So?" Ivy says.

"So I don't know how to do that stuff."

"You're going to have to learn sooner or later," Ivy says. Gently.

Dot changes the subject and we let her, but later, when

she and Ivy and I are at the sink, scraping plates, she says, "I just don't want to go and do a bad job. I don't want to do some half-assed version of what I was planning because I'm too tired or the meds are making me sick."

"It's not half assed," Ivy says. "Half assed implies you're not trying. This is just your reality now."

Dot doesn't say anything.

"You're still you," Ivy says.

"I know that. I don't… I'm getting used to it. It's just hard, okay?"

"Yeah, well, keep going, Spot." Ivy lowers her voice, but she sounds firm. "You need more than you used to. You have to forgive yourself for that."

"Okay," Dot says. "Well, you have to, too." And they just look at each other over the plates.

I don't really know what Dot means until late that night, when I'm woken up by another nightmare. I don't rush into Dot's room this time—Ivy is sleeping over in there, so I figure she has this under control—but once I'm awake, I have to pee, which takes me past their room.

And I stop, because it's not Ivy's voice I hear through the walls, comforting, soothing. It's Dot's.

"Shhh, it's okay. Everything's okay. I love you."

Ivy says something too quiet for me to hear.

"It wasn't your fault," Dot says. "I'm okay now. I'm here. You and Andie saved my life."

Ivy's been busy, obviously, and when she gets busy, she tends to suck at taking care of her space, so I go over on Sunday to help her clean. I don't know why she doesn't just throw things away. The trash can is right there.

"Do you need this electric bill?" I say.

"Isn't that all, like, autopay nowadays?"

"Uh, have you signed up for that?"

"Let's assume I have. Live on the edge."

It's easy hanging out one-on-one with her, which is funny when a few months ago I thought it never would be again. Who knew it only took a little heart failure to bring people together. Dot's macabre sense of humor about the whole thing is rubbing off on me. Yesterday I asked her to unload the dishwasher and she pretended to die on the kitchen floor.

"You've got like four unopened packages here," I say to Ivy.

"Uh, don't open those."

"What are they, sex toys?"

She gives me a look like *duh.*

"Wait, really? You can get sex toys on Amazon?"

"Oh, my sweet summer child."

"You're really shy about me seeing your vibrators? I'm relieved you seem to have developed some shame."

She rolls her eyes. "They're Dot's. She has them sent here."

"So you're saying *Dot* has shame? That sounds even less likely."

"I don't know. She's pretty shy about people seeing that scar."

One of the packages has the tape open and just a bunch of textbooks inside, so I unload those and stack them up on her coffee table. *Understanding Art. History of Art. Contemporary Issues in Art Education.*

"These Dot's, too?" I ask.

She glances over from the TV stand, where she's gathering up empty soda cans. "Uh, no, those are mine."

"Art textbooks?"

She shrugs and gives me this sheepish smile. "I'm picking up an art minor this semester."

"Oh yeah?"

She sighs heavily. "What can I say? The kid's persuasive."

I'm organizing a stack of papers later and I come across a few loose drawings sticking out of a sketch pad. Even if I didn't know Ivy's style, I'd recognize her fashion drawings anywhere. Dresses with crisscrossed straps on the back and flouncy skirts. Androgynous, perfectly tailored suits. Graphic tees tucked into tight, drop-crotch pants.

All drawn on a short Asian model. What a coincidence.

I smile to myself and close the book before Ivy sees me.

Dot's birthday is that Thursday, and then Ivy's the day after, so we all get together a few days before to figure out a joint birthday party. It's Dot's eighteenth, so it's a pretty big deal, but considering how her graduation party went, everyone's sort of tiptoeing around it.

"We can just go out," Dot says. "Do the Mama's and Kinetic circuit."

"That's not your scene anymore and you know it," Ivy says. We're all slouched around the living room, and Ivy's on the couch, braiding Dot's hair, since it's hard for her to do herself nowadays.

"My scene is sleeping," Dot says. "That's not a birthday party."

"We can just do something low-key," Alyssa says. "Hang out here. Cake. Presents."

"I like presents," Dot says, sounding remarkably like her old self, and Ivy smirks.

Melody gasps and claps her hands together, then whispers something in Diana's ear.

"Oh, hell yes," Diana says.

"What?" I say.

"Nothing, just my wife has the best ideas for low-key birthday parties ever," Diana says.

"Tell us!" Dot says.

"Nope. It's done. It's planned. See you then."

We have cake and sing "Happy Birthday" to Dot and she has lunch with her mom on Thursday, but the party is on Friday. Diana and Melody are already there when I get home from work. Melody's dressed like a fifties movie starlet, fake pearls and homemade cigarette holder and all, and Diana looks like...a cowboy.

"What," I say.

Diana solemnly hands me a booklet. "You are a California surfer," she says.

Melody shakes her thumb and pinkie at me. "Hang ten, bro."

It's a murder mystery party. Dot's an heiress (*aren't we supposed to be acting?* Ivy says), Alyssa's a chambermaid, and Ivy's an international spy. Our books have secrets about who we really are and where we were at the time of the murder, and even though Ivy is totally cynical and sarcastic at first, by the time we're done with the first half hour, we're all very, very invested, examining clues and making wild accusations and doing everything we can to prove that we're innocent. We eat our way through two pizzas and all the rest of the birthday cake, and at the end of it all, Diana totally gets away with murder.

"That was awesome," Dot says, giving Melody a squeeze.

"You were a natural," she says, and Dot beams.

We just lie around after that, watching stoner comedies on Netflix, and at around ten Dot gives Ivy a nudge. "You should go out," she says quietly. I only hear because I'm on Ivy's other side.

Ivy gives Dot a sideways look. "I'm fine here."

Dot snorts. "You are coming out of your skin. Go dance. Tell that bartender it's your birthday. I'm gonna go to bed soon anyway."

Ivy looks around the room, then at her phone to check the time. "You sure?"

"Are you actually asking me for permission right now?"

"Yikes. No." She kisses her. "Later."

"Later."

Ivy turns to me. "You coming?"

Well, what am I supposed to say, no? It *is* her birthday.

It's like Kinetic knows, too. The lights seem brighter, the glitter sparklier, the music faster. Or maybe I just really needed this. God, it's been a hell of a summer, but it feels like we're finding our footing again. It feels like we might actually be okay.

And if not, at least there's that bass beat. Our big gay collective heart pumping stronger than a person's ever could.

Ivy goes straight for that bartender, like a girl on a mission, and I guess that birthday line must work because they're making out over the bar in about a second, and not long after that, Ivy's leading her back to the couches by the collar of her uniform. I guess she finally decided Ivy's worth risking her job for. I can't say I'm surprised.

I dance by myself for a while, and then Ivy comes out and joins me, her arms around my neck, smiling up at the lights. "I needed this," she says, and she lets go of me to twirl around.

"I know."

She tucks her forehead against mine. "I love you."

I smile. "I love you, too." And for just a minute, it's like the last year never happened. We're back at Kinetic, the girls are beautiful, and Ivy is mine.

I know it's not real. I don't even really want it to be.

But it's a good story.

Ivy's sleepy as hell by the time we get home, and she heads straight up to Dot's room, but I notice the light in the kitchen and go to check out what's going on. My mom's standing by the stove. "Everything okay?" she says.

"Making some chamomile for your dad," she says.

"He okay?"

"Just having some trouble sleeping." She opens the cabinet where he keeps his meds. "Hmm. Can you go ask him if he took a Xanax already? I don't want to yell up and wake Dot."

"Sure," I say, but when I get upstairs, the door to Dot's room is open and the lights are on. Ivy's sitting on the foot of the bed, yawning and fastening a blood pressure cuff around Dot's arm.

"Did you have fun tonight?" Dot is asking her. I can't see most of her, but she sounds sleepy, happy.

"Yeah, did you?"

"Uh-huh. Did you fuck the bartender?"

"Sure did. Hold still."

"That's my girl."

"Fuck off." The machine beeps, and she says, "Hundred and two over seventy. Good. Where the hell's that log book…"

"I miss dancing," Dot says softly.

"We'll find a way," Ivy says. "You can still do everything. Just different now."

"I know. I'm okay, Ivy."

"I know you are. Ah. There it is."

"Quick question," Dot says.

"Hmm?"

"When did we get so fucking boring?" she says, and Ivy laughs, big and real.

It occurs to me right then, for some reason, that I'd always assumed that there were two Ivys. Fake Ivy, the one who makes girls crawl for her in the club, and Real Ivy, the one who cries in an abandoned street about her dad. But there's this Ivy, the Ivy who's carefully fastening a blood pressure cuff like it's the most precious thing in the world, who's laughing and tangling her legs up with Dot's.

Why did I think the only real Ivy was who she is when she's miserable?

I don't even remember to ask my dad about the meds.

I just go back downstairs and sit at the kitchen table, trying to sort through all the crap in my mind. Trying to figure out how the hell we got to here. Everything made so much more sense an hour ago, under the lights.

"What's wrong?" my mom says.

"I don't think I'm ever going to love anyone as much as Dot and Ivy love each other," I say.

I'm sure she'll instantly reassure me that I will, like Catherine did, but instead, she says, "What makes you say that?"

"I don't think I'm built to take care of another person like they are. Dot told Ivy to go out because she could tell that she needed it. Ivy's up there keeping a record of Dot's blood pressures. You're keeping track of Dad's meds."

"Well, not very well, clearly."

"I don't know if I can do that," I say. "And I don't know if I want to."

She turns around from the stove. "So don't," she says, like it's the simplest thing in the world.

"Then what am I supposed to do?"

"There is a lot more out there than falling in love," she says. "That's just one option. There are a million other things that you can be and do. And a million more ways to love people that you haven't even thought of yet."

"Aren't you disappointed in me?" I say. "I mean, I'm sitting here telling you that I'm not a good enough person to take care of someone else."

"Knowing your limits does not make you a bad person," she says firmly. "Not everyone has to be everything. Hell, if the world were only made up of Ivys, nothing would ever get done. No one would get out of bed." She shrugs. "And who knows. Maybe you'll never want to be responsible for another person. And that's okay. Or maybe you'll meet the right person and it won't sound like such a hardship anymore. And that's okay, too. You'll figure it out, Duck."

I cover my eyes and groan. "God. It's her."

"What's her?"

"For years, I thought Ivy and I couldn't be together because there was something fundamentally broken about Ivy and she couldn't be in a relationship," I explain. "And then she gets with Dot, and I think, okay, the problem is *me*; she just couldn't be in a relationship with me. But it's not about me, and it's not about Ivy. We're not the factor. It's Dot. It's *her*."

"Yes," my mom says. "It's her."

"God. I still don't get why. I don't think I ever really will."

Mom shrugs. "They see through each other's bullshit. And they think each other's bullshit is funny. I don't know, darling. She's just the lid to Ivy's pot. You can't fully explain these things. Sometimes two people just…"

"Orbit each other," I say.

"Yes. And by the way, honey?"

"Oh God, what did I do?"

She laughs a little. "I just thought you should know. You don't love someone who you think is fundamentally broken. That's not love."

I kind of just…sit with that.

"Imagine how Ivy would react if someone said Dot was broken now," she says.

"Yeah. I don't have to." I rub my hand over my mouth. "God, she really loves her."

My mom smiles at me. "This is her story. This big, once-in-a-lifetime love, it's Ivy's story this time. You'll get your own."

My own.

It's not that I'm the secondary character in my own story.

It's just that this one was never my story.

O n the last day of August, Dot comes down the stairs in brand-new clothes, her backpack on and stuffed with textbooks.

I jingle the keys. "You ready?"

She takes a deep breath. "I'm ready."

September

(Again)

"**D**o you have any other questions?" the admissions counselor asks me.

About a million, but I've already asked her a previous million and I have about ten brochures in my hands. *Imagine Yourself at Community College of Rhode Island. Student Life at CCRI. CCRI: English Department.* So I say, "I don't think so, not right now."

"Okay, well, you have our email address if you think of anything. Thank you for stopping by. Hope to see your application soon!"

I walk out of the administration building and into the midmorning sun. A couple of students brush past me on their way in, and a few more are on the sidewalk, chatting animatedly. It's not Brown's campus, isn't the manicured lawns and stone buildings I grew up picturing as the college experience, but look at Dot and Ivy. College isn't always what you expected it would be.

Dot and Ivy themselves are here, lying on their backs under a tree by the entrance, their heads against each other, laughing so hard I can see their stomachs moving. I make my way over and kick Ivy's shoe.

She sits up. "Got what you needed?"

"Yeah, I think so." I pull Dot off the ground.

"I still think you should apply to a four-year school,"

Dot says as we walk back to the car. "Dream big and all that."

"You are such a snob," Ivy says.

"You should talk."

"I can always transfer," I say. "But this is an easy drive. And it's *something*. I'm sick of being a tourist in my own life."

"And it's very close to my apartment," Ivy says.

"Yeah, Dot can do my makeup every day before class," I say. She's back to spending more time at Ivy's apartment than at my house.

Dot laughs. "Glitter eye shadow for first period."

"Cut creases."

"*Blinding* highlight."

"I'm sorry, what is this about every morning?" Ivy says. "Someone's got her own fucking classes to attend." She nudges Dot. "In Providence."

"Shut up," I say to Ivy. "I'm trying to have a conversation with your girlfriend."

"Don't worry about me," Dot says. "I'm an excellent multitasker." She tips down and does a cartwheel on the sidewalk.

For the first time in a year, the strip club makes money. So we celebrate in the natural way: a topless dance party. The dancers invite their friends, Catherine and I invite our friends, and we all crowd into Dav's after closing to blast music and drink our way back into the red.

I'm getting ready for it in the club dressing room after

the last customer leaves when my phone dings with an alert that a new video is up from someone I've subscribed to. And since I'm not a big YouTuber, that means one person.

I have to take a moment after I read the title.

Makeup When You're Sick.

Dot's in front of the white wall in Ivy's apartment, barefaced, her hair braided. She smiles at the camera—not her usual cheesy grin, just a little thing. Real.

"Hi, hi, what's up, it's your girl Dot. So I know I've been gone for a while, and I have a whole explanation video coming, but right now I just want to sit down with you guys and put a face on. So this is a tutorial on adaptive makeup, which means makeup for people with disabilities or chronic illnesses, but you can use it if you're just feeling sick or tired and you want to look good but you have trouble with the strength or dexterity you might need to follow a regular tutorial. Obviously the techniques I show here aren't going to be good for people with all illnesses or disabilities, so feel free to substitute or ignore anything that doesn't work for you, and I'm still learning all of this myself, so I'm *definitely* not an expert, but…let's dive in."

I get ready with her and watch the views roll in.

"Your makeup looks good," Alyssa says once the party's started and we're hanging by the bar. Hers does, too. I need to ask her how she always picks the perfect lipstick shade, because it makes her whole face glow.

"Thanks. Dot hauled me over and fixed my eyeliner as

soon as she got here."

The whole room is some kind of lesbian fantasy. Topless girl after topless girl, dancers, friends, strangers, gay girls, straight girls, cis girls, trans girls, mothers, daughters. Melody's hanging upside down on the pole. Dot's hanging out in one of the go-go cages, swinging her legs, playing with her scar with one hand. Ivy's…God knows where. Probably in the bathroom with her head between someone's thighs.

"I'm kind of drunk," Alyssa says.

I turn my face up to the disco ball. "Me too."

"Do you ever think about you and me getting together?"

I choke on my drink. "What?"

She shrugs. "I've had a crush on you for ages. I'm just wondering if you'd ever considered it."

I think my brain is broken.

"Um…no," I say truthfully. "I never really thought about it." Though it isn't escaping my notice that she has great tits. "Really? You like me?"

"No pressure or anything. But we're both single and I'm drunk enough to tell you, so I figured what the hell."

"This is *much* better than my drunken love confession," I say. "Can I go get something to write with? I want to take notes on this."

She laughs. "Just think it over, okay?"

"Yeah, I will," I say, and she kisses my cheek and climbs up on the stage to grind against Diana, and I pour myself another drink, because what a ridiculously strange year this has been.

Ivy sidles up to me at the bar a few moments later. "Yo."

"How was…whoever you were with?"

"Lovely." She scans the room until her eyes land on Dot, then abruptly pretends she wasn't.

"You're funny," I say.

"Shut up." She sighs. "God. She loved dancing."

"Yeah."

"It's hard," Ivy says. "It's just hard sometimes."

But they smile at each other across the room.

I think about what my mom said, that Ivy and Dot are some once-in-their-lifetime thing, and I'm not sure if that's exactly right. I think it's once in all our lifetimes. This is some once-in-a-generation shit. This is the kind of love they write poems about. They put up statues. They name holidays. Fifty years from now, schools will put on *Ivy and Dot: The Musical.*

"I'm so obsessed with you two," I say.

"Well, don't jump off a bridge if we break up."

"It doesn't matter if you break up," I say. "It matters that it happened." I hit my shoulder against hers. "Ivy Harlowe fell in love."

"You realize you're totally weird, right?"

"Yeah."

A slow song starts up, and Ivy says, "Gotta go." She cuts across the room and climbs into the cage with Dot, and Dot stands on her tiptoes and puts her arms around Ivy's neck. Ivy lays her fingers across her scars as they dance.

And I.... Fuck it. I go up to the stage and tap Alyssa on the shoulder.

She raises an eyebrow at me.

"I don't know if I'm ready," I say. "I don't know if I feel the same way you do."

"Okay," she says.

"And I'm still getting over Ivy and I don't know if I ever fully will."

"Okay."

"And I don't want to ruin our friendship and I'm scared of everything all the time."

"Okay," she says. She puts her arms around my waist. "Now shut up. Keep dancing."

So I do.

And I don't think this is going to last forever. I don't think this is my great love story. Maybe that's still to come.

Or maybe I won't have one. Maybe my story is about being a good friend or a good daughter. Saving a shitty strip club.

Saving a girl's life.

Or maybe I'm supposed to be a witness. To document. Maybe I'll write a book about two girls who meet, maybe in Italy. Maybe one of them needs a new heart. Maybe they fall desperately in love.

Maybe they'll live happily ever after.

Anything's possible.

Acknowledgments

Thank you so much to my incredibly supportive parents, my beautiful sister and brother-in-law and little nephew, to Benni, to Jessi, to Seth, to Parker, to Amanda, to Becca and Jen and Lydia and the whole Entangled team, to everyone who told me I was allowed to write this, to everyone who loves me at my most indulgent, to every girl who dreams of bigger things. You never know.

Friday Night Lights *meets* The Cutting Edge *in this pitch-perfect sports romance.*

IN THE
PENALTY
BOX

NYT & USA TODAY BESTSELLING AUTHOR
LYNN RUSH
USA TODAY BESTSELLING AUTHOR
KELLY ANNE BLOUNT

Willow
Figure skating was supposed to be my whole world. But one unlucky injury and now I'm down...but I'm definitely not out. I just need to rehab—a boatload of rehab—and who'd have thought I could do it on the boys' hockey team?

Of course, the infuriatingly hot captain of the team seems to think I'm nothing but sequins and twirls. What's a girl to do but put him in his place? Game on.

Brodie
Hockey is my whole world. I've worked my tail off getting my team in a position to win the championships—hopefully in front of major college scouts, too—so what's a guy to do when a figure skater ends up as our new goalie?

Of course, the distractingly sexy skater thinks I'm nothing but a testosterone-laced competitive streak. And surely she's only biding her time to heal, then she's gone. Game over.

Exploring issues of deafness, Deaf culture, and how we view others through our own lenses, Hear Me is also a beautiful romance about finally being seen and heard.

hear me

Listen with your heart.

dana faletti

When Margaret Star first meets Gray Trax, she instantly knows her whole world will change forever. Hard of hearing, she never really felt like anyone listened to her. Shy yet reserved, all Margaret has ever wanted was to share her music onstage. Lately, she'd settle for a minute of her parents' attention or even a friend who actually listens.

Gray Trax is that friend. Gray is often misunderstood. While others see him as deaf, troubled, an angry bad boy, Margaret sees another side to him. He's brilliant and caring. While neither of their lives is perfect, together Margaret might just be able to stop Gray from becoming another label, another statistic.

As Gray and Margaret are pulled closer together, they realize everyone, even those who are mislabeled, deserve to be heard.

Let's be friends!

🐦 @EntangledTeen

📷 @EntangledTeen

📘 @EntangledTeen

📰 bit.ly/TeenNewsletter

entangled teen

an imprint of Entangled Publishing LLC